Advance Praise for *The Ballad of Innes of Skara Skaill*

"Sometimes I read because I think I should. Like going to the gym. Or a museum. But sometimes a book hooks me and I think, 'Hey this is great, I should do this more often!'. Faulkner Hunt's *The Ballad of Innes of Skara Skaill* is absolutely one of those books."

—Owen Wilson

"Thrilling! I wish I'd had this book growing up, but I'm happy to have it now. As a coach, I was fascinated how this ragtag group bands together against the harshness of the land and the fierceness of their rivals. As a reader, I was enchanted by Hunt's ability to weave a world where nature and myth intertwine. *The Ballad of Innes of Skara Skaill* is a story you won't want to miss!"

—Andrew Rueb (Head Coach,
Harvard Men's Tennis)

"A thrilling mix of history, adventure, and high-stakes intrigue, *The Ballad of Innes of Skara Skaill* is a pulse-pounding mystery set against the rugged beauty of the North Atlantic islands. Seeping with atmosphere, the novel brings to life a small island community readers will easily lose themselves in. Alternating between taut, cinematic action and quiet evocative moments,

Hunt delivers a heart-racing journey through storm-lashed landscapes, forgotten relics, and the bonds of found family."

—Soman Chainani (Author, *The School for Good and Evil* series)

"If you like ancient legends built on the adventure of human drama, you will love this book!"

—Dr. Robert Ballard (Discoverer of the RMS *Titanic* and German battleship *Bismarck*)

THE BALLAD OF INNES OF SKARA SKAILL

FAULKNER HUNT

A REGALO PRESS BOOK
ISBN: 979-8-88845-804-4
ISBN (eBook): 979-8-88845-805-1

The Ballad of Innes of Skara Skaill

Cover Design by Georgiana Goodwin
Cover Art by Kathleen Littler

Publishing Team:
Founder and Publisher – Gretchen Young
Editor – Adriana Senior
Editorial Assistant – Caitlyn Limbaugh
Managing Editor – Aleigha Koss
Production Manager – Morgan Simpson
Production Editor – Courtney Michaelson

As part of the mission of Regalo Press, a donation is being made to the St. Jude Children's Research Hospital, as chosen by the author. Learn more about this organization at https://www.stjude.org/.

This book, as well as any other Regalo Press publications, may be purchased in bulk quantities at a special discounted rate. Contact orders@regalopress.com for more information.

Regalo Press
New York • Nashville
regalopress.com

Published in the United States of America
1 2 3 4 5 6 7 8 9 10

For Annie

I

A PALL OF PLASTER dust hung in the air like a veil. Down the hall in the dim light a figure worked steadily with a sledgehammer, tearing away at the walls, rubble gathering at his feet, his face half shrouded with a rag. Chalky powder had collected on the cloth at his nose and mouth. His ragged hair was dusted white as the bones of the old house slowly emerged from behind the walls. He moved easily. His back was made for work, his hands oversized from use. There was a mournful air about him. Continuing on, he worked without rest, but as he broke through a new section of wall, he stopped. Behind the opened plaster, sitting on a horizontal beam, was a pair of tiny shoes. A girl's shoes. They were robin's-egg blue and covered in dust. He took them down and held them a moment, small enough to fit in his hand. Not wanting to toss them onto the rubble heap, he set them out of the way on the staircase rising up through the dust in the hall. The man started again at his work until suddenly, through the din, he became aware of the sound of his own name being shouted from up the hall.

"Innes!"

The foreman was standing in a haze of light at the front door. Innes set his hammer down and walked up the hall, pulling the rag down from his face.

"Alright. That's it for today," said the foreman, fumbling through a ring of keys. Two other men were already out on the sidewalk patting the dust out of their clothes.

Innes headed out.

"You hang on," said the foreman. He pulled an envelope from his jacket. The envelope was layered with postmarks. *Last Known Address*. It had been forwarded many times. "And why would this have come to the office?"

Innes looked at the letter. It was addressed to him. "Right." He paused, recognizing the handwriting. "The last place I'd been staying wanted a forwarding address."

"And so you gave the office?"

Innes was slow to answer. "Well, it's only that I don't really have a proper home address just at the moment."

The foreman looked Innes over, then glanced into the house at a man coming down the stairs. "Jesus, Dickie, we hiring just anybody these days?"

"Why?" said the man coming up the hall. "He's a good demolition man."

The foreman looked at Innes again. "Alright then." He handed Innes the letter. "But don't be giving out my office address as your own, you understand me?" He thumbed Innes out the front door and began locking up.

Down on the street Innes drifted away a few steps. On the envelope, *Skara Skaill* was written as the return address. He opened it. The old handwriting, so familiar to him, was unsteady now, tremulous.

My dearest boy. By the time this letter reaches you…

As he read the letter a sudden coldness flowed through him. Turning his back to the others, he started it once more.

"Oy. What's the matter with you?" called the foreman from the top step.

Innes stared at the letter a moment, then turned to the foreman. "I'm going to be needing a few days off." His mind was already far away.

"Days off? What is that, a joke? You've only just started."

Innes stood, covered in dust.

"And you'd want this holiday starting when exactly?"

Innes's eyes slowly came back to him. "In the morning."

"The morning?" The foreman laughed. "Job's got to be done by the end of the week."

"It can't be helped."

"Oh, it can't be helped, can it? Now you listen to me. You take off on me tomorrow, you don't bother coming back." The foreman stood waiting a moment. "Suit yourself then." He turned angrily back to his ring of keys. "Find me another one, Dickie. No doubt there'll be another off the boat tomorrow."

Innes glanced down at the letter, then up at the foreman again. "Do you think I could get my pay though? Before I go?"

"Paydays are on Fridays," muttered the foreman without looking back.

"For the work I already did, I mean."

"Paydays are on Friday," he repeated, roughly locking the door.

Dickie looked at Innes standing in the middle of the sidewalk. He walked down to him and took out a few bills from his own wallet. "You can get what's owed when you get back."

Innes looked at him and nodded, and stuffing the bills into his pocket, he turned and started away up the street.

The foreman came down the steps. "Always the same old story with these types, eh, Dickie?" he said, watching him go.

At the far corner, Innes turned into a side alley. He stood a moment, still holding the letter. As the crowd flowed along the murmuring street behind him, Innes leaned against the wall to steady himself and read the words again.

* * *

The Northern Islands. Near Skara Skaill Village.
Kettleskaill House. Third Floor.

"Again, Tito? Why do we always go 'round and 'round with the same old story?" asked Rory, the older of the two boys. But Tito was already settling into his pillow, readying himself. Rory opened the book, its binding unbound, its pages laid loose. And he read.

"In ages old when—"

"Title too," interrupted Tito. Rory started again.

The Ballad of Innes of Skara Skaill.

In ages old when the world was new
And mists roamed dark and free
And Grendel stood on legs of two
And stalked men's company…

A prow slid silent 'pon the nameless shore
A hoard unloaded down
In the island's breast went the oaken chests
Hid deep beneath the ground.

Now on these northern isles, with hinterlands
Rare seen by civil men
Lived Norsemen old, the stories told
Where none came back again…

So to the north, a man sailed forth
To the island folk he came
To carry out his lord's command
And Innes was his name.

And the island folk found him thereon
And came and took him in
And filled his cup and bade him sup
And welcomed him as kin…

So he bent his sword to plowshares
For his warring days were done
And he found a love and married
And to him she bore a son.

But out upon the narrows dark
Sailed silent a marauder
With shackled men, chained down within
His lord's fresh cannon fodder…

A freebooter, a man looter
He saw the islands low
His mast nigh splintered from a storm
Spied timber past the shoal.

His anchor dropped near the shifting sands
And a bark was rowed ashore
While a mast-straight yew was being felled
Dread Marwick stalked the moor.

And the island folk found him thereon
And they came and took him in
And they filled his cup and they bade him sup
And they welcomed him as kin....

Tito listened as the story went on. He knew it by heart. When it was done, he lay on his bed, staring up at the yellow candlelight shifting around the ceiling. The fire burned quietly in the woodstove.

"Do you really not think it was true, Rory?"

"Other than the Marwicks still running everything?" Rory went over to a stack of books against the wall.

"I mean the rest of it?"

"I don't know, Tito." Rory considered the book a moment before setting it on the stack.

At the table along the wall, he turned the hand-crank of a radio until a blue light began to glow pale and steady. The static of a maritime weather report filled the room. *Winds out of the northeast, fifteen to twenty knots, with gusts up to thirty knots after midnight. Seas eight to ten feet.*

Kettleskaill House sat high, overlooking the open moors and the vast expanse of Skara Heath, and on nights when the wind blew up from the south, the radio might pick up a match from the mainland, or a music show from far-off somewhere, or the faint signal of a man reading straight from a book.

"Where's that one coming from, do you think, Rory?" Tito would ask about this program or that coming through the air, scudding low across the black water to the islands at night, all the way to them there, high up in their room.

Rory was fourteen, three years older than Tito, and his hair was a bit lighter and longer than Tito's, which was the color of a walnut shell and wasn't curly and wasn't straight and usually only the front got cut. Their eyes were blue and smart and their skin was fair and freckled where the thin northern sun angled across their faces. Rory's two front teeth crossed over each other a little, and Tito had a short, straight scar just beneath his bottom lip where he had fallen and bitten through it. He hadn't told anyone because he knew that stitches cost. One of the men in the village, the slow-talking one with the milky eye and the divot in his head, would always ask Tito, every time as if it were the first time, if he and Rory were brothers, which anyone could see they were.

Like most everything on the islands, Kettleskaill House had been used and reused, built and rebuilt, burnt, toppled down and built again, houses upon huts upon farms upon forts. Same stones, stacked and restacked, arranged and rearranged, from one time to the next, over and again.

Their room on the top floor had no closet, which Rory said was because Kettleskaill House was built back in the days when no one owned much of anything.

"And who needs a closet if you don't have anything to put in one?"

Tito thought this made great sense, as he did everything Rory said.

Electric lights had come to Kettleskaill long after it had been built, so the wires ran outside the walls, and the switches were heavy and ceramic. But the electricity at Kettleskaill had been shut off now, so when the sun went down, the house went dark. Tito had gotten used to doing everything he needed to do before night fell, navigating through the darkness in his mind. Up the steps. Down the hall. Sliding his hand along the wall, into their room. The soft step of the rug. The presence of solid objects all around him sitting heavily in the dark.

At night the boys let the radio play as long as the electricity from the cranking held out. Often they fell asleep to the sound of the match and the surges of the crowd. Rory said he liked listening to the matches best, but he never seemed to mind the program of the man reading from a book. Tito usually nodded off before the radio dimmed away, but some nights he lay awake.

Tucked up on the top floor, Tito had always been able to hear Mrs. Renfro down below as she closed down the kitchen for the night or called the cats in from the dark. When it was cold out, the wind rattling the house, Mrs. Renfro would ask Rory to make a fire in the small room with the oval rug, and they would eat dinner in front of the TV, each with their own little table. Sometimes they would play cards, and on Saturdays Mrs. Renfro would have a sherry, which she kept in the high cupboard. Just one. Maybe two, but never more.

Mrs. Renfro's laugh came out easy. It was hard to stop once it got going and was usually at something they'd done or said. A funny little dance or feat of strength Tito would do on the oval rug in the middle of the room. When it was over, she would lean back in her chair, wrung out as if she had just hurried up a flight of stairs. Whenever Tito happened across something particularly funny, he'd stop what he was doing and go straightaway to find her, and if she wasn't about, he'd always remember to tell it to her the next time he saw her, even before he'd said hello.

"You think this'd do it?" he'd ask Rory about something he thought might do the trick.

"It might," Rory would say, and Tito would scribble it down on a scrap of paper so he wouldn't forget.

Tito still scribbled things down on scraps of paper even though he didn't have Mrs. Renfro to say them to anymore.

Four months ago, arrangements had been made. They had watched Mrs. Renfro's funeral from a distance. A woman was coming on the ferry to find them a new home off-island. That night the boys slept out in the rocks on the ridge above Kettleskaill House, and in the morning when the car drove up, they had kept watch from above as the woman knocked on the door in her office clothes. She came again the next day and peered in through the windows, rattling the knobs. Walking to the front of the house, she had lit a cigarette and stood there looking up at the windows. When she was done, she dropped the cigarette in the gravel, twisted it out under the toe of her shoe, and climbed into her car and drove away. She took the ferry the next day and didn't come back to Skara Skaill anymore after that.

* * *

Tito lay awake listening to the rain thrumming on the roof. The radio had long gone out. In the silence, the darkness was so dark he felt as if he were floating, untethered, unsure which direction was the door or which direction was the window or how far away or how near Rory was to him. Rory was to turn fifteen that night while they slept.

* * *

Outside, the wind raced past the house. Beyond the bedroom window, far out in the blackness where the fields of Kettleskaill House gave way to the empty barrens, stood the skeleton shell of Skarahollow Chapel. From out of the ruins of the little stone church grew a solitary yew tree, long-limbed and knobby. As the winds blew through the bones of the chapel, a sudden thudding came from beneath the ground, as if something deep in the earth was letting go. The yew tree began reeling, slowly at first, then picking up speed, its branches snapping and shattering in the darkness as it crashed to the ground. The earth shuddered as the tree bounced once, then settled in silence. The old tree lay still, like a masted schooner run aground. Where the yew had stood, a hole was now wrenched open in the earth. The tree's ancient rootball was levered out of the ground, and held tight within its roots were clots of stones drawn up from deep beneath the sod. Vibrating in the wind, a tiny stone dangled from the thin tendril of a root before slipping soundlessly into the void. A second later the little stone sent up a clean clacking sound, echoing out of the blackness below.

II

IT WAS JUST BEFORE dawn. In the chill morning mist, a few men moved quietly along the wharf preparing their boats. Lights reflected on the wet cobbled streets. Innes walked slowly along the quay, a small duffel bag in his hand, a wool overcoat buttoned to his neck. In a low building at the far end of the wharf, the ferry office was just opening. Innes could see the fares for the crossing taped to the window there. He touched his thin wallet but left it in his pocket where it sat. Turning to the water, he looked out at the boats rocking along the quay. Down the wharf, a truck had arrived and was backing up to a small cargo boat tied along the dock. A new metal septic tank the size of a small car was being hoisted from the back of the truck onto the boat's deck. Two men guided the swinging tank lower, and as they tied it down Innes noticed the words *Skara Skaill* painted along the boat's hull. When the men were done they walked to the front of the truck and stood talking to the driver, who was gently blowing into a steaming cup. After a moment, the men walked across to the ferry office.

Innes moved behind a piling. From the quay he stood watching the men talking through the ticket window to a woman pouring coffees. As one of the men leaned to the window, Innes dropped lightly down onto the deck of the boat. Hurrying low along the railing, he reached the bow and tucked himself in between the septic tank and a stack of cargo lashed to the foredeck. A canvas tarp stretched tightly overhead made a low space for him to duck in. Wedging his duffel bag behind him, he drew his knees up close. A seagull standing nearby on the railing stared at him, its legs stick-straight as it unfolded and refolded its wings in the wind. From somewhere behind him, Innes heard voices approaching, then the sound of quick footsteps on metal rungs. After a moment came the thrum of engines vibrating deep within the hull beneath him. The boat lurched, then began slowly gliding away from the quay as the seagull leaped from the railing and banked away, screaming into the fog.

* * *

Sound asleep, Rory lay breathing. A downy fluff on his pillow vibrated against his inhale before suddenly releasing and disappearing down his throat. In a fit of coughing Rory sat up, blinking at the sight of two beady black eyes staring at him.

"Tito. What did I say about letting her in here?"

Tito opened his eyes to see a chicken of the brightest orange roosting on Rory's pillow. "I didn't let her in. She comes in when Sir Winston's not here," he said. "Must've been a frost last night." Rory tried to tip the hen off his pillow. "Here, I'll do it," said Tito, sliding out of bed. "You'll make her nervous. They lose their feathers when they're nervous." Tito lifted the chicken away with both hands. "C'mon, Honey. There's a good girl." Beneath her was a large egg denting Rory's pillow. "And you see what she's left you?"

Rory picked up the egg. "One egg doesn't do the two of us much good."

"Well, maybe it's a double yolker?"

Tito carried Honey to the window, then released the chicken straight out. Without a single flap, she plummeted, landing solidly into the hedge below before rolling onto the ground and waddling away toward the barn.

Downstairs in the kitchen, gray light came through the thickly settled glass in the windows. Dark timbers sagged across the ceiling, and a thin veil of dust covered everything. A barometer sat on a mahogany pedestal. Rory stared through its glass dome as the gauges steadily fell.

"It'll be getting colder soon."

From his back, Tito slid a tall canvas pack onto the floor. As he went to work adding bits of kindling to the coals, he practiced a thin whistle. He was always practicing it. He took quiet notice of the wood that Rory had stacked near the kitchen hearth: two broken chair legs, a few banisters from the stairs, and other wooden bits from around the house. Rory set a skillet onto the grate and cracked the egg into it.

"Double yolker," said Tito. "What'd I tell you?"

"Yeah, well, I still don't want her inside the house. She leaves squits all over the room." Rory laid two pieces of bread into the skillet and pinched a bit of salt onto the egg. As he waited for the eggs to cook, he watched Tito arrange and rearrange his belongings down inside his pack.

"You know you don't need to bring all that every time we leave the house, Tito."

"Well, what if we have to sleep out again?"

"We won't."

"It's happened three times already, Rory."

"Was twice."

"Three times. When those two broke in and slept downstairs, then came back the next night? That counts twice."

They sat eating quietly. A hard wind gusted outside. When they were done, Rory cleaned the plate with water from a tin bucket. Taking up his pack, Tito slid open the side window, and he and Rory climbed out into the cold morning air.

The front door of Kettleskaill House was boarded shut. A notice was tacked beneath the knocker. Ever since the county had posted it there, Tito had wanted to take it down, but Rory said they should leave it in case someone noticed it was gone.

> *Abandoned Property. Skara Skaill County Tax Authority.*

Across the dirt yard sat a stone barn. As they passed through its opening, a burst of swallows flushed up out of the dirt and resettled high in the rafters.

Tito whispered into the shadows. "Sir Winston?" He tried a thin whistle.

Rory stepped to the corner and pulled away a tarp uncovering two coils of copper wire. He stuffed one of the coils into Tito's pack.

"Sir Winston," Tito called again, as Rory adjusted the pack, then slung the heavier coil onto his own back.

Across the dirt yard, they passed through a low iron gate and started down the lowering path that led out to the fields below. At the bottom, the fog sat heavy. The path continued along a stone wall that cut across the center of two broad fields. As they passed along the wall, Rory slowed, then stopped, staring out beyond the far field toward the ruin of Skarahollow Chapel.

"Where's the tree gone?" asked Tito, coming alongside.

Rory stood staring at the yew tree lying within the ruins of the old chapel, before starting off again.

For a mile or more they continued along the path at the edge of the moors. Up ahead they saw an old broken camper on cinderblocks. It was white with faded blue trim. Brown rust streaks ran down its seams, and a goat stood atop a garbage mound at its back door. Inside the fence were scattered mechanical parts, a circle of bald tires holding down a tarp, stacks of scrap metal sorted into piles.

They passed through the gate and walked to a little shed. Hanging from it was a homemade scale that had been rigged using a square metal plate. A board listed the prices per pound for scrap metal. The goat hurried over and stared cockeyed at them as Rory loaded the wire from their packs onto the plate. After arranging the coils a little, Rory pulled the rope next to a sign that read *Ring for Service*. The goat put its front hooves on the scale and snuffed at the pile as the trailer door swung open. Inside, a lumpen man still seated in his chair held the door open with a stick. A miniature plastic Christmas tree sat on the desk. A TV was on in the background. Seeing the boys, the man dropped his head.

"Every time my program comes on," he said. As he hoisted himself to his feet, they could hear the relief in the chair springs. Otis Harslop, the proprietor, came muttering across the yard as if his feet hurt him. "So what stolen goods have you got for me today, eh?"

"They're not stolen," said Tito indignantly.

Otis passed the boys, ignoring them. He stopped at the copper coils splayed there on the metal plate. As he considered them, he took a lemon snap out of his pocket and popped it into his mouth. He squinted at the numbers on the scale, and as he did, he noticed the goat standing with one hoof on the metal plate.

"Oy," he said, shoving the goat off the plate. He glanced suspiciously at Rory.

"What? He's your goat."

Otis pulled a pad from his pocket, but Rory had already done the math in his head. "It's twenty-four and a half."

Otis stayed bent to his pad, then looked up. "I'll give you twelve quid even."

"Twelve quid? And how do you get that?" Rory pointed at the scale. "It's twenty-four and a half."

"Not for stolen goods it isn't."

"They're not stolen," said Tito.

"Oh no, they never are."

"They're not. All this came out of Kettleskaill House."

"Kettleskaill House?" Otis turned to them. "Are you telling me you stole the wire out of your own house?"

Rory paused. "Well…the power is out anyway, so…"

A smile spread across Otis's face. "Right out of your own house. Well, now that's a first. Either way it's still stealing. Twelve quid."

"And how do you figure that's stealing?"

"Because it's not your house now, is it? The county owns it. You two are just squatting in it. And since you don't own it, or anything else for that matter, everything you bring me from a brass button to a bent nail belongs to someone else, which makes you, and you, nothing more than a couple of little scroungers. To wit, twelve quid, or no deal." Otis popped in another lemon snap and stared at them, chewing.

Rory thought a moment. "Fine. We'll take the twelve."

"Yeah you will. It weren't ever a negotiation anyway." Otis wiped his hands on his pants, and taking out a wad of money, he counted off a few bills.

Rory took the bills and began carefully recounting them.

"You do know that's rude, don't you?" said Otis as Rory went right on counting. Otis nodded at their packs. "Got anything else today?"

Rory looked up at Otis. After hesitating a moment, he reached into his coat and drew out a folded cloth.

"Rory, what are you doing?"

"We need the money, Tito, so just—" He turned back to Otis. "And how much would you give for this?" He held out a blackened arrow point nestled within the cloth.

Otis leaned over it.

"It's a bodkin point," said Tito.

"Yeah I know what it is. And who'd you steal that from?"

"He didn't steal it. He found it."

"Found it where?"

"In the side field at Kettleskaill," said Rory. "Where they used to plow it."

"After a big rain, that's when you find them," added Tito.

Otis studied the arrow point.

"Probably Advanced Grade," said Rory. "Maybe High Advanced."

Otis straightened up casually. "I'll give you ten for it. And before you even start, you know how this works, yeah? I'm not a collector. I gotta leave some profit in it for me." He peeled off the bills.

Rory considered the money. "And two cigarettes."

"I don't smoke. It's a filthy habit." Otis jabbed the bills at him. "You want the deal or don't you?"

Rory took the bills and handed over the bodkin point. Otis beamed down at his new possession.

"Always a pleasure doing business with you boys. Now beat it so I can get back to my program." Otis glanced up from the bodkin, but the boys were already through the gate. As he reached for another lemon snap, he felt the goat chewing hard at his pants pocket. "Oy, get off." He shoved the goat away, then popped the lemon snap into his mouth. Groaning a fat man's groan, he bent to the scale, but as he lifted away the splay of copper, he saw a heavy stone sitting smack in the middle. Wheeling around, he looked out, but Rory and Tito were already hustling away on the moor path, disappearing beyond the rise.

III

INNES HUDDLED LOW WITHIN the cargo. The boat rose and fell over the North Sea swells that rolled beneath the ship in steady sets. What had been a gray morning was darkening fast. A constant spray of cold seawater began working its way deeper into Innes's clothes. Lashed all around him were crates bound for Skara Skaill. Among the cargo were wooden boxes of the highest-grade whiskey and wine and champagne and all manner of food packed in ice. On these crates a destination was stenciled: *Marwick Hall.* Innes considered the name a moment, marked in black.

"And wouldn't it have to be that?"

He gave one of the lids a little test, but it was nailed shut. From his coat pocket he pulled out a sandwich wrapped in paper. He ate it slowly, his mind far away. A hard wind vibrated the canvas above him, and a sweep of water now rushed back and forth across the deck. From a seam in the cargo, a gray mouse inched out into the clear. Innes watched the mouse lift its naked foot and shake away the icy water as it edged along the base of the crates. He tore a crust from his sandwich and flipped it into the corner.

As the sky continued to darken, the ocean turned from green to black. Off the port horizon Innes paused at the sight of a dark tower of clouds building high over the water. A bitter wind came pounding across the ship, and Innes turned up his collar against the cold.

* * *

The boys stepped along the concrete pipe that crossed the ditch. In the gulley a dead bird had blurred away into the icy mud. At the top of the hill sat Skara Skaill, a gray village of wet stone and slate. A single road passed through it, tracing away toward the sea cliffs beyond.

Clambering over a low wall, they passed the village square. A cobbled lane led sharply down to the wharf at the far end. They continued along a narrow back street, where water ran in the gutter from somewhere up the lane. As they walked along, Tito felt something hurrying beside him, and looking down, he saw the familiar markings of a little gray mutt, rib-thin, his tail twitching as he looked up at them.

"Sir Winston!" said Tito. He squatted down and patted the dog's smooth apple head. "And where have you been, eh? He looks hungry. Are you hungry?" He began rummaging through his pack and pulled out a slice of bread. The little dog instantly snapped it up. "Mrs. Renfro always said he was a rounder." Tito offered him another, and the little dog gulped it down in two quick lunges.

"Alright, Tito, that's enough." Rory took the bread bag and tied it closed.

Tito nodded at the little dog. "Come on then, you too." They started up the lane again, Tito making sure Sir Winston was following behind.

As they rounded the corner, Rory stopped short. A man came stepping out of the alley. This was Rat. Bug-eyed, razor-thin, sparse whiskers on his pockmarked face. He wore a pair of trainers that he kept spotless white. At the sight of him, Sir Winston immediately began vibrating a low growl.

"Shut it, you little mongrel," hissed Rat, but Sir Winston only lowered his eyes darkly. Rat faked a lunge at him, and the little dog let out a string of barking. "I said shut it." Rat flicked his lit cigarette at Sir Winston and stalked forward until the little dog finally turned and hurried away up the street, tight to the wall.

Rory grabbed Tito's arm and began leading him toward the alley.

"And what are you two little numpties sneakin' around about, eh?" Rat strutted back to them, still exhaling the last of his cigarette.

"Just going to the clinic," said Rory.

Rat looked down the alley. Above one of the back gates was a sign that read *County Clinic and Social Services.*

He eyed the boys. "And what scam are you two running now, eh? They giving stuff away or what?"

"No, Tito just has the squitters is all."

Rat looked at Tito with disgust. "Nasty." He pulled a pack of cigarettes from his pocket only to find it was empty. "You seen Otis?"

"Nope," Rory lied.

Rat considered them a moment. "Don't suppose you'd have a cigarette on you?"

"I don't smoke," said Rory.

Rat crumpled the cigarette pack and tossed it into the streaming gutter. "Me, I'm heading down to see the Badger."

He sniffed importantly. "At the wharf." The boys stared blankly at him. "With the Duffs," he added for effect. "You know Frankie's out?" The boys said nothing. And not getting the reaction he was hoping for, Rat waved them off. "Wasting my time with you two anyway," he said as he started again down the lane toward the wharf.

Tito hurried to the curb to see where Sir Winston had gone as Rory picked up the butt of Rat's still-smoking cigarette. He flicked out the ember, pinched off the filter, and tucked the stub into the cuff of his pants as they started again down the alley.

Tito fell quiet. "Do you think that's true? About Frankie Duff?"

"What, that he's back?"

"Not that." Tito glanced at Rory.

"Oh. Well if he only spent six months in prison for it then he must not have killed him."

"But almost?"

Halfway down the alley they stopped at a small fence. Through the slats they saw a metal bin sitting at the back step. Attached to it was a red flagstick.

"Is it up?" whispered Tito.

Rory nodded, and slipping through the gate, they stole quietly across the yard. At the bin, Rory raised the lid and lifted out a full paper sack. Carefully lowering the lid again, they started back across the yard. But as Rory neared the gate, he heard the clinic door open and a voice call out.

"Excuse me, is there something I can help you with?"

Rory hurriedly tried the latch, but the gate wouldn't open.

At the back door stood a young woman in her twenties. She had a cup of steaming tea in one hand and a bag of trash in the other. Tito stood stock-still in the middle of the yard.

"The latch is broken," she said. "You've got to reach through and lift it from both sides." She looked as if she'd just washed her face with very cold water. Her light-brown hair was knotted in a scarf. "I'm Aggie Allen, by the way." Tito stared silently at her. "You know it's OK to come during regular hours too, if you'd like. It's free, the clinic." She looked out at Rory, hiding the sack behind him. "The food too." She took a sip of tea. "So you've found what you needed then?"

"Yes, miss." Tito nodded finally.

"But you've only got just the one, for the both of you?"

"There only was one."

"Was there?" She set the bag of trash at the bottom of the stairs. "Sorry, one minute, they're just here. Don't go anywhere." Aggie set her mug on the railing and hurried up the steps. She immediately came down again carrying a cardboard box with sacks of food in it. "Here, these are better anyway. They're from this morning."

Tito looked hesitantly at the box. "And those ones, they're free too then?" He stepped tentatively over and took two sacks.

"Oh, I almost forgot, in the kitchen are little packs of lemon snaps, if you'd like." Tito didn't move. "Just on the counter there." She nodded.

Tito glanced back at Rory, then went up the steps.

Rory stood at the gate shifting his feet now that their numbers had gone from three to two.

Aggie considered him a moment. "So you're from here in the village?"

Rory nodded. "On the other side."

"So past the wharf road then?"

"No, the other way. Out toward the moors."

"OK, right. Still learning my way around. It's only my second week."

Rory looked past her, relieved to see Tito coming back down the steps.

"There was a cat," said Tito, passing widely around her. "On the counter."

"Was he up there?" she asked. "He was here when I got here." She looked at the boys standing there with their bags, very ready to go. "Alright, well, if you ever need anything? Or your family." Tito cut a glance at Rory, and Aggie studied him with a doctor's eye, taking note of his oversized clothes, the stray look about him. "I'm Aggie Allen, by the way. Did I say that already?"

Tito shifted his pack. "I'm Tito."

"Tito," she repeated.

"And that's Rory."

"Rory. OK. Well, nice to meet you both," she said, noticing the heavy pack on Tito's back. "That's quite a load you're carrying there, Tito."

"It's just my things."

Aggie considered him a moment more, then turned to Rory. "And it was out toward the moors you said? Where you're living?"

"Kettleskaill House," added Tito before Rory could stop him.

"Kettleskaill House," repeated Aggie, as if to remember it.

Tito kept his eyes on her as he slipped the lemon snaps into his pocket.

"Out toward the moors," she mentioned again, as if something had come to mind. "Sorry, you wouldn't by any chance know a Mr. Begbie, would you? I think he's supposed to live out that way?"

"Well, I wouldn't say we know him exactly," said Rory.

"Apparently he doesn't make it into town too very much, yeah?"

"I think never," said Tito.

"Never?"

"He lives a good ways out, miss."

Aggie thought a moment. "It's just that there was a prescription here for him when I arrived. Some months' worth now, actually. I'm thinking someone must've been taking it out to him."

Tito started to answer, but Rory cut him off. "Like I said, we don't know him really, not as such. But, well, we could take it for you."

"No. No, I couldn't ask you to do that. But maybe if you could just tell me the way?"

"Yeah, no." Rory took a step in from the gate. "The moors don't exactly work like that."

* * *

The pall of clouds had turned day into night. A towering thunderhead was building higher on the horizon, like a black galleon rising in the sky. The only light Innes could see came from the high wheelhouse at the aft of the ship. Heaving sets of waves were rolling in, and with each new wave Innes clung tighter to the cargo straps. As the ship rode up and crashed down again, he noticed some of the stacks of crates had begun to shift, their straps going slacker with each new wave. Through the wind Innes now heard muffled voices. He backed deeper in among the crates as the voices came closer, shouting over the storm.

"I told you we never should've sailed during Fhøghartide. Didn't I say that? Didn't I say?"

"The Badger said it had to be today."

"It could've bloody waited. I don't care what the Badger says."

"Oh, you don't, do you?"

"Well, it could've waited."

Rain came in sheets across the deck. Innes saw a pair of boots shuffling nearby, reaching high along the boxes. He backed tighter into the cargo.

"I can't find the end of the strap. Can you see it?"

From where Innes sat, the end of a strap came washing beneath him in the seawater. He quickly grabbed it and fed it back into the outbound wash.

"Here, I've got it," called one of the voices as the strap zipped tight. "It's for Marwick Hall, all this. For Lord Marwick's big to-do he's throwing."

"What big to-do?"

"And how would I know? What, you didn't get your invitation?"

"Yeah, well, we shouldn't be out here. Not on Fhøghartide. It's not right. And on the first night, no less."

"It's the last night you want to stay away from. That's when the tide's go wrong."

Innes could see the man's boots as they started away.

"Oh yeah, well, tell that to the storm we're sailing into."

* * *

The stonechats flitted low among the bushes, taking the hard red berries in their beaks before twitching away. Skara Heath turned purple in the evening half-light, and birds rose up from their cover as they headed home for the evening. Tito followed Rory along the thin path that led out across the moorlands.

Rory glanced back at him. "You didn't need to tell her Kettleskaill."

"What?"

"She works for the county, Tito. Which means the constable, which means the Badger and Frankie Duff. And if someone catches us at Kettleskaill again..."

"She seems nice enough."

"Just do what I tell you."

"OK."

"Unless you'd rather get put in a home off-island somewhere, yeah? Get separated?"

"I said OK."

After a while, the path disappeared, and they continued along a watery seam that cut deep into the heavy sod down the middle of the valley floor. On either side of them the moors stretched away in a long sloping climb toward the empty hills in the distance. Tito stayed close behind Rory. It unnerved him to be passing through a place as vast as this, so he passed the time daydreaming about what might lie sunk in the ground beneath their feet from times long past. Swords left to rust where they fell, a clutch of coins hidden but never returned to, a crucifix cast away in despair, the bones of a midnight traveler suspended down in a bog, lost and alone. He imagined them all floating above the ground, to be collected one by one.

As they came over a low rise, a tumbledown farmhouse lay below them in a shallow vale, its stones listing and disheveled as if slowly being reclaimed by the moors. Two round pigs rooted by the barn. Rory and Tito stopped and knelt in the high grass.

"You think he's in there?" whispered Tito.

"Well, there's smoke coming from the chimney."

Leaving their packs in the tall grass, they hurried to the top of the path.

"Wait here." But as Rory started up the path, he suddenly stopped at the sound of movement. Glancing behind, he saw the pigs burrowing through the tall grass, dragging something in their mouths.

"What have they got?"

"That's our packs!" called Tito as the pigs hurried toward the house. "That's all our food in there." At the front door the pigs rattled the door handle with their snouts until it opened, then disappeared into the house, one-two.

Rory ran to the door and peered in. "Hello?" he called into the darkened house. There was no answer. "Mr. Begbie?" But still no answer came. "I can hear them in there." Slowly he eased the door open and stepped inside.

In the dim light, Rory could see the house was hardly more than a single room. The ceiling was low, and the walls were of whitewashed plaster. A long table sat in the middle of the room. A shelf hung along the wall. From the far end of the room Rory heard a rustling, and as his eyes adjusted to the dark, he could now see the pigs in the corner rooting hard through the packs. Rory hurried over and wedged in between them, pulling the packs free while the pigs gorged on the trampled remains. Seeing that there was nothing left worth saving, Rory turned and started for the door, setting the prescription bottles on the table as he passed. But, as he did, he slowed, for along the wooden shelf sat a line of strange objects laid out in a row. In the low light he could make out what looked to be a jagged fishhook carved from an antler, and a clutch of charred pottery someone was puzzling back together, and a bone sewing needle, its eye packed with dirt. As he reached for the fishhook, the pigs suddenly startled and in a mad rush ran scrambling past him for the door.

Outside, the pigs came pouring past Tito and bolted straight across the yard, disappearing through a hole in the side of the barn, one-two.

"Rory?" whispered Tito into the house. "Rory, what're you doing in there? Why are the pigs running?"

From behind him came the answer.

"Because they know what'll happen to them if we find them in the house," came the voice, rickety and strange.

Tito wheeled around just as Rory appeared at the door.

The man tilted his head and looked past the boys into his house. "So is that it then, or will something else be coming outta there?"

The boys stared at him, unable to speak. He had a patchy gray beard, and his cheeks were hollow and toothless. He was wire thin and crooked. In one hand he held a clutch of wild turnips and in the other a dead partridge, its head lolling down. Out in the field behind him stood a massive gray mule, quietly grazing, still harnessed to its cart.

They all stood a moment, looking at each other.

Suddenly Tito straightened up, and a rush of words came pouring out. "Miss Aggie Allen, the new doctor at the clinic, had pills for you and she didn't know how to get them out to you so we told her we'd deliver them, also she had food for you but your pigs took it and ours too. They ran inside the house there and we knocked but no one answered and then my brother went in after them but—" Tito stopped.

Mr. Begbie considered the boys a moment. "Pigs are like that," he said finally. "One of them tried to eat my foot the other week. I was sleeping, but I think he figured I was dead."

He paused as if recollecting it. "Hadn't even been asleep too very long either." His eyes faded, and he began holding a silent conversation with himself.

"Well, we should be going." Rory shot a glance at Tito, and as Mr. Begbie continued muttering to himself, they started quickly up the path.

Mr. Begbie's eyes came back into focus. "Isn't it you two that live at Kettleskaill? There with Mrs. Renfro?"

Rory kept Tito moving up the path. "Just leave it."

When they reached the tall grass, Mr. Begbie called again. "It's Mrs. Renfro usually walks out our pills. She been busy, has she?" Tito stopped and looked back at Mr. Begbie standing at the front door, whose eyes were fading again in remembrance. "Feel like she was teaching one of you to whistle maybe?"

Tito thought to answer as the pigs poked their heads warily out of the barn.

"Can you tell me," asked Mr. Begbie, squinting out, "are we getting near to Fhøghartide?"

"It starts tonight," Tito called.

"Does it just?" Mr. Begbie nodded. "Felt like winter was coming." He looked up again. "Do you think you might could do something for us?"

"What kind of something?" asked Tito before Rory could stop him.

Mr. Begbie held up a finger, nodding as he shuffled into the house.

Rory held up his hands to Tito in annoyance.

"Well what?" Tito asked. "He knew Mrs. Renfro." He looked toward the open door. "Are we supposed to follow him in, do you think?"

In the house Rory and Tito stood just inside the front door. Mr. Begbie flopped the bloody partridge into the stone sink and laid the turnips on the counter. As they waited, Rory's eyes drifted to the line of objects sitting along the shelf behind him.

"We found all that," said Mr. Begbie over his shoulder. "My brothers and me. It's all from here on the island. Every bit of it."

"So you've got brothers then, have you?" asked Rory, looking around for any sign of them.

"Yep. Two of us are under the ground now. Me still above it. We were none, then one, then two, then three. Then two, now one. Soon none." He casually quick-twisted the head off the partridge. "And it's Fhøghartide starting tonight you said?" Mr. Begbie set the partridge on the counter. "And me with not one garlic put up. Not a single fish put up." He began stripping the leaves off the turnips.

"So you said you had a favor?" asked Rory.

"Oh. Right." Mr. Begbie nodded. "Just a minute, just a minute." He turned and went out the narrow door at the back of the kitchen. In the twilight they could see him through the window, stooping at the corner of a small stone shed.

Returning to the kitchen, Mr. Begbie laid a handful of little wildflowers on the counter, their petals peeking through tiny winter buds. As he caught his breath, he rummaged through the kitchen drawers, muttering until he found what he was after.

"You know what this is?" he asked, holding a small object of blackened metal in his hand.

"It's a Fhøghar lantern," answered Rory.

"That's right. And you know how it works?"

Rory nodded.

"OK then." Mr. Begbie handed Rory the lantern and two candle stubs. "Light the lantern from the town fires. That's tonight, yeah?"

"Yeah, and we should be getting there."

"Right. Then light those candles on my brothers' headstones, if you would. They're in the churchyard there, near Kettleskaill. You know the one?"

"We know it."

"They'll be the two small headstones along the back row. Marked *Begbie*. I'd do it myself, but I can't make it anymore." He chewed the place where his teeth would have been. "You can keep that, if you like. When you're done." Mr. Begbie nodded at the lantern. "Might come in useful sometime. Especially during Fhøghartide, eh? When the Little People are afoot? Closer even than usual." He looked at them earnestly now. "And it's fast-moving mists you'll want to watch out for. Or sudden darkenings in the sky. That's where they'll be, the Little People." Remembering the flowers, he handed them to Tito. "To nice up the graveside a bit. They're moonflowers. I pull them up because my mule eats them. They're poisonous."

Tito held the flowers loosely.

From outside came the wheezing bray of a mule. Mr. Begbie looked through the door at the giant mule staring in from the field. "Suppertime."

As the boys started up the path, the big mule, cart and all, rushed past them like a giant dog hurrying to meet Mr. Begbie shuffling across the yard.

"Alright, Eustice, alright."

From the edge of the moors, Tito looked back. In the fading light of evening, he could hear Mr. Begbie speaking softly to the mule as the two walked side by side to the barn.

* * *

High among the towering clouds, silent pulses of lightning flashed in the storm's upper reaches. Endless sprays of seawater blasted over the gunnels and across the deck, soaking Innes to the skin. Next to him, a crate bound for Marwick Hall sat wrenched open at the corner. Down within it remained eleven unopened bottles. Between waves Innes took quick sips from the twelfth to calm his nerves and fortify himself against the cold.

The whiskey was good and went down easy. At first it warmed him, but soon the wind and water began to leach from him whatever warmth remained. An iron coldness settled into his bones, and a hard shivering took hold of him and would not let go. The light in the pilot house began to flicker, then went out.

As the night passed in slow minutes, the temperature continued to drop and the wind came in harder. Innes shook uncontrollably from the cold, and his thoughts grew dark, turning in on themselves as the night wore on. He stared out into the darkness, keeping watch for the black mass of Skara Skaill whenever it should appear. It had been four years since he'd seen it last. For a fleeting moment, a gap appeared in the storm, and through it Innes saw a smudge of light hanging high in the night sky. Only the direction of its tail gave away the comet's heading. Pointing the way to Skara Skaill. Innes took a pull from the bottle, looking up as the swiftly moving clouds closed black over the comet.

"And why would I expect any different?"

As if by way of an answer, the boat began to slip steadily downward, riding deeper into a valley of black water. The water on the deck rushed into the hollow where Innes sat, pooling low around him. He quickly drew the soaked letter from his pants pocket and moved it to a higher spot in his coat. As he thought to check his other pockets, he suddenly saw his wallet floating past. He lunged for it, but it washed away out onto the deck. As the boat began its upward climb out of the trough, Innes struggled to his feet, now feeling the whiskey. Holding on to the cargo straps, he got to his feet, then, glancing quickly at the darkened wheelhouse, he staggered out onto the open deck. The wind blasted him head-on, and as the bow rode higher still, the wallet swept past him against the railing before finally rushing straight through a drain hole and disappearing over the side. Innes ran to the railing. Out in the empty blackness he at first saw nothing, but slowly his eyes began to sense a dark mass swelling beyond the bow as a black mountain of water began lifting the boat upward. As the wave's summit rolled beneath the hull, the boat hung suspended for the briefest moment in the void. And as it began its free fall into the empty blackness, Innes spun from the railing and dove toward his hole in the cargo. The iron hull impacted the icy water like concrete, hammering Innes's head down onto the ship's metal deck, glass shattering all around him, as everything went black.

Innes's eyes slowly opened. The deck was hard and cold against his cheek, and through the dull heaviness he noticed himself breathing. Slowly he sat up. He gently touched the side of his head. Beneath him the boat lifted and fell, lifted and fell. Heavy shards of thick bottle glass lay all around him. Seeing the glass, Innes raised his hands, inspecting them. They were corpse white, but untouched. Then he stopped. For at his side, in the slurry of shattered glass and seawater, bloomed red clouds of billowing blood.

IV

RORY CARRIED THE LITTLE lantern through the dark, a tiny flame burning within it. As he passed through the village, the faint sound of a dog barking carried in on the wind. Tito walked behind, looking up at the lit windows of the row houses, a low murmur of voices coming from somewhere within.

A radio playing low.

The sound of dishes being washed and put away.

Woodsmoke rising from the clay chimneys.

He thought of Mrs. Renfro, closing down the house for the night, he and Rory tucked away high up in their room.

Rory waited, watching him, and as Tito came alongside, they continued on together, leaving the sounds of the village behind.

At the low wall, they stared into the churchyard, the blackness of the endless moors at their backs. Out on the hillside beyond the village, the Fhøghartide fires died away as specks of lantern light were being carried homeward along the paths toward the village.

Tito looked warily over the wall. The headstones shone silver in the darkness. “Check if the lantern went out,” he said. “Then we couldn’t do it.”

Rory held up the lantern. Down within it the little candle burned bright.

Dropping down into the back of the churchyard, the boys began moving row by row. Etched on the stones, birthdates and deathdates rolled further back in time as the gravestones began listing over like old teeth, crooked and mossy, sinking into the earth until finally only stumps and corners remained above ground. Up ahead, newer rows of headstones stood straight and orderly in the dark. Rory began moving down the rows, the lantern in front of him.

“Begbie,” he said finally, stopping at two simple stones. He set his pack down while Tito stood facing the headstones. “Tito, you’re not supposed to stand on top of them like that.”

Tito quickly stepped around.

“Come on, let’s just do it and go. Here, cup your hands.” Rory lit the candles using the flame from the lantern, then lowered each one into a little windbreak of rocks stacked at the base of the stones. Tito laid the clutches of wildflowers next to them. As they stood watching the candles burning within the rocks, Tito looked beyond the headstones to a row behind. A name was etched darkly in the moonlight.

Mrs. Garnet Brown Renfro

“Should we light one for her, do you think?”

Rory said nothing for a moment. “She didn’t put any stock in all that.” He turned away and began searching out in the dark for his pack, his face hidden from view. “And we only brought two candles anyway, so.” He found his pack and shouldered it.

"But it doesn't seem right though. To just walk off. What with us being right here." Tito turned again to the grave. "Maybe we should take a couple of flowers from those other two? What do you think, Rory? You think we should do that?"

"I don't know, Tito. If you want, I suppose."

"But don't you think we should though?"

"Well, and what do I know about it, Tito?"

Tito looked back at him standing there in the darkness, coming no closer. Rory adjusted his coat. "Could we just go, please?" came his voice. Then, softening a little. "There's weather coming."

Stepping through the tall grass, and remembering to stand off to one side, Tito stooped down and laid two flowers at Mrs. Renfro's headstone. He stood there quietly a moment, then turned and walked back to where he knew Rory was waiting for him in the dark.

The chalky path to Kettleskaill stretched ahead of them, bone white in the blackness. Moving quietly along the stone wall separating the two broad fields, Rory suddenly stopped.

"What is that?" whispered Tito.

Out in the distance, radiant white, sat a luminous shape within the ruins of Skarahollow Chapel. "Isn't that where the tree's fallen?" They stared out at what they could now see was a large tent glowing bright in the blackness. "What's that doing there do you think?"

"I don't know." Rory began to step over the wall. "Maybe we should have a closer look. Might be something we could make use of in there."

"Like what?"

"What do you mean, like what? Like pretty much anything, Tito."

The ground was frozen and cloddy beneath their feet as they crossed the open field. The glowing tent sat shuddering in the wind, and the yew tree lay in freshly cut pieces. The light from the tent moved strangely across the ruins of Skarahollow Chapel. Rory listened for a moment, then started forward.

He parted the flap and peered in. A cable that had been laid from the far road snaked beneath the tent and lit a single bare bulb hanging inside. Seeing no one, Rory slipped through.

The bulb swayed slightly as the canvas walls sucked and billowed from the wind outside. Stacks of gear were piled in the corner. Picks and shovels, trunks and cases, a few large buckets, a pile of folded tarps. In the very center of the tent was a giant hole in the earth, wrenched open by the tree's massive roots, and angling down through it a ladder disappeared into the blackness below.

They sidled over to it. "What is that, do you think?" whispered Tito.

They leaned over the hole a moment, trying to see down in, then Rory turned back to the gear. As they rummaged through, Tito found a canvas roll tied with a cord. He worked open the knot. Inside were pencils and tools and assorted other items.

Rory looked over. "Take the batteries. And the pencils. Actually, just take all that." He tried the lock on a small trunk, but as he continued searching, he found himself repeatedly glancing over his shoulder at the hole in the ground.

He stepped over to the ladder. Tito came alongside and stared down into the perfect darkness. "Is it deep, do you think?"

"Not too." Rory squatted down to get a better view.

"Can you see the bottom?"

"It's too dark."

"Then how do you know it's not deep?"

Rory glanced at him. "You do realize the ladder's touching the bottom, Tito?"

"Yeah. Well," Tito muttered to himself. "Maybe it's a really tall ladder." He could feel a draft of cold air rising up out of the blackness. "Come on, Rory. Let's just go."

Rory walked over and unhooked the cord from the tent pole. Holding on to the cord, he slowly lowered the bulb down into the hole as layers of torn roots, then soil, then rocks became illuminated. But as the circle of light continued deeper down, something odd began to appear. A shaft of tightly fitted stones. Then from out of the void a stone floor came into view, and reaching the bottom, the bulb clinked and gently laid over.

Rory leaned in as far as he could. "Looks as if it opens out down there." He gave the ladder a little shake.

"Don't even think it, Rory."

"Well, they're not digging down there for no reason, Tito."

"And what if someone comes, while you're in there?"

"No one's coming out here this time of night."

"We did."

Rory paused. "Fine. You stay up here and keep watch. You hear anything, just whistle and I'll come up."

"Yeah, I don't really have it quite yet, a proper whistle."

"Alright, well, just do a warning call then."

Tito considered that. "What kind of warning call were you thinking?"

"I don't know, Tito, whatever you want."

"I could do an owl, I suppose. I can do an OK one."

"Fine, you see anything, just do the owl and I'll come up."

"Straight away?"

"Straight away."

"See, you say that."

"Straight away, Tito."

Rory stepped out onto the ladder and began lowering himself down. As he reached the bottom, Tito could see him guide the bulb around in a slow circle.

"Definitely opens out a bit," Rory called up. And before Tito could say a word otherwise, Rory began moving out of sight, the light dimming away behind him.

Beneath the ground, the sounds from above faded in the heavy stillness. Rory stepped through the low shaft. As he inched through the hollow, the bulb cast a swinging light, filling the shaft with movement and shadow. From floor to ceiling, tightly fitted stones arched over his head. Etched into the walls all around were whirling circular patterns, continuously feeding from one into the next. Farther down, as the shaft narrowed, a Celtic cross was painted thickly over the etchings in the wall, its pigment almost entirely flaked away. Its central nimbus circle incorporated the swirled etchings wherever it could. Up ahead, Rory could see that the passage ended in a heap of rubble. Above him the faint boom of thunder came rumbling through the ground. He held the bulb forward, his breathing the only sound within the deadened void. Suddenly from behind him came the scratch of a pebble, and movement, and then someone was in the shaft with him, and wheeling around Rory saw Tito standing there looking at him.

"Bloody hell, Tito!" he said, his heart banging in his chest.

"Well, you walked off with the light," said Tito, chewing, his mouth full.

"Are you eating something?"

"Oatcakes. I found them up in the stuff there." He held out the box. "You want one?"

"No, I don't want one," said Rory, then he took one anyway.

Tito looked around. "What was this place, do you think?"

"I don't know. The chapel cellar maybe." From above them, the deep rumble of thunder came again, pounding through the ground as a shower of sand sifted around them. Tito instantly turned and went for the ladder, but as Rory raised the light, a veil of dust hung like powder in the air, illuminating the bulb like a halo. The dust hung motionless a moment, then slowly began to move, floating down the passage, picking up speed before finally sucking away through the rubble at the blocked end of the shaft.

"Come on, Rory," called Tito, already halfway up the ladder. But Rory and the light were heading away again down the shaft.

In the bare light, Rory could see that the rubble had slumped lower, revealing a gap at the top of an arched opening. He tried to peer in, but the light's cord reached no farther. Carefully he set the bulb down onto the rubble and began climbing through.

"Oh, what are we doing, Rory," called Tito, scrambling back down the ladder.

The lower chamber was cold and almost entirely caved in. Above them, the remaining ceiling rose to a point in the center, like a stone beehive. The walls were curved, and on one side a dark hollow was built into the stone. Rory stepped over to it and looked in. As he did, another boom of thunder came rumbling through the ground, and suddenly the bulb dimmed, then sizzled, then popped. Everything went black.

"Rory?" called Tito, reaching blindly into the blackness. "Rory?!"

"I'm here, Tito," came Rory's voice.

Tito swept his arms in front of him until he fell into Rory.

"Alright, just hold on to me." But as Rory began inching slowly forward, a cold pocket of air settled over them.

"Why've we stopped?" asked Tito, still clutching blindly at Rory in the blackness.

"I'm just a little turned around is all. And you climbing on me like that isn't helping things any. Would you just—OK Tito that was my eye."

"Well, I can't see anything."

"And what is that you're banging me with?" Rory paused. "Tito? By any chance would that be the lantern you've got there?"

"The lantern? Yeah, why?"

Rory sighed. A moment later a match snapped to life. Tito raised the lantern, and as one flame became two, the little lantern lit their faces golden in the blackness. Rory held up the light, and there, dead ahead, was the way out.

"And to think it was right there all along," said Tito. But as he started to go, Rory turned again to the hollow in the wall. "Rory?"

"Just while we're here." Rory stepped to the little hollow and raised the lantern. Inside were shelves carved straight into the stone wall. He moved the lantern close. On the top shelf were several tufts of fur and the desiccated remains of a small animal. Next to it, little twists of leather lay in a field of mouse droppings. Rory slowly lowered the lantern down, passing empty shelves. But as the light fell across the bottom shelf, a scattering of pottery shards came into view, and in among them was a little figure, no bigger than a chess piece, tipped over on its side. He picked it up. It was a bone carving of an elk. Its tiny eyes were scored black. The light from the lantern flickered across the carving, animating the elk's shadow against the wall. Rory bent to the shelf once more, and in the very back lay a flat square of thickly folded leather, darkened and hardened with age. As Tito squeezed in beside him, another rumbling of thunder sent dust showering down around them, and as the lantern's flame began to falter and gutter out, they turned and hurried for the ladder.

Out in the open air, the storm had come in hard off the sea. The boys leaned across the field and up the climbing path. Sheets of cold rain swept over them as the dark mass of Kettleskaill House sat high above them on the hillside.

V

THE SKARA SKAILL HARBOR bell gonged softly in the morning mist. The storm had passed during the night, leaving behind a hard winter chill. Two men climbed down from the wheelhouse while another hurried along the wharf tying off the boat. In the middle of the boatyard sat a little warming shack, smoke rising from its chimney. The door swung open, and a few men came sleepily out, looking up at the boat.

"You get caught out in it then, did you?" called one of the men, scratching his belly.

"I told him we shouldn't make the crossing during Fhøghartide. Didn't I tell him?"

"How about you get up here and give us a hand before the Badger comes walking up out of nowhere. You know how he does." The two men dropped down from the wheelhouse ladder as the others came up the gangway. "He said he wants all this up at the Marwick Hall as soon as we tie up. Where's Frankie?"

"I don't know. The Badger has him and Munro off doing something."

The two men led the others along the foredeck, checking the cargo after the storm.

"Looks like everything came through alright." But as they came around the septic tank, they stopped at Innes's hollow in the cargo.

"What the hell's this?" All around the deck, chunks of shattered glass were everywhere. Only a few bottles within the opened wooden crate remained unbroken. And there, among the glass and seawater, was half a shoe print smeared across a dark stain of blood.

"Somebody'd better go and find the Badger. And it's sure as hell not gonna be me."

* * *

Tito slipped quietly out of bed. Gray dawn came slowly through the window. Making sure Rory was still asleep, he padded across the room in his underwear to a sink that no longer worked.

"Don't pee in the sink, Tito," muttered Rory, shifting in bed.

Tito stopped. "I wasn't," he lied.

Balled up on the floor were his clothes from the night before, still wet from the rain.

Out the door and down the hall, Tito drew open the double doors of a large wardrobe crammed with cast-off clothes. He pulled out a pair of dark gray trousers that were too big and a sweater that was too small. He pulled them on, cinched up his belt, and wedged his feet into his shoes.

Outside, the cold morning air was damp on his face. Last night's rain had stopped, and a mist settled heavily in the fields below. Beneath the eaves, a bowl of food he had left for Sir Winston sat untouched. At the corner of the house, Tito peed sleepily in the dirt, then crossed the yard, practicing a thin, airy whistle as he went.

At the chicken coop, Honey pecked around in the gravel while Tito went nest to nest, feeling beneath the straw. Nothing. At the back of the coop, he saw a frenzy of little stoat prints and a broken eggshell. He followed the prints out of the coop and across the dirt yard. Then something caught his eye. Lights. Barely visible out in the fog. He stopped at the low gate, and looking out at the far fields, he could see headlights and a red roof light shining faintly in the gloom at Skarahollow Chapel. As he drifted forward, the lights suddenly blinked off, and at the bottom of the hill, two dark figures were slowly making their way up the path.

* * *

"Rory. Rory, wake up. There's men coming up the path."

Rory opened one eye. "What?" He squinted up at Tito. "Can you see who?"

"I don't know. But the constable's parked down in the field."

Rory swept off his blanket. "Are you sure?" Hurrying to the window, he saw two hulking figures in flat caps and dark jackets coming through the gate. He drew back from the window.

"Is it the Duffs?" whispered Tito.

Rory put his finger to his lips and nodded. After a moment they could hear the deep murmur of men's voices below the window. They stared at each other, listening. Then the silence was shattered as the boards across the front door began wrenching loose.

Rory turned to Tito. "Get your pack."

No sooner had Rory started pulling on his clothes than Tito was standing in front of him again, pack on his shoulder.

They hurried to the bedroom door, but as they started down the hall, they heard the sudden blast of the front door being kicked in and movement within the house below. At the end of the hall, they eased open a window and climbed through. Out on the flat roof, Rory inched to the edge and looked down. At the corner of the house he could see the broad back of Frankie Duff's brother Munro looking in the downstairs windows. As Munro disappeared around back, Rory waved Tito out.

Dangling their packs, Rory released them into the bushes, then slid down the post, with Tito right behind. Grabbing up their packs, they hurried to the front corner of the house. Rory peered around, then looked Tito in the face. "OK. Stay with me, yeah? Right with me."

Tito nodded, and after leaning around for one last look, they burst from the corner and started across the yard.

Tito's pack jerked him back and forth as he ran through the gate and down the slope, his legs flying pell-mell down the path. Reaching the bottom, he could see Rory ahead running through the bands of the mist until finally Rory came to a stop.

Tito came alongside him. "Do you hear them?" he whispered.

Rory shook his head. As they stood listening into the silence, the sky suddenly opened up, and a wall of cold rain began to hiss down.

"What do we do now?"

Rory kept his eyes fixed on the direction they had come. Then, turning to the open moors, he squinted out through the rain.

As Tito hurried along, the only thing visible in the rain was the circle at his feet. The thin moor path gradually disappeared, giving way to moss and cloudberry and brambles. After some time, the land began to rise slowly beneath them. Just ahead, Tito could see a broad field slowly come into view. Across it, boulders were scattered as if tossed there by giants. The mist divided itself as it moved its way among the rocks. Rory paused, but seeing no way around, he started slowly forward, stepping in through the shoulder-high rocks. All around, tight knots of wildflowers were tucked in the stoney ground, vibrating low in the wind. As the rain came heavier, Rory stopped.

Tito dropped his pack to the ground. "Where are we?" His arms, still feeling the phantom weight of the pack, rose up on their own.

Rory climbed to a higher spot to get his bearings. The cold wind battered him. Looking back, he saw Tito sitting down among the rocks, his coat over his head, soaked to the skin. "We need to get out of this weather," he called.

But then from somewhere out in the rain came a strange sound carrying in on the wind. Tito hurried to where Rory stood. "What is that?" he whispered. The sound came again, low at first, then building into a long, piercing cry.

Something was slowly approaching out of the gloom. They stood perfectly still, and as the fog slowly thinned away, they saw it. A bull elk, moving evenly through the rain, its shoulders as tall as a man.

"Stay still," breathed Rory, his eyes straight ahead as the massive elk clambered up the rocks. It stood there a moment, resetting its hooves, rain dripping from its antlers, its ears lifted to catch whatever sounds might come in on the wind. After a long moment, it turned and started slowly away, before vanishing again into the mist.

Rory drifted forward in the direction the elk had gone. All around him, gorse bushes began appearing, thorny and low. He stopped. Just ahead, emerging from the murk, was a small stone hut built directly into the base of a ridge, its opening just tall enough for a man to stoop inside. Across its rock face, moss and lichen had grown so thick that hut and hill were indistinguishable from one another. Rory glanced back at Tito, then stepped to the opening.

"Looks dry enough," he called back.

"What, you're not thinking in there?" Tito stood shivering in the rain.

"Tito, we need to get out of this weather."

"Yeah, well, I'll not be going in there."

"And why not?"

"You know why not."

"Oh, would you stop it. All that talk about these places is just talk."

"Well, you can believe what you want. I'll not be going in there."

"Are you telling me you'd rather just stay out here in the rain?"

"Yes, that's exactly what I'm telling you. I'd rather stay out here in the rain, yes I would."

But from somewhere still nearby, the high bugle of the elk came again, keening out of the rain and echoing off the ridge above them. Tito turned and stared in the direction the sound had come.

"Alright then." Rory shrugged. "Suit yourself." And stepping to the opening, he looked in once more, then disappeared inside.

* * *

In his foul-weather gear, Constable Tulloch, burly and round-headed, stood beneath the tent staring out through the rain, waiting. He took off his hat, knocked the water from it, then fitted it back on his head. In the distance, he watched as the Duff brothers slowly made their way down the path from Kettleskaill House, crossed the field, and ducked in out of the rain.

"Well? What'd you find?"

Frankie, the larger of the two brothers, ignored the question entirely. Keeping a dismissive eye on the constable, he slid out a cigarette and cupped it in his giant fist against the wind. He had a head like an anvil and a roll of muscles at the base of his skull like a pack of franks. He was built for violence. As Frankie shook out the match, a white Rover turned off the dirt road at the high end of the field.

"It's the Badger," said Munro, a half head shorter but a full foot broader-backed than Frankie.

"Well, now." Frankie turned to the constable. "I suppose I'll just tell him myself then, won't I?"

The Rover moved slowly across the muddy two-track and came to a stop. *Marwick Hall* was stenciled in black letters on the driver-side door. The Badger stepped into the rain and strode quickly across to the tent. He was lean, and his face was mallet-flat. One of his ears was crumpled and cauliflowered. His pants were belted tight, and he wore a well-worn macintosh over his clothes. He glanced around the tent, bantam-sharp, taking it all in.

"So what all was taken?" There was something of the street in his voice.

"Nothing," said the constable, turning to the gear and lock boxes.

The Badger nodded to the Duffs for a cigarette. Munro quickly handed him one. Lighting it, the Badger stepped over to the cord that had been hauled up out of the hole. He toed the charred bulb lying on the ground.

"Me and Munro had a walk around," said Frankie. "Those two scroungers were squatting at the house up top there. But they'd run off."

"Found these though." Munro held out the little canvas roll of tools.

The Badger glanced at the constable. "Nothing was taken, eh?"

At the ladder, one of the crew climbed up through the hole and poured a bucket of rubble out onto the ground. The Badger turned to the constable. "Didn't I say no one was to go down in until I'd seen the cave-in? Didn't I say that?"

"Oy. You watch your tone. I'm not one of your bloody crew."

"It's Lord Marwick who'll be wanting to know." The Badger eyed the constable as he took a long pull from his cigarette. "And it's gonna be me who has to tell him." The Badger walked over to the hole in the ground, and as the man hurried off the ladder, the Badger started down in, staring at the constable as he went. "I'd ask what else was taken if I thought I'd get a straight answer."

Underground, the Badger stood in the silence. The air was heavy with the smell of damp earth. Moving down the shaft, he passed the painted cross on the wall, then stopped at the opening in the rubble. He shone his flashlight into the lower chamber, then clambered in.

Sweeping his light around the room, he lingered on the tightly fitted stonework of the walls and ceiling. Around the slope of rubble, he came to the hollow nook built into the wall, shining his light across its empty shelves. Backing out again, he swung his light along the top of the rubble heap. At the very back of the chamber, barely visible above the rubble, his light fell upon the edge of a stone embedded in the top of the wall. He held his beam on it. It was larger and whiter and more finely worked than the others. Climbing up the pile, he wedged himself into the space where the rubble met the slant of the ceiling. When he could go no farther, he stretched his arm forward and began raking the debris away. As the stone came more fully into view, he saw that something was etched upon it. He brought his flashlight in close. Little puffs of dust disturbed by his breath rose into the beam of light as he suddenly stopped, staring in silence at the markings carved thereon: three interlocking circles made from a single continuous line.

* * *

Tito sat inside the stone hut, quietly staring out at the rain. The clouds were dark, and he could no longer tell if it was afternoon or night. After a long while he turned to Rory.

"What're we gonna do, Rory?"

Tito waited for an answer.

Rory glanced at him, then looked back into the hut where it opened out into a small cave.

"I'll see if there's something we can't burn back there."

From his pack, Tito took out a flashlight and the batteries he had stolen from the tent. He slid in the batteries, then pounded the butt end of the flashlight until it came on.

"You think Sir Winston will be alright?" he asked, shining the flashlight for Rory at the back of the cave.

"I think he's the last one you need to worry about. And save those batteries, I can see well enough."

"Well, don't you think he'll wonder where we've gone to?" Tito pounded the flashlight until it went off again.

"I really don't think dogs do a lot of wondering. Food—not food. That's pretty much it." Rory stopped in the middle of the cave. In the center of the floor was a shallow fire pit scratched into the ground. Directly above it, the ceiling was charred black. A pile of loose sticks and broken wood that had been something once lay along the back wall. A half dozen peat bricks, dusty and dry, were scattered nearby. In the far corner, a mound of old mussel shells was mixed in with broken shards of pottery. And on the wall above them, a cluster of odd swirls and scratchings were etched into the stone.

"What's that you're looking at?" called Tito.

"Nothing." Rory hurriedly gathered up the wood as the sound of the rain outside came to him echoey and strange.

Rory arranged some twigs in the fire pit and lit them. Carefully he added more twigs, then sticks, then broken pieces of wood, until finally the fire's heat and light filled the cave. But as the fire grew, the smoke began slowly pooling at the top of the cave. They sat watching as it spread deeper and wider across the ceiling until it began to slip through an unseen crack in the rock, drawn out from somewhere deep in the earthen hillside above them.

Rory set a can of beans from his pack down into the coals. In the firelight, Tito could now clearly see the discarded mussel shells and the strange wall carvings at the back cave.

"Rory."

"Just don't say it, Tito. It's a roof over our heads, alright?"

Tito stared at the back of the cave. "So how long until we can go home, Rory? To Kettleskaill?"

"I don't know. Until they're done digging down at the chapel, I guess."

"And you're sure that was the Duffs then?"

Rory nodded. "Which means the Badger."

Tito sat thinking about that for a moment, then he opened his pack and began nervously organizing and reorganizing his things down inside it.

They ate in silence as the rain fell outside. When they were done, Rory took from his pocket the little carved elk he had found beneath the chapel ruins. It was pitted with age, and in the firelight, he could see the tiny clefts carved into its hooves and the delicate notches at its nose.

Tito leaned close. "Better than a bodkin." He pulled out the hardened leather pouch from his pack. "What do you think it is anyway?"

"I think like a purse maybe."

"What, like a lady's purse?"

"No, that's just what they called them."

Tito studied the rectangular fold of leather. "So you get the elk and I get a purse?"

"Well, I don't know, maybe there's something in it?"

Tito opened the stiff leather flap. "Empty." The inside of the purse was decorated in faded pigments of gold and purple and blue.

Through the seam in the roof, Tito watched warily as the smoke puffed back in a moment like a dragon exhaling, before quickly sucking away again.

"And wouldn't it just have to be during Fhøghartide no less."

"Yeah, well, if the Little People come, you'll just have to budge over."

"Oh, very funny." Tito fell silent a long moment. "Rory. What're we gonna do?"

Rory started to answer, then said nothing.

"But we'll be home by Christmas though, right?"

"I don't know, Tito. Just eat your beans."

Rory prepared a place for them to sleep. As the fire settled down and the rain fell steadily outside, Tito thought of Kettleskaill, and of his bed, and of the woodstove glowing in the middle of their room, and of the man on the radio reading quietly from a book, and of Sir Winston, and Honey, and whether she had found some bugs to eat, and...

It was deep in the night when Rory opened his eyes. Tito's moon-white face lay an inch from his own, steadily breathing. The fire had died all the way down, and the cave had gone cold. Rory placed a stick of wood onto the last of the coals and watched sleepily as the little fire flickered back to life. Wrapping his blanket around him, he stepped to the cave opening, the ground cold beneath his feet. Outside, the rain had cleared, and the moon was a white hole punched in the blackness. Its stark light shone down upon the field of stones, and the open moors, and the hills beyond, all moonlit silver like a stage awaiting its play. Rory could see the comet hanging fixed in the night sky, its tail jetting away, motionless, behind. As quickly as they'd gone, the dark clouds closed again, and a bitter rain came hissing across the plain. Suddenly Rory stopped cold. Standing out in the rain was the dark silhouette of a man looking in toward the cave.

Rory scrambled out of view, his heart hammering in his chest. As Tito sat up blinking, Rory covered Tito's mouth with one hand and shoveled handfuls of dirt on the fire with the other.

"There's someone out there," he whispered, slowly taking his hand from Tito's mouth. Rory peered around the corner again, and there, exactly as before, was the dark figure, standing perfectly still.

"Is it the Duffs?" whispered Tito.

"I don't know. There's only one."

Tito thought a moment. "He's not—well, he's not little, is he?"

"Oh, would you stop that? He's normal sized." Rory looked around again, but as the figure tried to take a step forward, his leg buckled oddly. Dropping to one knee, the man slumped backward, then collapsed to the ground. Still.

"Is he dead?" asked Tito.

Rory considered the man a moment. "Drunk maybe."

"Do you think we should go out and check him?"

"We don't know who that is, Tito."

"Well, we can't just leave him like that."

Rory looked out at the man lying in the rain. "Alright. Fine. But you stay here."

Tito nodded, then scrambled to the back of the cave, quickly returning with a heavy stick. "In case we don't know him." He handed it to Rory.

Rory stepped out into the rain. As he came nearer, he could see the man's chest rising and falling beneath his clothes. On the ground next to him was a little duffel bag lying in the mud. Rory looked back at Tito.

"He's breathing. And not a Duff." Rory took a half step closer. "Hello?" The man didn't move. "Hello? Can you hear me?"

Tito hurried out into the rain and bunched in close behind Rory. The man's soaked clothes clung tightly to him.

"He's shivering, see?" Rory said. "I think he's feverish."

The man's brown hair was shaggy and longish and flat across his forehead from the rain. He had a thin beard, and his skin was stone pale. His lips were red with fever.

"What's that smell?" asked Tito.

"He's got sick all over him." Rory studied the man a little closer, the rain pouring heavily over his face.

"Should we get him inside?"

Rory assessed the distance. "He's too big to carry. We should at least try and sit him up."

Moving closer, the boys each took a sleeve of the man's coat, and as they pulled him to a seated position, a clap of thunder crashed high across the ridge. The man's eyes flickered. "Sir. Can you hear me? Can you stand up?" shouted Rory, but the man only stared blankly.

"What day is it?" asked Tito. "Do you know your name?" The sky flashed white, and thunder again boomed across the valley.

The man looked up at them a moment. "Innes," he said finally at a whisper.

"Do you think you can stand?"

From somewhere deep within his fever, Innes bent one knee. They could feel his hands close around their arms, and with all they had they hoisted him to his feet.

"Step," called Tito. Innes took one heavy step forward. "Step again," he shouted. Innes took another step. "And again." And one shaky step at a time, they led Innes across the rocky ground into the opening of the hut, then carefully laid him down by the wall.

"I'll get his pack," said Tito, running out into the rain and back again, setting Innes's belongings by the fire. Innes's eyes had already closed again. His breathing was thin, and he was shivering hard. The boys knelt by the fire and stared at the stranger. Outside a moment ago. Inside with them now. Tito grabbed up a blanket, and from a little distance, he carefully draped it over Innes and backed away while Rory began stoking the fire as hot and as high as he could make it.

* * *

The cave was warm and dry, and the fire had settled low. The boys lay propped against their packs, staring at Innes, studying him as he slept.

"Maybe he's a hermit?" whispered Tito. "Maybe this is his hut we're in?"

"He doesn't really look like a hermit," said Rory.

Tito thought a moment. "Well, maybe he's an escaped convict? You don't think he could be that, do you, Rory? An escaped convict?"

"There's no prison on these islands, Tito."

"How do you know that? We've never been to any islands other than this one."

After some time, the fire dimmed lower still, and Tito's eyes began to grow heavy.

"You can go back to sleep if you want. I'll keep watch."

"Watch?" Tito looked at Rory. "What, you mean for outside or for in here?"

"Well, for both now, I guess," said Rory, and glancing over, Tito saw that Rory still had the stick he'd given him from before, tight at his side.

VI

Marwick Hall. Outside Skara Skaill Village, Northern Islands.

THE WARM POLISH OF the library's wooden walls shone golden in the firelight. A brass firewood bin flickered near the hearth. In the middle of the great room, at a desk of blond wood, sat Lord Marwick, the fifteenth Earl of Skara Skaill, bent to his work. The classic Marwick skull shone bare in the light of the desk lamp. His skin was blotched with veiny blooms, his lips thin and bloodless. His jaw worked with obsessive purpose as he ran his finger along the page. Across his desk were scattered piles of old sketches and folders and tattered charts covered with notations and markings. At Lord Marwick's right hand sat an open folder of new photographs marked *Skarahollow Chapel Site*. A broken yew tree lay on its side—a hole torn in the earth—the murky image of a chamber beneath the ground. He moved one of the new photos slowly across the desk, comparing it carefully to a collection of old drawings and sketches lit brightly beneath the lamp, each depicting a crude version of the same symbol—three conjoined circles made from a single continuous line. Placing the photograph in the center of them all, Lord Marwick leaned back in exhaustion, pressing his fingers to his eyes. He ran his hands over his forehead, flattening the few strands of hair on his shining pate. From the darkened anteroom just outside the door, the pendulum clock clicked, then struck two chimes. The earl stared at the photo a moment more, then slipped it back into its folder and switched off the light.

* * *

Tito opened his eyes in the predawn. Next to him, Rory lay asleep against his pack, his hand closed on the heavy stick at his side as Innes slept soundly by the wall. Tito reached for a sip of water, but the drinking can was empty. Taking up his shoes, he stepped silently through the hut and slipped outside.

The rain had stopped again overnight. The air was fresh. Above him on the ridge, he saw a rocky outcrop where the water squeezed through the rocks. Tito scrambled up to it and could see that the water ran clear. Putting his lips to the icy rock, he breathed in a long, cool drink. He let out a little belch, then set the lip of the can against the rock as he practiced his thin whistle. Across the way, he could see the smoke from their campfire venting out through the sodden hillside above their cave. A black bird flew raucously past. Tito stood watching the smoke float lazily higher. Hearing the rising pitch of his water can, he screwed the lid back on, but as he did he suddenly flattened himself hard against the rocks. Below him in the distance, standing on a little knob, a man stood staring up at the column of woodsmoke rising into the sky.

* * *

Tito rushed into the hut and quickly sat down.

Rory opened his eyes. "Were you outside just now?" he asked, forcing himself awake. "You should've woken me."

But as Tito started to answer, the sound of a rock being trod upon came from outside the door. Rory sat straight up as a voice came through the opening.

"Hello in the cave?"

The boys sat perfectly still.

Another footfall came closer, and the voice came again. "Hello? Anyone at home?"

Rory quickly pulled Tito into the shadows at the back of the cave as a massive head with a giant man attached to it came peering through the door.

"Hello?" he said again. "Not an intruder."

Seeing no one, the man ducked into the cave, and from the shadows Rory and Tito saw that he wore a flat wool cap and a long, heavy coat colored every shade of earth. Stooping beneath the ceiling, the man glanced around, and in the firelight, he saw the cache of food Rory had laid out to inventory the night before. With a light step, he eased over to have a look. The boys stayed very still in the shadows, but at the sight of the man sizing up their only food, an indignancy overtook Tito.

"Actually there is someone at home and you're not at all welcome."

Startled, the man jerked upright, smacked his granite head against the stone ceiling, and stumbled backward into the middle of the campfire. "Bloody hell!" A stream of curses and obscenities came pouring out of him as he frantically beat out the sparks on his pants. Upon realizing that he was not in fact on fire, he turned to the darkness at the back of the cave. "Sorry," he called, squinting blindly into the dark. "Very sorry, my apologies. Only saw the smoke from your fire there is all." He tilted his head, trying to see into the shadows. "Name's Ham, by the way. Camping just down the way there. Didn't mean to walk up on you like that."

Rory and Tito stayed silent in the shadows. In the firelight, they could see he was a giant of a man. He had a woolly head of dark-red hair and a matching beard. His face was raw from the wind. "Just thought I'd say hello. Like I said, not an intruder." And after still getting no response, he bowed his head a little and gave an apologetic wave. "Alright. Well, I guess I'll be going then. Apologies again." But as he turned to go, there came a weak cough from the other side of the cave. Ham turned to see Innes lying against the wall, pale and shivering. "So what's the matter with your friend there?" He studied Innes a moment. "He doesn't look too good."

"He's not our friend," came Rory's voice finally.

"Oh. Well, who is he then?"

"We don't know. We just found him like that."

"You found him?"

"Last night." Tito paused. "He's possibly a drunkard."

Ham looked more curiously into the dark. "So how many of you are back there exactly?" He glanced back at Innes. "I mean, he really doesn't look very good at all." He took a half step toward him. "Doesn't smell so great either. Look, I'm no doctor, but that's more than just too much drink. This fella doesn't look right."

After a moment, Rory's voice came again. "Well, what do people usually do in such a situation?"

"Way out here?" Ham thought about that. "I suppose you'd go for the constable."

At the mention of the constable, there came a longer pause. "Is there anything else people do in such a situation?"

Ham studied the shadows more carefully now. "Sorry, and how many did you say were back there?"

"Maybe he'll get better on his own?" came Tito's voice. "Last night we thought he might be dead at first."

"Dead? Look, whoever he is you can't just leave him like this. And could someone come out of there, please? This is a little ridiculous."

Rory and Tito stepped slowly into view.

"Is that it then? Just the two of you?" Ham looked past them into the shadows. "Alright, well, this fella here needs a doctor, and since there's not one on Skara Skaill, and apparently you two seem less than eager to get the constable involved—"

"No, there is one now," interrupted Tito. "In the village. A lady doctor."

"A lady doctor?" Ham considered that a moment. "Well, I guess that'll have to do, I suppose."

"No, no, she's a regular doctor," said Rory.

"Oh, right. Yeah, well, that's where he needs to be then." Ham turned to Innes, assessing him. "I don't think we'll get him there on foot though. That's a long walk. What we really need is something to haul him in."

"Rory, wasn't there a mule and cart at Mr. Begbie's?"

"Yeah, that'd do it." Ham nodded.

Rory ignored the question. "Look, we don't really know Mr. Begbie. Not enough to borrow something anyway. And could a cart even make it out this far? Through the rocks and that."

"What if I can get him on his feet?" asked Ham. "Get him up to the flats there? You think you could get there maybe?"

"I don't know, what do I know about it? I mean how does this even fall to us anyway?"

"Well, who then?" asked Tito.

"Look," said Ham, "it's either that, or someone needs to start for the village. See about bringing someone out to your camp here. The doctor, maybe the constable. But someone."

VII

HAM LOOKED OUT BEYOND the ridge, waiting, as banks of cold fog slid past. He glanced over at Innes sitting on the hard ground, a blanket wrapped around him.

"Shouldn't be too long now." Ham nodded. "Shouldn't be too long." He could see that Innes was pale as paper, shivering in the wind. "So I'm just gonna keep talking if that's alright? Probably best we keep you awake." He scanned out for the boys, then back at Innes. "I'm Ham, by the way." He rubbed his hands together from the cold. "And it was Innes, yeah?" Innes opened a bleary eye and nodded. Ham turned and scanned out again. "Shouldn't be too long."

Suddenly the wind changed directions, and riding in on the breeze came a faint jangling sound. "Do you hear that?" Ham stared into the mist. As he listened, a massive gray mule came tromping out of the fog. Hitched behind him was an old truck frame with nothing on it but a front bench seat and four bald tires. Rory reined the mule to a stop as Ham hurried over. "Well done, lads. Well done, indeed." Ham looked the big mule in the face. "And look at you. You're as ugly as I am."

"That's Eustice," said Tito, and as Ham reached out to pet the mule's forehead, it snapped its yellow teeth at him. "He bites."

"I can see that."

Ham eased Innes up into the cart, and giving the mule a wide berth, he climbed aboard, the springs of the cart groaning heavily over to one side. As Rory flicked the reins, the big mule slowly started forward, and the four headed off, wobbling and squeaking away into the mist.

* * *

The village was empty. In the center of the square stood a statue of the first Earl of Skara Skaill. Innes and Ham sat in the cart. Ham held the reins, looking nervously at the mule's massive rump, nicked and scarred.

"Was never much of a horseman, me." Ham looked up the sidewalk, then checked on Innes huddled in the front seat. Up the curb a door suddenly swung open as Tito led Rory and Aggie Allen out onto the sidewalk.

Ham and Rory guided Innes down the hall into the low-ceilinged room. A thin curtain hung across a door leading into the kitchen.

Aggie quickly cleared off the table. "Let's have him here, please." Ham helped Innes onto the table, then backed away. "What's your name?" she asked, feeling his head and neck.

"His name's Innes," said Ham.

Innes nodded, steadying himself.

"You've got an extremely high fever," said Aggie. "Did he have any other symptoms?"

"No," said Rory. "Just shivering like that."

"Plus he had vomit on himself," added Tito.

Without a word, Innes leaned to one side and lifted the edge of his shirt. Just below his ribs was the jagged line of a hard wound, blood-black and swollen hot.

"Jesus," whispered Ham. "He's had that this whole time?"

Aggie leaned close to the wound. "And how did you get this?"

Innes tried to clear his throat. "On the crossing," he said weakly.

She touched around it gently. "Well, it's become infected. It should be cleaned out immediately." Aggie quickly set a few items on the table, and after washing the wound thoroughly, she brought a light up close. "Feels like there's something still in there." Touching carefully around the wound she took up a pair of large tweezers. She looked at Innes. "This is going to hurt a bit, I'm afraid." She bent closer to the wound. "Actually, this might hurt a lot."

Ham's face mirrored Innes's with a sharp inhale from the bright pain. Carefully Aggie drew out a bloody object the size of a half deck of cards, tapered to a point. She clinked it heavily into a metal bowl.

Tito whispered close to Rory. "That's not a bodkin, is it?"

"Looks to be a chunk of glass," said Aggie, rinsing the blood away. "From a bottle, maybe. See, some of the label's still on it."

She sewed the wound closed, snipped it clean, then stuck a needle neatly into Innes's arm. "For the infection. He'll need to rest now." She looked at Innes quietly. "You'll need to rest, alright?" Innes nodded, his eyes already half closed again.

Aggie turned to the others. "So which of you does he belong to?"

"Well, none of us," said Ham, glancing at the boys. "These two, they found him last night."

"Found him?"

"Outside our door," said Rory. "He was just lying there."

"So none of you even know him then?" They shook their heads. "Well, you were right to bring him in. It could've been very much worse."

The bell in the village square began to toll.

"No, is it seven o'clock already?" Aggie glanced at Innes, who appeared to already be sleeping. "Right, good. I'll be back to check on him in a bit." She passed through the curtain. "Anyone care for breakfast?" she called from the kitchen. They watched as she took up a large pot from the stove, pushed open the back door with her foot, and hurried down the steps.

Ham shrugged. "I could eat."

As Ham and Rory followed her out, Tito stopped to look at Innes a moment, his eyes closed, his breathing steady, and as the last village bell peeled away, Tito turned and hurried after the others.

* * *

The dull sun angled through the curtains. Innes slowly opened his eyes, staring blankly up at the ceiling. From outside he heard the murmur of voices. Taking a long breath, he sat up, wincing hard at the pain in his side. Parting the curtain, he could see the dirt yard through the kitchen window. People were sitting around a long table, bowls of food steaming up into their faces. He saw Aggie working around the table, pouring tea, listening as she went, a word here, a nod there. Innes watched her a moment, then carefully slid down off the table. Looking around the room, he found his bag and coat. He slipped it on. The cat on the kitchen counter sat staring at him. Through the curtain, cans of food were stacked along the shelves. Innes reached in and took down two cans and slipped them into his pockets. As he turned to go, he paused and put one of the cans back on the shelf before starting again down the hall and out the front door.

* * *

As the village bell rang once for the half hour, they stood on the curb looking down the street.

"I can't believe he'd just leave like that," said Tito.

"Can't you?" asked Rory. "What with him being such an upstanding sort and all?"

"Well, where do you think he's gone?"

"Don't know. Don't care," said Rory, stuffing a few items of food Aggie had given them into his pack. "Come on. I don't want to be hanging around the village too very long just at the moment." But as Rory started up the sidewalk, he suddenly stopped in his tracks. "Where's the mule?" He hurried to the corner. "Where's the mule gone?"

Ham looked out toward the edge of the village. "I'm sure he's fine. He's probably halfway home by now. My uncle had a horse like that. Every time you'd turn your back on him, he'd head straight back to his hay."

"No, I tied him." Rory stepped into the road. "I tied him good, I'm sure of it." Suddenly a thought came over him. "He must've taken him."

"Who?" asked Tito.

"Him. Innes." Rory put his hands on his head as he looked out at the empty square.

"He wouldn't have," said Tito. "Maybe Eustice untied himself?"

"Untied himself?"

"They can do it with their teeth."

Rory stared down the alley. "Well this is just great. Not what we need right now. Really not." He shook his head. "Well, we'll just have to find him. They'll have us for stealing if we don't."

"Come on now," said Ham. "You're alright. I mean you asked to borrow him." He saw Tito shoot a glance at Rory. "You did ask him, didn't you?"

"Well, we knocked," said Tito. "And we called into the house, but—" Just then from up the street a voice called out.

"You lose something?" It was Rat, stepping duck-footed out of a doorway, shaking out a match.

"Have you seen a mule?" called Tito before Rory could stop him.

"A mule, or a man?" Rat took a pull from his cigarette. "'Cause I seen both. And if I'm not mistaken, that was Innes Mackie come stumbling out of that clinic. The Badger will most certainly be interested in that."

"And who's the Badger then?" asked Ham.

Rat looked up at Ham. "Well, now, would you get a load of the size of you. You must've been dropped from a square womb? What are you then, Innes's new crew?"

"Sorry, what?"

"Look, did you see them or not?" snapped Rory.

"Oy. Don't forget who you're talking to, boy." Rat took a threatening step toward Rory before Ham cut him off.

"I believe he asked which way they went."

"Alright, alright, no need to get hostile." Rat pointed his cigarette out toward the moors. "He went that way, straight out."

"The mule too?" asked Rory.

"I don't know. What am I, the information desk? I seen 'em both, then I didn't see neither." Rat cocked a suspicious eye at Rory. "But wasn't that old Begbie's mule? He's not usually one for lending things out."

"Come on, Tito. Let's go."

As they started up the sidewalk, a thin rain began to fall over the cobbled streets of the square. Rat stepped off the curb and into the street, taking a thoughtful pull from his cigarette as he watched them go.

* * *

The wipers flicked double-time as the driver navigated the narrow roadway in the rain. The long sweep of Skara Heath sloped away in the distance. Lord Marwick sat in the back of the car alone.

"Get me Mr. Croy."

"Who, sir?" asked the driver.

"The Badger. Get me the bloody Badger."

"Oh, right, sir." The driver passed back the radio handset. Lord Marwick took it and began speaking as if he were already in the middle of a conversation.

"And tell me again, you're the only one that's gone below since this morning, yes?" The car surged over the last rise. The village lay dead ahead, slate gray and rain slick. "I told Constable Tulloch I want a guard posted around the clock. And you tell that crew of yours at the wharf to keep their eyes open for anything out of the ordinary. Coming or going. This break-in at my dig site has me troubled, Mr. Croy. Quite troubled." Lord Marwick checked the driver, then turned and spoke quietly into the handset. "And you're the only one I want down in that hole, are we clear? I want you living at that site until it's done, do you understand me?" The car sped through the village streets. Out the window, Lord Marwick saw a cluster of villagers gathered down a side alley at the clinic gate. His eyes stayed on them as the car streamed past. "And where are we with the village cleanup? We've had this discussion once already, have we not? The closing ceremony will be held in the square, and I won't have the other members looking at us like we're the poor relations. It's been a hundred years since Skara Skaill last hosted the Order of Albion, so get it done, Mr. Croy. Just get it done." He clicked off and tapped the handset impatiently on the seat back for the driver.

"Bloody stuffy in here," he muttered, leaning back.

"Shall I crack a window, sir?"

"It's raining, man." He smoothed the few strands of hair on his glistening head. "Anyway, I prefer my air *conditioned*."

"The air is out of order, sir, remember? Would you like me to have the car serviced? There's been quite a lot wrong with it."

"No, I would not like you to have the car serviced." Lord Marwick looked around at the shabby interior of his once grand car. "We'll hold off on that for now." As he gazed out the window, the car suddenly swerved hard as three figures in the rain scrambled off the road and down the embankment. "What the hell?" said Lord Marwick as the car righted itself again.

"Sorry, sir. People on the road."

Lord Marwick collected himself. "You know in my grandfather's day he wouldn't have swerved for the likes of them." The driver smiled in the rearview. "What, you think I'm joking?" Lord Marwick sniffed and turned again to the window as the car sped on.

Down below the road, Rory, Ham, and Tito came stumbling to a stop as the big car hissed away into the distance, its red taillights glaring back at them through the rain.

* * *

Moving slowly, the village far behind, Innes picked up the thinnest ghost of a path heading out across the moors. The rain was cold, and the sky was leaden. With every heartbeat, the pain pulsed hard against his side where Aggie had stitched it closed. For a moment his thoughts went to the cool of her hand as she tended the wound. At his feet, little flowers grew tight down among the rocks. Stitchwort. Woodsage. Bindweed. As the ground started to rise before him, his head began to reel and his legs went elastic. He stopped to steady himself. A chill had come over him from the lingering fever, and his clothes were soaked cold from the inside. He took a deep breath, then readied himself to begin again, when from behind him there came a sound in the distance, chaotic and rattletrap, approaching at a high rate of speed. He turned and looked out. From a quarter mile off, appearing out of the rain came the sight of a mule galloping wildly across the moors, the black truck frame clattering behind him, the reins dragging along the ground. Innes watched as Eustice powered across the ridgeline, then disappeared into the fog, the sound slowly fading again to silence.

* * *

Rory and Ham stopped at the top of the rise.

"I'm too fat for all this tramping around," said Ham, out of breath, his hands on his knees. "So what was that fella back in the village saying anyway? About Innes and that?"

"Who, Rat?" Rory waited as Tito caught up. "I dunno, just that the Badger, he sorta runs things down at the wharf."

Tito dropped his pack. "And for the county too he does it. Him and his crew down there." He squinted up at them through the rain. "Why've we stopped?"

"Rory needed a rest," said Ham. "You know, with all this rain I'm thinking the huts will be shot through with water. It runs straight through the middle of mine."

"Well, ours is dry," said Tito before Rory could stop him. "We've got room, if you'd like?"

"No, no," said Ham, not meaning it. "No, I couldn't ask you."

"At least 'til the rain stops. It's no trouble."

"Well, I do have some canned peaches I've been saving. Willing to share."

"Yeah." Rory shook his head. "I'm thinking it's better we just keep things separate, if you don't mind."

"Oh, sure." Ham lifted his hand in understanding. "I mean, I could just give you a whole can of your own if you'd rather. Oh. Wait, was it the food you were you meaning to keep separate?"

"Rory, look." Tito suddenly pointed to the valley below. "Is that Innes?"

"It's not him," said Rory, squinting out at a tiny figure moving across the valley floor. "Why would he be walking back in the same direction he'd just come?"

"How can you tell if he's coming or going from this distance?" asked Ham. The figure stopped and gave a slow wave over his head.

"That's him," said Tito, waving back. "That's him. And look, Rory, no mule." He started down the hill with Rory and Ham trailing after him. When they reached the bottom, Innes was sitting on his pack.

"You lose your mule?" he asked, struggling to his feet.

"We did," said Rory. "Why, did you see him?"

Innes pointed to the far rise. "Passed me about a quarter mile back."

"That's the way to Mr. Begbie's, Rory."

"Just what I said he'd do," said Ham. "Didn't I say that?"

"He must've untied himself. They can do that."

"They can't do that, Tito."

Tito turned to Innes. "So where were you heading anyway?" he asked. "You left without saying."

"Come on, Tito. Everyone's got places to go."

"And do you?" asked Ham. "Have someplace to go, I mean?"

"I do, yeah." Innes nodded. "Was just trying to beat the weather."

"So it's far then, where you're going?" asked Tito.

"C'mon, Tito." Rory took up Tito's pack. "We've got to go the long way now, past Mr. Begbie's."

"But should he be walking? What with his new stitches and that?"

"Tito." Rory reached for him.

"Yeah, I should be heading on too." Innes looked at them a moment. "But. Well, thanks for your help, you know, with all that from before."

"Oh, sure," said Ham with a wave.

Innes nodded his thanks again, but as he readied himself to go, he watched as Tito hefted the rain-soaked pack onto his shoulders, the cold rain pouring down on him, water squeezing from his shoes. "And so it's the cave huts you're heading back to then, is it?"

"That's right," said Rory.

Innes considered them all a moment. "You know. There's a house there, where I'm heading. And a barn. And what with the temperature dropping. Well, it'd be dry, at least."

"We'll be alright where we are, thanks. Me and Tito anyway. Come on, Tito." Rory started away, but Tito didn't move. "Tito. Come on." But Tito still didn't move. Rory dropped his head and stepped over to him, his back to the others.

"OK, what is it?"

"A house. There's a house there, Rory."

"No. Come on, we're going." But as Rory started again to go, Tito stood unmoving in the rain, the water streaming down his face, his feet planted in the mud. Rory sighed, and knowing where this was going, shook his head and turned to Innes. "So this house of yours. It's far then, is it?"

* * *

The snap of sea air came in on the wind. Below them, a long slope led down to a stretch of tall grass running straight out to the cliff's edge and to the green sea beyond. Along the flats, drystone walls were patchworked into three small fields. A stone farmhouse and a barn sat low and gray and heavy on the earth. Far out along the cliffs, where the land dropped away to the shore, a stone fisherman's shack was built into the slope itself, facing out to sea.

For a long moment, Innes took in the sight of it all. He slowly started down. But as he approached the farmhouse, he stopped. As the others came alongside him, they could see that the roof was burned through, half open to the sky. A chimney, charred and blackened, rose out of it, and the wind moved unchecked through the broken windows. Innes stood watching the rain fall into the house. Slowly he drifted forward. Tito started to follow, but Rory held him back. From the front path, they could see a notice nailed to the door, faded and bleached.

Inside, the house was still. Innes closed the door behind him. At his feet lay a collection of notices from the county slid beneath the door. The back wall was scorched to the roof, and rain fell in through the beams. Near the fireplace, two wooden chairs were placed around a table. A cold kettle sat on the stove. Along the shelf were tins of canned food, a half-empty bottle of dish soap, a bowl of shrunken onions with dead shoots growing out of them.

He walked across the room and stopped at an open door. Inside sat a double bed. A sheet on a string divided the room, and behind it was a twin bed in the corner, its thin blanket soaked through. On the dresser, a collection of books was neatly stacked. Taking one down, Innes opened it. Pressed within each page were dried wildflowers, the names carefully written out in a woman's handwriting. He slowly turned a few pages, then closed the book again. Above the dresser hung a small shaving mirror mottled with age. He looked at himself. The reflection of his face framed within the house. In the seam of the mirror frame was wedged a little scrap of paper. On it an address was written in an unsteady hand. A hand that he knew. It was an old address. One that had been his for a while, on the mainland. Two years ago. Maybe three. Next to the table, a coat hung loosely on a peg. Its tweed was coarse. It smelled of wood-smoke and damp salt air, but also of tobacco still and shave cream. Innes reached into the pockets. There was a little book of matches, and flecks of pipe tobacco. A small coil of twine. A hard candy in clear yellow paper. And he was with him again now. Leaning small against his side, tucked in against the wool, listening as his father talked to other men about the weather or the prices of things. The resonance of his voice coming through the coat, through the chest beneath it, before the house had become too small, too filled with that which they did not know how to contend.

* * *

From the barn door, Tito stood in his bare feet staring out through the wall of rain at the farmhouse. Lines of rainwater came in through the roof all around the barn. Innes walked across and appeared at the barn doors, a bucket in each hand. They stared at him, not knowing what to say. He turned to a shelf and began quietly unloading items from the buckets, his back to them.

"No one had been living there at the time. If that's what you're wondering." From the buckets he drew out a few cans of food, a trowel, a plastic bottle of cooking oil. "And it's been some years since I've been back, so." He tucked a few of the books from the house down into his pack, then turned and noticed the rain leaking all around, and the tattered roof. Tito stood in his wet clothes. Along the slats of a stall their socks were hung like drying fish. "Well, I suppose we should have a fire then," said Innes, and looking into the back of the barn, he pulled a book of matches from his pocket. "Burn whatever's dry."

VIII

TITO SAT IN THE circle around the fire, eating from a bean can. He poked at the embers, adding little sticks here and there. A thin blanket from the house hung by the fire.

"Tito, will you stop monkeying with it?" said Rory.

"Well, I don't want it to die out."

"It's going fine."

The dampness from their clothes steamed in the warmth of the fire. Rain fell across the open door.

"Beans are good," said Innes.

"Ah, you're nice to say so," said Ham, and when it was clear no further compliments were coming, he continued. "Most people just dump the beans in the pot and leave it at that, but I doctored these up a bit." He pulled a few tiny bottles from his pack.

"You carry kitchen spices with you?" asked Tito.

"Just your basics. Your salt, your pepper, your garlic powder. A chili powder is nice as well." Ham leaned forward and seasoned four fat potatoes that were tucked at the edge of the fire. They ate the steaming potatoes like apples on a stick. When Ham was done, he lay back against his suitcase and moved his blanched feet as close as he could to the fire. "Don't listen to them, Tito, that very well might be the best fire ever made. I think I must be using damp wood back at the cave huts."

"So how is it you're living out there anyway, at the caves?" asked Tito.

"Oh, it's just a temporary situation." Rory listened without looking up. "The boat I was working on broke down halfway through the season. They pay you at the end, which left me a little short. That would've been a few weeks ago now."

"So where'd you been working the rest of the year?" asked Rory.

"Down south. A cousin of mine's a roofer down there."

Innes finished his potato and pitched the stick into the fire. "Yeah, well, if I were you, I'd think about heading right back down there. There's nothing out here but wind."

"Oh, I don't know. I gave the mainland a try. Not sure I'm cut out for it though, really. But I like it out here. I do. I'm tired of moving around. I'm just looking for the usual, me. Wife, kids, a dog. The full catastrophe." Ham considered the boys a moment. "And what about you two, eh? How is it you came to be out at the caves, if you don't mind me asking?"

"Well, actually, we live at Kettleskaill House," said Tito. "But they—"

"It's only for a couple of days," said Rory, cutting him off. "We live near the village there, with Mrs. Renfro."

"And who's Mrs. Renfro then?"

"The lady whose house it is."

"And what, she doesn't mind you being out here alone, your Mrs. Renfro?" asked Ham.

"No." Rory kept his eyes fixed on the fire. "Like I said, it's only for a couple of days."

Ham thought to ask more, then left it alone. "How about you, Innes? You were working back on the mainland you said?"

"Yeah, odd jobs. Some construction."

"Oh yeah?"

"Demolition mostly."

"What, like with a wrecking ball?" asked Tito.

"More like with a crowbar."

Rory stirred the fire, not looking up. "So what's that pay anyway, demolition?"

"Not near enough." Innes glanced at Rory. "But you'd be on the young side for that type of work."

"He's just turned fifteen," added Tito.

Ham leaned forward and felt his socks drying, a question on his mind. "So, the fellow back there in the square, with the big eyes?"

"Rat?" asked Tito.

"Him, yeah. He seemed to think he knew you, Innes, from before."

"Did he?"

"He did, yeah. Had your last name as Mackie."

Innes took up his bean can again. "Rat always did make it a point of knowing everybody's business."

"Also said something about, what, the Badger, was it?" Ham glanced at Innes. "Like he'd known you as well?"

"Yeah, well." Innes quietly studied his bean can a moment. "That would've been a while ago now." He offered nothing more, and a silence passed over the conversation.

Ham looked through the barn door at the farmhouse. "So will you fix it up, do you think?"

"What, the house? No."

"It's not so bad. Definitely seen worse. It belongs to you though, yeah?"

"Was my father's."

Ham nodded gently. "And is he, I mean, so your da, is he still—?"

"No." Innes spooned around at the bottom of his can.

Rory tried to stop Tito, but it was too late. "And your mam?"

Innes shook his head. "When I was a boy. My da last year."

"Oh," said Tito quietly. "But you've only come home now though?"

"Tito," whispered Rory.

Innes quietly poured a line of water onto his spoon. "It took a while for the news to reach me." He thumbed the spoon clean. "My da wrote that he was—well, he said he'd be leaving me the house. But seems like it's the county owns it now. What's left of it." He flicked the last of the water into the dirt. "Anyway, I didn't come back here for this place."

"No?" Tito asked. "Why did you come back?"

Innes leaned against his pack. "I left Skara Skaill four years ago." The fire made a loud snap as a single spark popped out and landed in the dirt, cooling from orange to black. "I guess you could say my da and me, we hadn't always had the easiest time of it."

"Well, you were right to come." Ham nodded. "Pay your respects. In my experience you never really leave home, not all the way anyway."

Innes started to speak again, then reached for his blanket drying near the fire. "Yeah, well, I lost all my money coming over on the crossing, and as soon as I get another piece together, I'll be leaving again, so."

"As soon as that?" asked Tito.

"As soon as that." Innes shook the dirt from his blanket as the rain shifted angles outside.

* * *

New weather had come in overnight. The morning air was sharp, and the fire was cold. The clothes Rory had laid out the night before were still wet from the rain, but he collected them anyway, stuffing them into his pack while the others slept. At the back of the barn, a hatch suddenly blew open and began thumping mindlessly against the wall outside. Rory went to close it. In the mist beyond the far field, he saw Innes standing in a little plot hemmed in by a stone wall, two buckets at his feet. Rory watched him as he stood stone-still among the gravestones. Frost covered the ground. Innes reached down, and picking up the buckets, he started for the barn. Rory quickly pulled the hatch closed.

Tito opened his eyes and yawned, staring blankly.

"OK, Tito, time to go."

Ham propped up on one elbow and scratched his woolly head as Innes walked in out of the wind, a metal bucket hanging in each hand.

"What's in the buckets?"

"Mussels." Innes set the buckets down. "The only thing I ever missed about living out here."

Soon the fire was going again, and they were reaching into the buckets, taking out the steaming mussels, wrenching apart the shells.

"They taste like ocean," said Tito. "Are they hard to find?"

"What, have you never gotten any?" asked Ham.

"No." Tito reached in for another.

"Well, there's nothing to it really, you just have to know where to look."

"And where *do* you look?" asked Rory.

"Has no one really ever taken you?" asked Innes.

The boys shook their heads.

Innes considered them a moment. "Yeah, well, I guess I could show you a spot." He turned to the fire. "When we head back."

Tito looked up. "What, so you're not staying out here then?"

Innes pitched a shell into the fire and stood up. "Not enough left of this place, really." He picked his blanket out of the dirt. "And if the county owns it now…well, I've certainly got no interest in the constable coming around." A cold wind suddenly snatched the hatch open again, beating it against the wall. "I just have one stop to make before we go."

* * *

A black crow stood on the stone wall, cawing loudly at them. From the tall grass, Rory and Tito stood looking in at the little plot where Innes had been earlier that morning. In the middle of the plot was an old stone cross. All around it, gravestones were gathered. *Sinclairs. Mackies. Fletts.* Here and there a tiny headstone was tucked down among the others. Looking out, Rory could see that Innes and Ham had already reached the cliffs. Ham was gazing out at the water, his hands on his hips, but Innes stared straight back at them there at the cemetery wall.

* * *

Down below the fishermen's shack, waves crashed white against the rocks. From the cliff above, Ham stared warily down at the stone shack, its roof covered thick with sod.

"So what kind of an errand is this anyway?" he called in the wind.

"A quick one," said Innes, already picking his way down as Rory and Tito followed.

"You know, if I'm honest"—Ham started after them—"I really don't care much for heights."

Innes stopped at the opening of the little shack. A tin bucket with the bottom rusted out sat in the corner. A snarl of old ropes lay in a heap. In the middle of the floor, a single stool sat facing out to sea. For a moment, Innes considered the stool, then ducking into the shack, he immediately stumbled backward as a seabird roosting in the shadows shrieked angrily past him before launching itself off the ledge.

Ham chuckled to himself. "Loud bird."

At the back wall, a pile of rubble had cascaded down, and at its base sat a large stone the size of a breadbox. Innes began to clear away the rubble, but as he tried to move the stone, he winced in pain at the stitches in his side.

Ham tapped him on the shoulder. "If I might?" Picking up the stone, Ham swung it easily out the front door into the open air where it flew far from view, finally sending up the sound of crashing rocks below.

The boys stared in disbelief.

"I was a mason for a while." He shrugged, clapping the dirt from his hands.

In the spot where the stone had been was a gap in the wall. Innes knelt to it, and reaching in, hc pulled out a small whiskey bottle, half empty.

"Tell me that's not the errand?" whispered Rory to Tito.

Innes reached in again, this time drawing out a metal coffee can covered in rust.

Tito tried to see in.

"Nothing to get too excited about." Innes pulled a little sack out of the can, and from it he drew a thin fold of paper money. He put the bills in his pocket, and turning the can upside down, he banged it until a single clump, the exact size and shape of the bottom of the can, fell to the ground with a thud.

"What is that?" asked Ham.

"Well, it used to be spare coins."

"Looks more like a cowpat," said Ham. Leaning over it, they could all see it was in fact a cluster of corroded coins fused together into a single green clot.

Innes picked up the clump. "The salt air must've got to it." He held it a moment, then passed it to Ham. "My father said he liked to keep a little stash of money somewhere other than the house. Just in case."

"In case of what?"

"Well, I'd say fire for one, Tito." Rory watched as Ham managed to snap a solid green coin off the clump.

"So did he used to come out here a lot then?" Tito asked.

In the corner of the window, a spider's web being pushed by the wind glistened in the sea air. Innes considered the empty stool, and the window facing the open ocean, and the half-drunk bottle in the corner. "He did, yeah."

Flashing across the opening, a gull came screaming past, breaking Innes's thoughts. Picking up the bottle, he slipped it into his pocket and ducked out again through the door.

Leaving the farm and the sea cliffs behind, Innes led the way out onto the moors. A thin rain started down, then stopped, then started again, and after a while, they came upon a narrow footpath scattered with sheep pellets. As they made their way along, and having little else to occupy their minds, each of them became aware of the sound of Ham's boots, still soaked with rain, squashing with every step.

"Is that me?" he asked. "I was thinking that was Rory this whole time." Setting his bucket down, he pulled off his boots, poured a little water out, and began hopping in a circle to wrestle them on again. "Ready."

But from somewhere far behind them came the slow clop of a horse plodding up the path. On its bare back sat two riders, a girl in front and a boy in back, both having recently received identical haircuts. As the horse tromped slowly past, the girl held on to the horse's mane while the boy stared dully at them, chewing on an apple core, his feet dangling loose. Tito stood and watched as horse and riders slowly stumped away before finally disappearing over the hill. As the four started off again, they soon crested a little rise and could see the riders in the distance. Out beyond them, in a low field, was a line of white tents and string lights just beginning to glow in the twilight.

"Rory," called Tito, turning to him. "The Fhøghar Fair. I'd forgotten what day it was with all this."

The faint smell of fried food carried in on the air, and up ahead, cars were parked along the narrow road. As they approached the tents, they stopped and stared at the lights and sounds of the fair. A drunken man with a divot in his head and one milky eye came wobbling out through the gates. Seeing Innes, he stopped, and seeming to recognize him, he swayed back a little, tipped his hat very formally, then staggered away again into the dark.

"And what was that about?" asked Rory. But Innes gave no answer, only scanning out toward the entrance of the fair.

Ham rubbed his hands together. "Who's for getting some food, eh? Real food. No beans for us tonight, eh, lads?"

Rory was slow to answer. "We'll just wait until later, me and Tito."

"What? You haven't had a thing since this morning; you've gotta be starving."

"We're alright. We'll wait," said Rory again, and as he and Tito started toward the entrance, Innes held Ham back.

"At the end of the night, some of the food sellers will give a handout of whatever's left over. Instead of throwing it away. You understand?"

"Oh. Right." Ham began digging in his pockets. "Well, I'm sure I've got enough here for the both of them." As he drifted toward the entrance, counting his coins, he stopped and looked back at Innes. "Aren't you coming?"

"You go on ahead." Innes nodded. "I'll catch up." Ham waved and walked away, still counting his coins, the little green coin there among them. Innes watched as Ham headed into the fair, and drawing the little amber bottle from his pocket, he took a sip. Casting a wary eye into the crowd, he started a wide path out behind the lights and the tents, disappearing into the dark.

IX

A MAN ON LONG stilts came striding past as Rory and Tito entered the hurly-burly of the fair. Every item of clothing he wore was dyed homemade red, from his shoes and socks to his stovepipe hat, which he tipped at Tito as he passed. Just ahead was a large tent, and inside it were all manner of chickens and rabbits and ducks housed in stacked cages. In the next pens over, newborn goats and lambs lay in the straw being tended to by a group of girls in folding chairs, their pants tucked into their rubber boots. At the sight of the girls, Rory brushed the dirt from his clothes and tried to flatten his hair.

"What're you doing?" asked Tito.

"Me? Nothing."

The boys walked along the midway between the tents. Clusters of children ran freely about, weaving among the crowd. Teenagers snuck out to the edges of the darkness. Across the matted grass was a string of tents steaming with food. Twists of wax paper were being handed out as money was handed in. The beer tent was packed with florid-faced men debating loudly or bursting in unison with laughter. Tito watched a child toddling past carrying a paper plate of hot food, which Tito hoped might drop into the dirt, good-side up. On a post nearby hung a sign.

Tonight. Stone Put Competition.
Open to All Comers.

"Rory." Tito pointed at the sign.

"What, you want to watch it?"

"No. Look at the prize. Four pies."

"Yeah, so, same as last year."

"No. Four of us. Four pies."

"Oh, like we could win it, Tito."

"Not us." Tito nodded back at Ham walking toward them. "Him."

Tito led Rory and Ham through the crowd to a folding table. They stood patiently until a bespectacled man looked up from his clipboard to see what had thrown a shadow over him.

"Well, now, I presume you'll be wanting to join the competition?"

"I would," said Ham. "So long as this is the one where the winner receives the pies?"

"It is, it is." The man slid the clipboard to Ham. "Just your name here for me if you would, please. Last name, first name."

Ham bent down to the clipboard. "And might you be able to tell me what kind of pies are on offer?" he asked as Rory and Tito looked expectantly at the man.

"I believe two meat and two berry."

"That'll do." Ham wrote his name with a flourish. The man squinted down at it.

"Last name Little. First name Ham?"

"That's right."

Rory leaned to Tito. "Sounds like a pork dish." Tito tried not to laugh.

"Excellent. You'll be contestant number sixteen. Please pin this somewhere on your person." He handed Ham a safety pin and a square paper with his number on it. "Just behind the rope there, if you would, please. We'll be starting in a few minutes. You can leave your coat with your people." Ham nodded, and they all walked over to where the other contestants were readying themselves. Ham stepped inside the rope and stood nervously trying to pin the number to his shirt.

"Here, I'll do it," said Tito as Rory took Ham's coat.

Out in the darkness, Innes stood at the back of the crowd. Spectators assembled thickly along the ropes, bundled against the cold. Across the way, Innes saw Tito and Rory tucking in close at the front. The PA crackled to life as the bespectacled man thumped the microphone.

"Can we clear the field, please? Clear the field. Thank you." He clicked the microphone off, then on again. "And may we please have any remaining participants sign in so we can commence? Last call for participants."

Innes stayed deep in the crowd. He took a sip from the bottle. Down the ropes on the opposite side, he noticed a group of men wading forward through the crowd. At the front of the pack strode Frankie and Munro Duff, their crew following along behind laughing and sloshing beer as they forced their way to the front. Innes kept his eyes fixed on them as he took a step back, deeper into the crowd.

"Ladies and gentlemen, good evening and welcome to the annual Skara Skaill Stone Put Competition. We've a fine group of lads competing this year, so let's get started shall we? Can we have Contestant Number One come forward and toe the line, please. Contestant Number One." The announcer clicked off the microphone as a stout lad of no more than eighteen stepped nervously forward. The applause from the crowd died down as he walked over to a wooden rack, upon which sat a round stone the size of a large melon. Wiping his hands on his pants, he lifted the stone to his shoulder, then backed up four measured paces. Squaring himself, he focused his eyes straight ahead, exhaled long and slow, then lumbered forward before heaving the stone downfield, where it landed with a thud in the thick sod. Four men hurried out. The first man stuck a little white flag in the ground, while the second quickly measured the distance. "Eleven feet, seven inches!" he called to the scorer's table. The crowd clapped politely as the Duffs and their crew laughed with derision, grabbing at each other as they fell out.

Two men hoisted the stone into a little wooden cart and dollied it back to the starting line. The next contestant approached the line. He was larger than the first and was covered from his neck to his knuckles in hair like a dark-red bristle brush. He glanced nervously at his bristle-brush family, who were bunched tightly together along the ropes, silently urging him on. Stepping over to the rack, he took the stone in hand, backed up a few paces, breathed deep, then rushed forward, letting the stone fly. As before, the four men hurried out. "Twelve feet, one inch" was called, and upon hearing his score, the contestant hurried over and burrowed back in with his clan as they grabbed him by the neck and shoulders and shook him with violent affection. Contestant after contestant came forward, and throw after throw was made and measured, and as each contestant left the field, some shrugged contentedly to their people while others slipped silently behind the crowds in private disappointment.

Far out in the darkness, the Badger leaned against his car watching the lights of the fair, his cigarette glowing orange. Off the narrow road, a car turned and crossed the field, slowly rolling to a stop. Constable Tulloch stepped out.

"Passed by the dig site on the way out here," he said, walking up. "My man says everything's been quiet."

"Right." The Badger took a hard pull on his cigarette and leaned away from his car. "About that. Starting tomorrow I'll be having my own man down there. Just so you know."

"Lord Marwick didn't say anything to me about it."

"No, he wouldn't have. And for the next few days my crew will be doing a bit of security work around the village as well."

"Security?" The constable glanced up from buttoning his overcoat. "What are you talking about, security?"

"Lord Marwick says he wants Skara Skaill to have its best foot forward. For when his guests arrive. Nothing for you to worry about."

"Oh, nothing for me to worry about, is it? And what, that'd be your crew from the wharf then now, would it? Is that a joke?"

"Not a joke. And before I forget." The Badger reached into his coat and pulled out a fat envelope.

"And what's this then?" asked the constable.

"I think you know what it is."

The constable eyed the envelope. He shifted his feet.

"What, you didn't think I knew about that?" asked the Badger, tapping the envelope. "From now on all this'll be coming through me. Your little monthly extra." The Badger peeked inside the envelope. "Lord Marwick wanted me to let you know."

"Oh, he wanted you to let me know, did he?"

"That's right. Said he wants his hands clean of it now." The Badger studied the lights of the fair in the distance. "But you just keep looking the other way, yeah, and we shouldn't have any problems, you and me."

"Problems?" Constable Tulloch studied the Badger, and a slow recognition came into his eyes. "Well now, I see you've been quite a busy man. Been scheming this up for some time then, have you?"

"It's just how Lord Marwick wants it."

"Is it just?" The constable nodded darkly, rolling things over in his mind. "Like how it was you came to be Lord Marwick's man down at the wharf to begin with, eh?" The noise from the crowd rose in the distance. "Funny about that though. I suppose you heard Innes Mackie's back on Skara Skaill, yeah? Come back to pay you a visit, has he?"

The Badger took a draw off his cigarette. "And I assume you'll have no problem remembering where your loyalties lie, yeah?" He held out the envelope. "We wouldn't want to be biting the hand that's feeding you now, would we?"

"I've got my own reasons for tracking Innes Mackie. And it's not because of this." He took the envelope and tucked it into his coat. "How Lord Marwick wants it," he repeated to himself. "And what's next, eh? Lord Marwick gonna make a gentleman out of you? Is that it? That what you think? With the gutter written all over you?" The constable took his hat off, picking at it. "Well, I hope it's worth it, the little scraps he throws you. Squeezing people off their land now, is it? And God knows what else." He fitted his hat back on. "Well, here's bit of advice for you. I'd watch your back if I were you. Because you may be his man for now, but if you think Lord Marwick gives a damn about the likes of you, think again."

"I'll take that under advisement."

"You should do. And if Innes Mackie's back on the island, you'd do well to keep your own crew in line as well, because if you ask me, Frankie Duff seems like a man with ambition."

"Is that right?"

"Oh, it most surely is."

The Badger spit a fleck of tobacco off his tongue as the noise from the crowd rose again in the distance. "You might want to head on, make sure the drunks are behaving themselves, yeah?"

Constable Tulloch eyed him evenly.

"Unless you've got something else to say?" asked the Badger.

The constable eyed him a moment more, then without another word, he turned and headed off toward the lights of the fair.

The Duffs' crew cheered violently as Munro Duff swaggered belly first toward the line. Clapping once, he took up the stone, exhaled hard, and started forward in a violent rush. At the line he barked out a grunt that sent the stone flying high through the air until it embedded in the sod well down the field. The four men hurried out.

"Fifteen feet, three inches" was called.

Above the thin applause of the crowd, the Duffs' crew shouted and pumped their fists, pouring their beers down their throats. Munro bayed at them from the line as the man at the table leaned forward into the microphone.

"And will our final contestant, Contestant Number Sixteen, please toe the line? Contestant Sixteen."

Hearing his number called, Ham awkwardly stooped under the rope. The stone was set back into place. As Ham stepped to the rack, Munro eased back directly into his path and stood there, his eyes on the ground.

"Pardon me, mate," said Ham. But Munro only smirked a glance over at his crew. "Excuse me, I'll just be needing the stone there." Ham nodded toward the rack.

Munro smiled to himself, then finally backed away, gesturing grandly toward the stone. "All yours," he said, strutting back to the howling delight of his crew.

Ham took up the stone and backed to the very edge of the crowd. Along the ropes, two elderly sisters stood looking enthusiastically up at him.

Ham glanced over his shoulder. "Sorry, ladies, not meaning to crowd you."

"Don't you worry yourself, lad, we've plenty of room back here. Plenty of room." They nodded hard at him. "But you just go to it. You just go right to it."

Ham could see the keenness in their eyes, and glancing out at the crowd, he saw the same look in the faces all around him. He nervously turned to the runway, balancing the stone in his hand. Taking a last breath, he started forward, not lumbering like the others but fast and light, and as he reached the line, his right arm flashed out, bidding the stone farewell. The stone flew above the little white flags like a bird looking down on a sheep's meadow until at last it began its downward arc, finally auguring into the emerald sod with a thud so deep the crowd felt it in their feet. The men with the measuring tape rushed onto the field, but Ham's stone had traveled well past the last chalked line, and having no measurement to call out, they could only look back at the announcer and shrug.

From all directions Ham was overrun by the jubilant crowd. Yet some in the audience, having grown emboldened by Ham's victory, rushed past the Duffs too fast and too close, jostling the brothers as they went. Grabbing the first man within reach, Frankie Duff shook him and threw him to the ground. Seeing Ham being presented with the trophy, Frankie began to bull his way through the crowd. His crew dropped their beers and hurried after him.

Rory and Tito reached Ham just as the bespectacled man placed four boxed pies in his arms. "Do you want us to carry those?" asked Tito, calling up to Ham through the din. But suddenly Tito felt himself being yanked away.

Rory pulled Tito farther into the crowd. "The Duffs." He pointed.

As the Duffs' crew surged out of the crowd, Ham was jostled hard, and the pies tumbled to the ground. He tried to reach down beneath the mass of trampling feet, but as he did, the trophy was suddenly knocked from his hand. He turned around to see Frankie Duff standing squarely in front of him.

"You should be more careful." Frankie smiled darkly. "A nice trophy like that."

Ham eyed Frankie warily as Munro and the rest of the crew appeared. "No harm done," he said after a moment. "Not looking for any trouble."

"Well, but you see," Munro replied, stepping in next to Frankie, "you've managed to find it just the same, haven't you, friendo?"

Ham considered their numbers as they pressed in closer. Then feeling someone at his side he turned to see Innes appear out of the crowd.

"I believe he said he wasn't looking for any trouble."

At the sight of Innes, Frankie and Munro stopped still.

"Well, now," said Frankie. "We'd heard something about this."

"The Badger knows too," added Munro.

"I have no doubt. I'm sure you two saw to that," said Innes. "What with you being as loyal as you are."

Frankie looked at him evenly. "Was you that left, Innes. Me and Munro, we just seen which way the wind was blowing, is all." He set his feet. "Course we can sort out any hard feelings you might have right now, if you'd like."

From behind the Duffs, some of their crew had recovered the pies and were eating drunken handfuls out of them.

"Oy," said Ham. "You pass those over."

"How about you come and get 'em?" laughed the men. But as Ham started to reach through, Munro shoved him back.

"Don't be coming through me like that," and before Munro's sucker punch was halfway home, Innes flashed across, striking Munro flat in the ear, knocking him to the ground. The Duffs' crew instantly came boiling forward in a rage, but as they did, a voice rang out over the crowd.

"Alright, break it up!" The constable was wading toward them through the chaos. "Let's go. Everyone break it the hell up. It's a family occasion."

Seeing the constable heading their way, Innes immediately ducked low into the crowd. "Go, Ham!"

"But where are the boys?" asked Ham.

"Already gone. Go." And staying low, the two disappeared together through the crowd as the constable stepped directly into Frankie's path.

"I said break it up, Frankie."

"The hell I will. Did you not see who that was?"

"All I seen was you and your brother up to the usual. Time to go home, Frankie."

"Is that right? I'm to go home am I?" Frankie smiled at the constable. "And what exactly are you gonna do about it, eh? It's the Badger calls the tune now."

"Oh yeah? And how about you try me then, eh? Today the day, Frankie?" The constable waited. "Just give me one reason to throw you back into lockup. Just one."

From behind them, Munro let out a little whistle. Out beyond the crowd, the Badger stood staring in at them, nodding the Duffs toward the parking lot.

Frankie slowly backed away, eyeing the constable as he went.

"Alright then, Tulloch. Next time, yeah? Next time."

As the Duffs and their crew began to clear off, the constable turned and scanned out over the fair, but the crowd all around him had closed in again.

* * *

Night settled over the fairgrounds. The muted sounds and colors of the evening filled the air. A town band played brightly from a little stage. Stopping beneath the string lights, Ham and Innes watched as couples moved each other around the dance floor.

Ham noticed Innes staying back from the lights. "So did I mention I saw the constable drive off?"

"Did he?" Innes kept one eye on the crowd.

"Aye, and those others too." Ham considered Innes a moment. "Seemed like you were in a bit of a hurry back there. Couldn't help but notice."

"Is that how it seemed?" Innes glanced at him. "Yeah, well, me and the constable, we have a bit of a history."

"And with those brothers too, sounds like?" Innes didn't answer. Ham turned again to the dance floor. "Anyway. I wanted to say thanks, you know, for your help with all that."

"I'm sure you didn't need it."

"See, people always think that, you know, because of my size."

"Let's just call it even then. For getting me to the clinic and that."

They stood watching as the couples moved around the dance floor in a slow-turning spiral. Through the light and space, Innes's eyes suddenly fell upon Aggie Allen standing in the crowd at the far side of the floor. She was eating popcorn from a paper sack and laughing at a group of children dancing wildly near the stage. She had an easy, crooked smile, and her face was lit warm in the lights, and as Innes watched her, he felt a tightness rise within his chest. Pairs of dancers pinwheeled between them, but his eyes stayed on her.

The music stopped, and the fiddler mopped his brow before starting in on a simple waltz as the dancers began anew. Down the line, Ham saw the two elderly sisters he'd seen in the crowd at the stone put. He took a polite step toward them.

"Excuse me, sorry. Hello, just wanted to say thanks for cheering me on back there."

"Oh, and it was well done too, lad." They nodded ardently at him. "Well done indeed."

"It helped more than you'd think, the cheering." Ham nodded, then turned quietly back to Innes. "Come on, we should have a dance. It'll do us some good."

"Ah, Ham, you're not really my type." But Ham had already stepped down the line again and was giving the ladies a courtly bow.

"May we have the pleasure?" he asked, offering his elbow. Innes came alongside. The ladies smiled up at the sight of the two wild-haired men before them, and glancing at each other, they gently took the men's arms and allowed themselves to be led out onto the dance floor. As the band played in waltz-time, Ham and Innes danced the sisters carefully around the floor, but the ladies knew the old steps well, and Innes and Ham tried their best for them. From where she stood, Aggie caught sight of Innes as he tried to follow the steps, the elderly sister smiling patiently up at him as they went. Through her gloves, Innes could feel the strength in her thin hands. When the tune was over, they turned and clapped for the band. Innes walked his partner slowly back to the side as Aggie watched him all the while.

The crowd began to thin away. Innes and Ham saw Tito standing among a group of children just beyond the lights.

When they reached Tito, he was peering into a shoebox a little girl was holding. Inside it, a tiny pipit lay dead on a bed of grass. The perfect fan of its wing was folded against its side. Its feet were clutched closed.

Ham peered into the box. "Where's your brother gone to, Tito?"

"He went looking for food."

As the little girl wandered away with the box, Ham now saw Aggie in the crowd. "It's the doctor." He waved.

Aggie stepped over, greeting them all. "Good evening, hello. Hello, Tito."

"Hello, miss."

Innes nodded. "Evening."

"And so you're feeling better then?" she asked him.

"Much better, yes. Thank you."

Rory appeared out of the dark. He had no food, but he held Ham's trophy, dented and dusty.

"Wait, I think I heard about this," said Aggie. "Was that you then?"

"Ham won it," said Tito.

"And I understand a few folks didn't take it too very well?"

"They did not," said Ham.

"The Duffs tried to start a fight, miss," said Tito. "But the constable, he sent them off."

"Well, that's good at least."

"Innes did have to punch one of them though."

"Did he now?" she asked. Innes silently reset his feet.

"In the ear." Tito nodded. "But he deserved it quite a lot."

From out in the darkness toward the edge of the fairgrounds, an orange glow began slowly rising in the meadow.

"Bonfires are lit," said Rory, and before he'd finished saying it, Tito was already weaving away through the crowd as the others followed behind.

Stepping out into the meadow, Innes and Aggie found themselves walking alone together in the dark.

"And so you're really feeling better then?" she asked after a moment.

"I am, yes, thank you."

"And no fever?"

"No. Nothing."

"Good."

A silence fell over them.

"So you're settling in alright then, are you?" Innes asked.

"I am, yes."

Innes nodded. "You know, I'd meant to say so before, but I am going to pay you for your help with all that."

"No, there's no need; it's a free clinic. But it was good they brought you in when they did though."

Innes watched the boys up ahead, walking side by side in the dark. "You know, there'd never been a full-time doctor out here before. On the island."

"Yes, I'd heard that." She nodded.

The dewy field grass grabbed at their feet. All around them, silhouettes moved along in the darkness. "And you say you're settling in alright then?"

"I am." She glanced at him. "I've been doing a bit of walking as well. Trying to learn my way around. I thought I might walk out to Kettleskaill House here next week. Hoping to get to know some of the families outside the village as well." A young couple hurried past them toward the orange glow in the darkness. "I even walked a little way out on the heath this morning."

"Did you?"

"I did. I kind of lost my way a little. Actually, I definitely lost my way."

"Yeah, well, this time of year if you ever get turned around you can always just put the sun at your back and start walking. You'll hit the village every time."

Just ahead, two bonfires burned side by side, rising twenty feet up into the night sky, their sparks swirling away into the blackness. As Innes and Aggie caught up with the others, a young couple took each other by the hand, bowed, curtsied, then hurried between the fires before disappearing into the darkness on the other side.

Rory turned to Tito, pretending to take his hand. "For luck, or for love?"

"Oh, very funny." Tito snatched his hand away. "Let's go see the pigs after. There's one as big as a cow," he said as they took off between the fires.

Ham considered the fires warily. "Nope. I think I'll just go have a look at the food," he said, heading away toward the tents.

Aggie and Innes stood there awkwardly, suddenly alone. Another couple hurried around them hand in hand, bowing and curtsying, kissing clumsily on the run as they went.

Aggie looked at Innes and shrugged. "For luck, at least?" she asked, the firelight glowing golden in her face. She curtsied to him. He paused a moment, then nodding a little bow, he took her hand. In the night air, he could feel its warmth in his.

Passing through the fires, the heat overwhelmed them for a moment before they were out again in the cool of the evening, the vast sweep of the moors stretching out beyond them in the emptiness. Aggie continued a little out into the dark, where the outlines of other young women stood to their waists in the wet grass, and doing as they did, she, too, drew her hands gently through the grass, touching the dew to her face three times. Nearby, a pipit twitched into the night air, its under-feathers flashing white in the firelight before vanishing into the blackness above. Aggie returned to Innes just as a little girl came up to them holding out a braided-grass garland.

"How lovely," said Aggie. But the little girl offered it only to Innes, and before he could refuse it, she shoved the garland into his hand. "What, only for the boys?" Aggie smiled as the girl turned and ran away.

"Well, traditionally," Innes paused awkwardly. "Traditionally it would be the man who places it on the lady's head. For luck." He stopped short, looking for the words.

"For luck then," Aggie said, bowing her head to him.

At first Innes did not move, but when Aggie didn't rise, he stepped forward and carefully placed the garland on her head. She straightened up and smiled at him. Her pale cheeks flushed from the heat of the fire and the coolness of the dew. Innes looked at her a moment, then glanced away as Rory and Tito came walking up.

"You got the garland, miss?" asked Tito.

"I did," she said, adjusting it on her head. "Can't have too much luck."

Rory glanced at Innes, then back at Aggie. "Well, yeah, it's for luck, but..." He paused. "Well, for over the winter, when..." He stopped again.

Tito looked up at Aggie. "It's for luck making a family, miss, you know, during the winter." He nodded earnestly.

"Oh." Aggie froze as Innes smiled hard at the ground. "Well, that's not really the kind of luck I'm looking for just at the moment."

* * *

The sounds of the darkening fair faded away behind them as Innes led Ham and the boys down the slope toward the moors.

"Anyone hungry?" asked Ham. "Because I happen to have a little surprise." He drew a large golden-brown pie out of a bag tucked in his coat.

"I thought all the pies got ruined?" asked Rory.

"They did. I bought another one at the tent." Ham held out the pie. "Willing to share."

"Meat or berry?" asked Tito, stepping in close.

"Meat. And she's cut it for us."

"You should save your money," said Innes, still carrying his buckets. "We've got all these cans of food from the house."

"Nope, no beans tonight. And besides, I didn't spend my money. I spent yours."

"Mine?"

"One very green coin." Ham nodded. "The one you gave me."

"What, she took that as payment? What was that, fifty pence?"

"Who could even tell? She wanted to give me the pie for nothing because she'd seen what happened with the other ones. I tried to make her take something, but she only took the coin. She said she liked it." Ham offered the pie around, and the boys each took a wedge. "Her name's Ada. She works at the Vat and Fiddle." They all started walking again, eating as they went.

"Good, isn't it?" said Ham. "Come on, Innes, get some of this."

"When we get back to the cave huts."

They went on eating quietly as they walked along.

"She said she works in the kitchens mostly," said Ham. "Which would explain the pies, but then I guess sometimes on busy nights they have her up front too, waiting tables, and…"

Ham and the boys continued ahead as Innes stopped and set his buckets down to rebalance them. When he straightened up, he stood searching in the darkness until he saw them again, their silhouettes moving steadily away onto the moors, Ham's voice fading in the wind, while high above, moonlit clouds sailed across the night sky.

"Works evenings mostly, which she…but sometimes…able to…and fill apparently."

X

THE BADGER OPENED HIS eyes just before sunup. His coat lay over his chest like a blanket. The inside of the windshield was frozen over. A gray mist blew cold across the field. On the dashboard, a half-smoked cigarette sat cold. He tapped away the ash from the night before and lit it. On the seat next to him lay a thermos of coffee. He filled a Styrofoam cup and climbed out of the vehicle. A man half sleeping in a chair stood up as the Badger stepped inside the tent.

"You sure you don't want any help down there, boss?" asked the man.

The Badger walked over to the hole, taking little sips from the steaming coffee.

"No. You can go. Just get to the wharf and tell Frankie to send someone else." Stepping wearily onto the top rung, his cigarette between his teeth, the Badger climbed in.

Down in the shaft, he passed the painted cross on the wall and stooped beneath the archway into the lower chamber. He switched on the light. The room was half dug out now. Along the walls were newly exposed stones, longer and smoother than the others. On some of the stones were crude paintings. The pigment, cracked and faded, barely clung to the rock. They were simple scenes of the moorlands—wild boar among the crowberry—salmon running in the streams—an elk on the ridgeline—a flock of sheep on the hill. The Badger looked quietly around the room, then pulling off his coat, he picked up a shovel and dug.

* * *

Innes led the others scrambling up the embankment, soaked to their waists in sand and seawater. In the tall grass, they set their buckets down as Innes stared out in confusion at the dark tide rushing in from every direction. Seabirds wheeled in the gray sky overhead.

"I'd forgotten it was Fhøghartide," he said, catching his breath. "These tides used to be so familiar to me." Far out in the tide, the rock where they had been collecting mussels all afternoon sat pocked and ancient, quickly sinking beneath the waves.

"What does he mean about Fhøghartide, Rory?" Tito whispered.

"Just that the tides are strange this time of year."

Tito watched the tides swirling over the last of the mud flats that had shone that afternoon like scattered mirrors. "And you say it's the moon that controls it, the tide?" He looked up at the cold moon in the twilight, the faint smudge of the comet hanging motionless in the sky.

Ham tried to brush the wet sand off his clothes. "Am I the only one who stepped in that bloody hole?" He was soaked with seawater up to his beard. "You know how some people have natural buoyancy? Well, I don't have that."

Smiling to himself, Tito pulled a scrap of paper from his pack and scribbled something down, then shoved it back into his pack.

"We'd better make a fire," said Innes. "We can dry out while we clean them."

They set a fire and started in on their work.

Tito stared into his bucket of mussels. "Look at this one, he's huge."

"Actually, it's the medium ones you want," said Innes. "The big ones can be nasty."

"Yeah, look at the beard on that big fella." Tito squatted down. "Disgusting."

"You know, if I didn't know you were talking about mussels," said Ham.

Innes went over to Rory's bucket. "Come on, we'll need to get some seawater on those. And you'll want to make sure and pick out the ones with a cracked shell."

"Definitely don't want those," said Ham. "Or else you'll be sitting on the hoop for a week."

Rory followed Innes down to the water's edge.

Tito reached into his bucket. "Cracked one." Standing up, he turned and chucked the broken mussel out toward the water, but before it could hit the surface a gull flashed low, and snatching it in its beak it banked away as two gulls screamed after it. "See that?" asked Tito kneeling again to his bucket, practicing a thin whistle.

"So, where does the name Tito come from anyway?" asked Ham.

"That's just a nickname. My real name's Theodore."

"And how'd you come by Tito then?"

"I don't know, was just in my paperwork." Ham glanced thoughtfully at Tito digging in his bucket. "It means *pigeon* in Latin. Rory looked it up. But I don't know who gave it to me. My last name is Hay though. Rory's is Corrigal."

"What, are you not brothers then?"

"We're halfs. We had the same mum, but different da." Swallows darted homeward as evening began falling over the water. "Rory says I can't have remembered her, but I do." Tito reached his arm deep into the bottom. "Mrs. Renfro said some people just have a harder time of it, is all."

"That's true enough, Tito."

Tito went back to his work, practicing his whistle. After a moment, he stopped and listened as the faintest sound, a jangling sound, came carrying in on the wind.

Rory and Innes came stepping up the bank just as Eustice, fully harnessed, trotted past them out in the twilight. But as the big mule disappeared over a low rise, a horrifying scream suddenly pierced the wind, loud and shrill.

Ham jumped to his feet. "That didn't sound like Eustice."

The scream came again, desperate and piteous.

"This way," said Innes, hurrying up the hill, the boys following behind.

Ham called out after them. "And so it's toward the terrifying sound you think we should be heading then?"

From the top of the rise, they could see the dark shape of Eustice standing in the swale below.

"Well, he looks alright," said Rory, starting down. But as they reached the bottom, the scream came again, and this time Innes saw all too well from where it had come. The others saw it too. A moor pony, half buried in a bog, its head and forelegs barely visible above the surface of the mud. A short way off, gathered in a row, stood the rest of the herd, their eyes fixed hard upon the pony.

"I'll grab Eustice," whispered Rory, but as he started forward, Innes pulled him back.

"The mire," he said quietly. "It's all around us. Right where we're standing." As they eased back toward solid ground, the scream came again as the pony struggled weakly in the mud before exhausting itself and lying still.

Innes turned to Rory. "I think if we go the long way around we might get to Eustice from the other side."

"And what about the pony?" asked Tito.

Innes was slow to answer. "Well, he's in the mire, Tito, and I mean, well once you're in it—"

"What? Are you saying we're just gonna leave him in there?" Tito turned to Rory. "We can't just leave him in there, Rory."

"Maybe he's close to the edge?" suggested Rory.

"Even if we could reach him—" Innes looked out. "I mean, he's fifteen stone easy. Maybe twenty. And that's if we could even get close to him, what with his herd right there. Those horses are wild, Tito. They are no joke."

As the pony began thrashing again, it slipped lower into the bog, weakening, until finally laying its cheek softly down, it fell quiet.

Ham set his buckets down.

"Nope. That's it. I can't take that. I really cannot. I'm just gonna go and—well, I don't know what I'm gonna do exactly, but I'm going in." Ham began swinging his arms side to side to ready himself. "Innes, if you wouldn't mind just calling out to me which way I should go. Left. Right. Stop, of course."

"But what about you not having the natural buoyancy?" asked Tito.

"Not planning on needing it. Actually, I'm hoping some of this bog has already dried into peat anyway."

"Hang on," said Innes. "Just hang on a minute."

"Nope." Ham stood facing the bog. "I know what you're gonna say, and you'll not talk me out of it."

"What I was gonna say was, if we're gonna do this, and I still say it won't help any, but if we are then it should be me that goes. I know the mires. Plus, you're the biggest one here in case I need pulling out."

Ham nodded immediately. "Works for me."

"Well, you certainly jumped on that pretty quick."

"Yeah, well, you made a fine argument."

Innes turned and stared out at the mire. Reaching down, he selected a few small stones.

"I'm just gonna see how close I can get, alright? Not promising anything more than that."

Tito nodded at him.

As Innes started forward, he would every so often drop one of the stones at his feet until finally, he came to a stop a short distance from the pony. He glanced quickly over at the herd, and their eyes were on him. Stepping to the very edge of the bog, he leaned out for a closer look, but upon seeing Innes, the pony's eyes flashed and it again began thrashing against the grip of the mire. With every movement, it sank deeper, crying out more loudly than before. The herd whinnied back their reply, shuffling their hooves at the edge of the bog but coming no closer, as the pony exhausted itself again and lay still once more. In its struggles, the pony had slid farther and deeper from the edge and was now well beyond Innes's reach. Its big eyes, white with terror, stared up at him.

Glancing back, Innes saw Ham now stepping slowly out to meet him, with Rory and Tito right behind. "What're you doing?" he called, waving them back.

"We're coming out, is what."

"No. Go back." But Ham kept inching forward, his eyes locked on the ground. "Can you at least see the stones I dropped?"

"You mean the stones that look the same as all the other stones?"

"They're the whiter ones. Are you seeing them?"

"I wouldn't say I'm exactly seeing them, but I am most surely looking for them."

"Well, just go slow."

"This *is* slow," called Ham as he and the boys hurried the last few steps to where Innes stood. "Well," Ham looked nervously at the ground around them, "here we all are."

"Yes, here we all are," repeated Innes.

"Well, and what good could you have done out here by yourself anyway?"

Rory looked at the pony. "He seems calmer, at least."

Innes shook his head. "Not calmer, he's—well, I'd say he's maybe been in there a day or two already. And with no water except what's rained on him." They could see the pony's ribs showing through its hide, its eyes wide with fear. It tried to lift itself but slowly laid its cheek down again in the mud.

Ham stretched out his arm. The pony's hoof was still a foot or more beyond his grasp. He inched closer, but his boot immediately began to sink in the mud.

"What if we hold on to you, Ham? Lean you out?" asked Tito.

"Lean him?" said Rory. "I think once he starts leaning there'll be no bringing him back."

Innes studied the pony a moment. “I don’t know. I mean if we had some rope maybe.”

Tito dropped his pack and immediately produced a coil of thin rope.

Innes took the rope and tied a little slipknot in it. “So what I’m thinking is—here, Rory, you take this end and I’ll try and lean out, see if I can’t get the loop on him.” Innes stepped carefully to the edge of the bog and reached back for Ham.

Ham took Innes’s hand and dug in. “OK.” He nodded.

Innes struggled a little with Ham’s grip. “I can’t really get a good—hang on, OK my wrist is—hang on a minute.”

“Sorry,” said Ham.

Innes readied himself once more and slowly began leaning out over the bog.

“More. A little more. OK, that’s good right there.” Stretching out as far as he could reach, Innes carefully draped the loop of rope over the pony’s front hoof. But just as the rope grazed its foreleg, the pony twitched with terror and began thrashing in violent panic. And this time it didn’t stop. With each convulsion it slipped deeper into the bog as its legs and neck and finally its terrified eyes slipped away beneath the mud. They stared in stunned silence at the loop of rope lying empty on the surface of the mire. Suddenly Innes jerked loose from Ham’s grip and lunged forward onto the bog.

“Innes!”

“Just hold the rope.” Innes grabbed for the loop of rope, and as his lower half began sinking below the mud, he worked frantically beneath the surface. “Alright, take out the slack.”

The rope snapped taut as Innes hauled himself hand over hand and scrambled out onto solid ground.

"OK, now let's all pull, but gently." The thin rope quivered arrow-straight into the bog. "Easy. Don't snap it." For a long moment, the rope didn't budge, but finally it began to move, and slowly breaking the surface of the mire, the pony's front leg came into view, then its head and the curve of its chest, and then all in a rush the pony slipped out of the bog onto dry land.

Caked with mud, it lay motionless on the ground.

"Is he alive?" whispered Tito.

"He's breathing," said Rory. "See."

The pony's ribs rose and fell weakly. After lying a long moment, the pony suddenly shuddered, and drawing its legs beneath itself, it struggled to its feet and stood there, its big eyes staring wide at them.

"Everyone be very still," whispered Innes. "He's wanting to run, and if he does he's going to end up right back in it." The pony's back hooves stood at the very edge of the mire. The rope lay on the ground.

"I think we should all take a step back," whispered Rory. "He looks like he needs some room." They took a single step back. But the pony didn't move. "And again." For a moment, the pony only stared at them, but then his ears flicked and with a little shake of his head, he took a wary step toward them, and step by halting step, he followed them slowly out onto solid ground.

"Well done, Rory," exhaled Ham. "Well done."

Innes quickly moved around between the bog and the pony and raised his arms. "Alright you. Go on." But the pony only stood blinking at them all. "Go on then."

"Innes," whispered Rory suddenly, an urgency in his voice.

From the corner of Innes's eye, he now saw the herd, heads low, moving straight toward Tito standing alone between the herd and the pony.

"Tito," whispered Innes. "Do not move. Hold perfectly still."

The herd approached uneasily. Tito could feel their hooves thudding into the ground. As they passed around him, he could smell the cold coming off their matted manes and could see the hard scars in their hides. Their marble eyes were on him, and slowly surrounding the little pony now hidden deep among them, they headed steadily away.

From behind him, Rory heard Eustice jangling forward to follow after the herd, but grabbing hold of the bridle, he held the big mule tight as they all stood watching the gray mass of the herd slowly fade into the darkness.

XI

THE SQUARE OF WINDOW light burned orange. Rory and Tito stood at Mr. Begbie's front door, while Innes and Ham held Eustice at the top of the path. Through the door, Rory could hear movement inside the house. He knocked and took a step back. Suddenly the window went dark, and the house fell silent. Rory glanced back at the others, then stepped forward and knocked again.

"Hello?" he called through the door. "Mr. Begbie?" But there was no answer. "We have Eustice here." In an instant, the window lit orange again, and the hardware of the door rattled open. Mr. Begbie stood in the rectangle of light, squinting out. Upon seeing the big mule at the top of the path, he hurried out across the threshold.

"Ahh, Eustice, look at you. You're a delinquent," he said, shuffling past Rory and Tito. "We turn our back on you for a minute, gone again. He was with those moor ponies, wasn't he?"

"How did you know?" asked Tito.

"Because that's what he does. He wants to be one of them. He's besotted, aren't you, boy? Always knows exactly where to find them too. Unties himself, if you can believe that. With his teeth he does it." Rory turned away from Tito, ignoring him.

"Sorry we didn't let you in right away. We thought you were one of them other fellas that's been coming around." As he reached the mule, Mr. Begbie began gently thumping Eustice's long face. He took the bridle in his knobby hands and started Eustice toward the barn, lecturing the big mule as they went. "It's hard for us to stay angry with you, but if you keep this up…"

Innes and Ham stood watching them go.

"Are we meant to wait for him, do you think?" asked Ham.

Innes could see the old man's stooped silhouette in the light of the barn door. "Let's give him a minute."

"He's chatting up a mule, Innes. There won't be any minute about it."

After a little while, Mr. Begbie stepped out of the barn again and labored back across the yard, mumbling to himself. As he reached the path, he looked up at the four of them still standing there.

"Oh. Right. We'd almost forgotten about you lot."

"Well, we were just leaving," said Innes. "Just wanted to make sure you were all set with your mule there."

Mr. Begbie looked up at Innes, noticing for the first time that he was covered head to toe in bog mud. "Look like you just crawled out of the grave." Suddenly Mr. Begbie stopped and stared at something out beyond them in the blackness. "Now that's passing strange."

The herd of moor ponies were standing out in the dark, grazing in the wind.

"Never seen them in this close before."

The ponies lifted their heads a moment, then went back to their grazing. All except the little one, who stood stiffly on his thin legs, looking in at them.

"Just never seen them in this close before," repeated Mr. Begbie, before starting up the path. "Should get out of this wind though. Got a good fire going inside." And before they could answer, he was already at the front door. "How 'bout a cup a tea? I've got no milk, mind you."

Inside, they stood along the wall, nearly filling the little house. Mr. Begbie went to the end of the front room, where a cast-iron stove sat next to a sink at the window. Centered along the wall was a stone hearth. A little bed of coals glowed faintly, and nestled down within the embers sat a steaming iron pot.

Mr. Begbie rummaged through the kitchen. "I could've sworn we had tea left. The family that lives upstairs sometimes borrows it. They do that." Tito looked curiously up at the ceiling of the one-story cottage. "Well, and who's for a cup of hot water and honey?" asked Mr. Begbie. "It's old, the honey, but it should break up in water alright."

"Thank you, no. We've still a bit of a walk ahead of us," said Innes.

Ham nodded toward the pot on the fire. "And we wouldn't want to interrupt your supper there."

"My supper? Oh that, that's just water for the wash. We already had our supper." Mr. Begbie's eyes dropped in confusion. "At least, I think we had. My appetite's been leaving me of late."

Innes considered the old man a moment, standing alone in the dim kitchen. He turned, but Ham was already nodding at him, and they set their buckets down.

"Eh, Mr. Begbie?" asked Ham. "We were wondering if it might be alright if we used your fire there? To cook our supper? Plenty to share, if you'd like."

"You want to cook it here?" asked Mr. Begbie, shuffling out of the kitchen.

"It's mussels," said Tito.

"Oh, well, of course you can. Of course." Then a thought came to him, and he snapped his fingers. "And we have a garlic, we have a wild garlic. Hanging in the shed." With his finger still in the air, Mr. Begbie started for the back door.

"A garlic, you said?" asked Ham, following him out. "Would you mind if I have a look? I've actually been wanting to see what a wild one looks like."

The fire settled low, and a single candle lit the room. They sat, well fed, a heap of empty shells piled in the middle of the wooden table. Being that there were only three chairs, Tito and Rory shared a square metal tub tipped on its end. From out of a dark corner, a thin gray cat stepped smoothly around the base of the wall, then slipped beneath the table. Tito peered underneath as the cat intertwined itself among the legs of Mr. Begbie's chair and sat down between the old man's boots. The boots were worn through, and Tito could see that Mr. Begbie's ankles were bare and scabrous and swollen so purple they could hardly fit down into them. Tito stared a moment, then the cat sprang lightly into Mr. Begbie's lap, stepped gingerly out across the table, and hunched down at the pile of empty mussel shells.

"You can find piles of old shells like that all over the islands." Mr. Begbie nodded. "Wherever people were."

"Innes showed us where to find these ones," said Tito.

"Easy enough to catch, am I right, Tito? Not too quick on their feet, eh?" Mr. Begbie shifted in his chair and turned very deliberately toward Innes. "And so it's *Innes* then, is it?"

"It is."

"And did you say you're from the islands?"

"I am, yeah. Well, I was anyway."

"He's been gone for a while," said Tito.

"And whereabouts on the islands are you from then, lad?"

"Out by the western cliffs."

"Innes of Skara Skaill. That's quite a name they give ya."

"Yeah, well, that would be my father," said Innes. "He put stock in all that. The old stories. Said he thought the name might bring me some luck out there."

"Out where?" asked Tito.

"Just out in the world, I guess. He knew all the old stories though. The ballads." A remembrance came across Innes's eyes. "He had them by heart."

"And so you've been away then, have you?" asked Mr. Begbie, studying him. "Out in the world?"

"I have."

"And what did you find out there?"

Innes adjusted his plate. "Oh, this and that."

"Emm, Mr. Begbie?" asked Ham. "Can I ask, earlier you said that you didn't answer the door because some other fellas had been coming around?"

"Aye." Mr. Begbie nodded. "That'd be the county boys."

"The county? And what would the county be wanting with you?" asked Ham. Innes listened, but kept his eyes on his plate.

"Our land is what. The county says we owe on it, and the Badger, he does the county's business. The earl's business. It's him that wants it."

"The earl?" asked Ham as politely as he could manage. "The earl wants this place, does he?"

“What the earl wants is how things used to be,” said Mr. Begbie. “The Marwicks, they used to own all this land, all around. Used to, they did. But now this one, he wants it back.”

“Why?” asked Tito. “With him having so much already.”

“Because some men want to own the world, lad. Of that you can be certain.” Mr. Begbie looked over and saw Rory glancing at the objects laid across the shelf. “Go ahead, have a look, have a look.”

As Rory and Tito went to the shelf, Mr. Begbie again turned to Innes. “So you’ve come back, have you? And you’ve got family here then?”

“No,” said Innes, sweeping something off his lap. “Just passing through.”

“Ah, well, and aren’t we all, Innes of Skara Skaill. Aren’t we all.” Mr. Begbie nodded. “For fast falls the eventide, I can tell you.” He looked over at the boys at the shelf. “All that came from here. From Skara Skaill. We’ve been walking these islands a long time now.”

“Sorry, and when you say ‘we’?” asked Ham. “You’ve got family do you?”

“Brothers.” Begbie nodded. “Two under the ground. Me still above it. Like I was telling the boys here, we were none, then one, then two, then three. Then two, now one. Soon none.”

At the shelf, Tito picked up a rounded stone. He could see that it was fashioned into what looked to be a small child. It had two indentions for eyes, and etched on its middle was a faint marking, three circles made from a single continuous line.

“That one there, he’s from the beginning,” said Mr. Begbie. “The First People would’ve made him. The Little People. Just a lad like you, eh, Tito?” Mr. Begbie squinted fondly at the little stone boy. “But life would’ve been short for him. Dying was closer in them days. Much closer than now. That's why they made him outta stone."

"Why?" asked Tito.

"Because they were saying to Death, 'Here, take my boy from me if you must. I can't stop you. But bloody choke on him.' And so Death spat him out and let him be. And there he sits."

Tito studied the stone boy, the fire flickering across its face. Glancing over, he saw that Rory was holding a flat metal object in his hand, pitted with age.

"What's that?"

"An ax-head," said Rory.

"That's right," nodded Mr. Begbie. "That's right."

"And who would've made that one, do you think?" asked Ham.

"That one? Oh, hard to say. Picts. Northmen maybe. Look at the edge on it though. Could still fell a tree, that."

"Wouldn't have had much need for that out here, I suppose," said Ham. "There's hardly a tree on this island."

"Well, no, not now maybe, not now. But these shores used to be full of them. Have you not read your sagas, lad?" Mr. Begbie leaned toward Ham. "*In ages old, when the world was new, and mists roamed dark and free, and Grendel stood on legs of two, and stalked men's company.*" Mr. Begbie saw the confusion on Ham's face. He turned to the others. "What, has the whole world forgotten its yesterdays?"

"We've read them," said Tito. "Me and Rory. Do you know the rest?" He lowered himself onto the metal tub as Ham adjusted his chair, waiting.

"What, you want me to tell it?" asked Mr. Begbie. Rory went over and set another brick of peat onto the embers. "Well, alright then." Mr. Begbie glanced at Innes. "Me, I've got them by heart too."

And taking a sip of warm water, he began…

In ages old, when the world was new
And mists roamed dark and free
And Grendel stood on legs of two
And stalked men's company.

Two cousins from the northern lands
Raised up as kith and kin
Yet one became the crown'ed king
The other jailed within.

Now locked away he sat alone
And bewept his outcast state
Yet did befriend imprisoned men
And dreamt of better fate.

But the night-watch guard was good of heart
And knew his ward was true
And leaving late his post one night
Prince Harald he let through.

Into the stores of the false king's hoards
Did steal the outcast one
And take by right the gold that night
And board his ship anon.

A following sea drove him westerly
Through the dark his ship did fly
As gray dawn came, with an iron rain
An island he did spy.

The prow slid silent 'pon the nameless shore
Harald's hoard unloaded down
In the island's breast went the oaken chests
Hid deep beneath the ground

Then the island folk that lived thereon
They came and took him in
And filled his cup and bade him sup
And welcomed him as kin.

Now the snow-white moon did die and bloom
Four years and then one more
And he dwelt with them most happily
His soul aggrieved no more.

But one cold day a ship it came
The impostor king was dead
His heart proved black, his mind 'twas slack
The crown sought its rightful head.

So with heavy heart did the prince depart
Yet a gift he left behind
Worth such a cost, yet can't be lost
Then he vowed return in time.

As for the hoard, 'twas left ashore
Still hid beneath the ground
For wary was he of what schemes may be
Still plotting for the crown.

But as the wind did once again
Return him eastward home
Upon the rocks his ship was lost
And dragged beneath the foam.

Now lo, three hundred years did pass
The white moon bloom'ed still
And from the south a man set out
An order to fulfill.

For his wanton lord, now long at war
In need of men and treasure
Sent rangers out, all roundabout
For all to pay full measure.

So to the north, this man sailed forth
To the island folk he came
To carry out his lord's command
And Innes was his name.

Now these northern isles, with hinterlands
Rare seen by civil men
Lived norsemen old, the stories told
Where none came back again.

But the island folk he found thereon
They came and took him in
And filled his cup and bade him sup
And welcomed him as kin.

No warriors here, nor swordsmen
And of riches they had none
Just farmers and fishers and keepers of bees
and a little church of stone.

On the breeze the smell of gathered wheat
Warmed in the slanting sun
And the motes drifted to the bee-drone
When the working day was done.

And his sword was bent to plowshares
For his warring days were done
And Innes found a love, and married
And to him she bore a son.

And the snow-white moon did die and bloom
Two years and then one more
And Innes dwelt most happily
His soul aggrieved no more.

But out upon the narrows dark
Sailed silent a marauder
With shackled men, chained down within
His lord's fresh cannon fodder.

A freebooter, a man looter
He saw the islands low
His mast nigh splintered from a storm
Spied timber past the shoal.

The anchor dropped near the shifting sands
And the bark was rowed ashore
While a mast-straight yew was being felled
Dread Maerwicke stalked the moor.

But the island folk found him thereon
And came and took him in
And filled his cup and bade him sup
And welcomed him as kin.

Back from the fields came lads and men
Amongst them Innes too
But his eyes stayed low in the firelight glow
For this viper Innes knew.

As he crossed the floor to bar the door
In burst the villain's band
Broadswords held tight within their fists
Short daggers in their hands.

Then young and old were rounded up
Against the longhouse wall
When a gaffer he came stooping out
And spoke squarely to them all.

"These lads here are but farm boys
And these men not made for war
I pray don't carry them 'cross the sea
To die in fields afar."

"It's true your lads are farm boys
And your men not trained for war
But they will draw the cannon fire
Away from those who are."

"Dear sir, I beg, release them
For a bargain I'd propose
If you'd only leave them here this day
You'll have their weight in gold."

The bandit grinned and looked askance
At the gaffer's mean array
Then turned and laughed and shook his head
As he led them all away.

But a golden coin dropped in the dust
In the path the gaffer stood
"Five hundred pounds of the very like
In chests of oak heartwood."

"Very well," agreed Dread Maerwicke
"You have until the dawn
But when the morning sun comes up
Your kin will be chained and gone."

So the gaffer had the stable boy
Bring lamps and oxcart 'round
For the oaken chests in the island's breast
Lay hid beneath the ground.

And guarded in the gloaming dark
Lads' eyes full-wide and white
With dew upon their woolen clothes
They huddled through the night.

While quietly, so quietly
Spoke Innes to them all
And calmed them in a soldier's voice
As they sat against the wall.

At dawn's first break the pipit spake
As the oxcart made the rise
Ten oaken boxes 'pon the cart
The thief he had his prize.

A look within, a wolfish grin
Then he cast his eyes about
And before one word was spoken
His broadsword was drawn out.

"On your feet when your captain speaks!
Bid farewell to your dear old mam.
For the only promise I'll keep this morn
Won't be to this old man.

"For my lord has offered titles high
And my lord has offered land
To him who brings back men and gold
Now tie them by the hands!"

How piteous came the women's cries
Bereft upon the wind
As the men and boys were led away
Their poor hearts broke within.

The winds picked up, and the mists they ran
As they marched them 'cross the plain
But Innes bided patiently
As he slowly worked the chain.

"Step lively now!" Dread Maerwicke called
As they hurried through the glade
While a gale shrieked 'round the wildwood
And his men were sore afraid.

But then a bugle call, a bull elk's cry
Came bawling through the trees
And in a moment's mayhem
Brave Innes stood there, free.

A bloodied sword tight in his hands
Two soldiers slain and still
The island folk now fled the wildwood
And scattered t'ward the hills.

"A choice now lies before you,"
Said Innes, standing ground
"Leave them that's fled amongst the rocks
And I'll lay my broadsword down.

"For surely you remember me?
Sent we for men and gold
I went north while you went east
To seize good men. To fill our holds.

"And your ship rocks full at anchor
And the hoard is in your hand
And a bountied traitor in your grasp
Worth ten that tattered band."

Now the outlaw eyed the bearded face
Three winters spent from home
And a fiendish smile bent 'cross his lips
As Innes set his broadsword down.

But one thin lad still stood hard by
Too afeared to turn and run
And to Innes they did bind him fast
Then ox and cart moved on.

But lo, a squall most foul rolled in
And bewitched their muddled minds
And a fever did befall them
As they staggered on, half blind.

Out from the bending woods they passed
Out 'pon the spit of land
The black waves crashing toward them
As they leaned across the strand.

From the blinding storm, dread howls arose
The wails of ox and men
And the haunted gang gone mad with fright
Fled the cries upon the wind.

The ship's bell banged in the roiling sea
And the men swam for the sound
But some had filled their pockets full
And were weighted and dragged down,

While others reached the heaving ship
And fell upon their knees
As the tempest ripped the anchor's grip
And blew them out to sea.

Upon the new morn's daybreak
The sea lay flat and calm
Rent trees bumped gently 'gainst the hull
But ox and men were gone.

Three days they sailed the shifted shore
Their minds bewildered still
Drifting past each shoal and headland
Marking every hill.

But of cart, or ox, or stranded men
No traces there remained
The mists did shroud the island 'round
Its hoard it had reclaimed.

So Dread Maerwicke raised his sails for home
To be earled with titled lands
"To what realm, pray tell, do you aspire?"
"My Lord, the North Islands."

For the heartwood chests yet ever rest
On Skara Skaill within
And forevermore did he search her shores
To find them once again.

And the snow-white moon still dies and blooms
Above the barren winter moors
Where Innes roams o'er frost and stone
In silence, evermore
With the island folk that live thereon
Who'd come and took him in
And filled his cup and bade him sup
And welcomed him as kin.

The room was silent except for the wind rushing outside and the fire hissing low. Mr. Begbie watched as their eyes slowly returned from the story.

"And Innes?" asked Ham. "And the boy? Were they never found then?"

Mr. Begbie shook his head. "Nor good King Harald's hoard neither. But Dread Maerwicke, he was made the first Earl of Skara Skaill. Granted all these Northern Islands. The *great* Lord Maerwicke. And all the Marwicks after him." He spat angrily on the floor. "They've been searching for the hoard ever since, on every spit of land they've looked. But they never found it. Not a single fleck of gold. Nothing." He leaned in close. "Truth is, Skara Skaill took back what was hers." He nodded for good measure. "She took it back."

Tito looked up. "Could that have been the Little People, do you think? That took it back?"

"It's just a story, Tito," said Innes.

"Oh, just a story, is it?" asked Mr. Begbie. "And do you put so little faith in stories then, Innes of Skara Skaill?"

"I can't say I put too much faith in anything anymore, I'm afraid." Innes slid his plate politely away. "But it's gotten late. And we should be going."

"Right. Yes, of course, of course. We forget ourselves sometimes with all our talk. Comes from living alone too long."

"But thank you, though." Innes nodded to the old man. "For the story, and the fire. It's been some time since I heard it told so well."

The boys set the items back on the shelf, and as the table was cleared, Mr. Begbie stayed seated, suddenly looking very pale and tired.

"I think we'll just say goodnight from our chair, if that's alright." He held up his hand as they said goodbye and stepped out into the cool night air.

Outside, the sky was clear. As Innes started away up the path, he stopped and glanced back through the window. Through the gap in the curtain, he could see Mr. Begbie sitting alone at the table, his hands in his lap. The gray cat took up a shell in her mouth, went to the edge of the table, and jumped.

XII

THE MORNING KETTLE WHISTLED. Aggie came down the hall, tying back her hair. She poured the steaming water into a teacup and leaned against the counter. Breathing in sips of tea, she noticed the garland from the fair still sitting on the kitchen table. She looked at it a moment. She picked it up, and placing it on her head, she tilted a glance at herself in the mirror on the wall. At the sound of the cat scratching at the back door, she opened it and stepped out into the gray dawn. From the top step she saw a man quickly slipping through the back gate.

"Excuse me?" she called. "Excuse me, can I help you?"

"Sorry." The man stopped. "Sorry, I didn't think you'd be awake yet."

As the man took an apologetic step back into the yard Aggie could see that it was Innes, a bucket in each hand.

"Oh. No, I didn't mean to—well, I think I may have shouted at you just now."

"Hardly a shout."

Aggie stepped down into the yard. She felt the packed earth cold beneath her bare feet. "I'm afraid breakfast doesn't start for a few minutes yet, but if you'd like to come in?"

"No, no, I wasn't needing breakfast."

Aggie noticed something odd sitting on the long table in the yard. Heaped in the middle of it were two large mounds of mussels, glistening black. Next to them was an even larger pile of gray-shelled oysters shining fresh with seawater.

Aggie looked at Innes. "Is this from you?"

"I thought maybe you could use it for the clinic." Aggie walked to the table. "Since I hadn't had a chance to pay you." Innes watched her pick up an oyster. "I would've brought more, but they can get a little heavy after a while."

"I can imagine." Aggie set the oyster back on the pile. "Innes, I don't know what to say. But thank you."

"It's nothing."

"It's hardly nothing. To be honest, I don't really have an actual budget for the kitchen." Aggie now noticed a large walking stick leaning against the bench. "And you almost forgot your stick there."

"Oh. Actually," Innes shifted the buckets in his hands, "you'd said you'd been doing some walking, so I just thought. Well, that's for you."

Aggie smiled a little. She went over and picked it up. It was solid and heavy, and its knots were whittled smooth.

"It's beautiful."

"Yeah, well, now you're a proper local." Aggie felt the weight of the stick in her hand. "It's hazelwood," he said. "Good for whatever needs warding off."

"And what am I meant to be warding off exactly?"

"I'm sure nothing." They fell silent a moment.

"Actually, this week I thought I'd walk out to Kettleskaill. I've been trying to visit some of the families farther out."

"You'd said so, yeah."

"There's just something about the older one. Rory. Seems like he's got a weight on him, you know what I mean, for only fifteen."

"Well, I'm guessing you're not used to a place like Skara Skaill. Given where you must be from and all?"

"Me? No, I'm from a place very much like this. Not quite as beautiful but, do you know Dalaray?"

"I do. And your family's there?"

"They are. My father, he's a mason. My mother a math teacher. And I've got two older brothers."

"And you a doctor."

Aggie nodded. "On scholarship. So after, you go where they send you."

"And you got Skara Skaill."

"And I got Skara Skaill," she said. "And you? You're from here then?"

"I was, yeah." Innes paused. "But I'll be leaving again soon."

"Oh." Aggie nodded.

They stood awkwardly a moment.

"They're lucky to have you here, you know. On the island. A full-time doctor, I mean."

"Yes, I was surprised when you'd told me that," she said, only now noticing the morning chill. "But won't you come in? A cup of tea maybe?"

"Thank you, no." Innes put his buckets in one hand. The church bell rang once for the half hour.

"Yeah I should probably get the kitchen started anyway. People will be arriving soon."

Innes stood at the gate a moment more, not seeming quite ready to go.

"And you're sure I can't offer you something?" she asked again.

"No." He nodded politely. "I should be going." And giving her a little wave, he started for the gate.

Turning back to the house, Aggie smoothed her hair with her hand, realizing that the garland from the fair had been sitting atop her head the entire time.

"Ah, Jesus." She snatched the garland down. "Well, that's just lovely." She started toward the back steps just as a knock came again from the alley gate.

"Sorry, it's the latch." Aggie started back across the yard. "Breakfast isn't for a few minutes yet, but you're very welcome to wait in the—" She opened the gate. The Badger was standing in the opening.

"Thank you, miss, but we've already eaten." He took a sip from a Styrofoam cup and looked past her into the yard. "Hope we haven't called too early?" The Badger noticed her holding the garland in her hand. "And we had a nice time at the fair, did we?"

Aggie now saw the two Duff brothers standing in the alley behind him. "I'm sorry, is there something I can help you with?"

"Quite right. Right down to business then, are we?" The Badger gave her a look asking to come in, then stepped through the gate. "And the business, I'm afraid, well, it would be about your permit."

"My permit?" She eyed the Duffs in the alley as the Badger looked around the courtyard. "Sorry, and you are who again?"

His eyes lingered a moment on the piles of mussels on the table. "My name's Croy. I do a bit of work for the county. And what it comes down to, miss, is that in three days' time, Marwick Hall is hosting quite a big event here on Skara Skaill. In fact, the closing ceremony will be held just around front there in the square."

"Sorry, and that has something to do with the clinic, you're saying?" Aggie noticed a few villagers arriving in the alley.

"It does. You see, Marwick Hall is quite eager for the village to put its best foot forward." The Badger glanced back at the lineup forming in the alley. "Right. So let me put it to you plain, miss. We're going to need to make sure all that right there"—the Badger thumbed toward the alley—"stays out of sight."

"Sorry, what?"

"To be honest, miss, the county actually sent me to shut you down for a few days. But if you could just keep the alley clear, yes? I'm sure we can look the other way with the rest."

"It's a clinic." A disbelief came into her eyes. "And a community pantry."

"Yes, I'm aware of what it is."

"You realize we've got people coming and going here all day?" Aggie stared at him. "Sorry, and you're with the county, you said? Well, perhaps you could tell me who I'm supposed to speak with up there because I'm receiving half the budget I was supposed to. County business runs through Marwick Hall, yes?"

"That's right."

"Well, from what I understand, the Marwicks own half the island and most of the village, and yet no one up at the hall can seem to find the time to get back to me."

"They're a bit shorthanded just at the moment."

"Well, they were certainly quick to send you out though, weren't they?"

"Look, miss, I understand your position."

"And what would Marwick Hall know about a place like this, I wonder?"

"Well, me, I know plenty. Let me assure you of that." The Badger collected himself. "Look. Here's a bit of advice for you, and you can do with it what you like. If I were you, I'd be doing everything I could to hang on to what little budget the county's already given you. You understand what I'm telling you?"

Aggie looked beyond him to the villagers gathering quietly in the alley. She flicked the dregs of her tea onto the ground.

"I'm late. So if there's nothing else?"

"Right then." The Badger nodded. "One of my associates here may be dropping by now and again in case there's anything you might need clarification on." He touched the place where a cap would have been. "Miss." The Badger started away up the alley. Munro and Frankie followed after him, nodding dark smiles back at Aggie as she welcomed the queue of villagers through the gate.

The alley sat empty and still. From behind a small cut in the wall, Innes stepped quietly into view. He stood a moment, staring in the direction the Badger and the Duffs had gone, then turning away, he started for the far end of the alley, buckets in hand.

XIII

Ashenrose Museum. Office of Antiquities.
Oxford, England.

THE MAIL CART CAME rolling quietly down the carpeted hall. At a little desk in the outer office, Jameson Hewitt, all knees and elbows, sat bent over his work, his cheap necktie disheveled, his foot wiggling in concentration as a fat letter dropped into his inbox.

"Thanks, Tommy." Without looking up, Jameson reached for the letter.

In the inner office, Alastair Clements, long and angular, his hair thinning, sat reading a stack of papers as he unwrapped a tuna sandwich. His coat and tweed hat hung on the rack by the door. On either side of his desk were two long tables, upon which sat photographs and folders, annotated, stapled, and stacked. With great anticipation, Alastair carefully separated the two triangles of his sandwich as a paper slid beneath his door, and then another, and as more pages started coming through, Alastair sat back.

"Come in, Jameson," he sighed. The door slowly opened and Jameson leaned around it, a large green reference book under his arm.

"Sorry, sir, I know this is lunchtime, but this seemed important, so I thought I'd..."

"No, no. Come in." Alastair slid his sandwich away. Gathering up the papers, Jameson hurried over and set the dusty reference book on the desk. It was already opened to a grainy black-and-white photo of a coin. Alastair leaned to the book, covering the photo's caption with his hand, testing himself.

"Dirham coin. Late eighth-century Byzantium. From the Black Sea basin. This one is silver, but they were sometimes minted in gold. Also in electrum, I believe."

"Yes, sir," said Jameson, laying the stack of papers along with a letter and a color photo of a coin on the desk. "Well, apparently one has been found."

Alastair considered the photo. "Interesting. Nice find. Nothing earth-shattering, but a nice find," he said. "And where was it found?" he asked, scanning the accompanying letter.

"Well, that's the thing, sir." Jameson waited as Alastair finished the letter.

Suddenly Alastair looked up, before quickly scanning the letter again. "Skara Skaill?" he asked, taking a magnifying glass from his desk. "And at a county fair?" He bent close to the photograph.

"Shall I open a file on it, sir?"

Alastair sat up. "Actually, no." He thought a long moment. "No. Get the motor pool on the phone. Tell them we'll be needing a car."

"A car. Right, sir." Jameson hurried out the door.

From a cabinet behind his desk, Alastair pulled out a small duffel, already packed. In the outer office, Jameson covered the phone with his hand.

"And what shall I say is the destination, sir?"

"Tell them..." Alastair paused. "Tell them we're heading to the Northern Islands. And we'll be needing reservations on the first ferry from Aberdeen as well."

"Right." Jameson stopped, then covered the phone again. "And when you say *we*, sir?"

"Yes, Jameson, you'll be coming as well."

"Yes, sir. Right, sir. I've got my go bag right here."

Making sure Jameson was still occupied on the phone, Alastair opened the bottom desk drawer and lifted out a metal lockbox. From within it, he took out a large roll of cash bound with a rubber band. Burying the money and the papers deep inside a worn leather satchel on his desk, he hurried across the carpet, snatched his hat and coat from the rack, and headed out the door.

* * *

Innes walked along the cobbled streets beyond the square. He stopped at the top of the lane that led down to the wharf. From here he could see the Duffs' long copper sedan parked below. The harbor buoy gonged gently in the distance. In the middle of the boatyard sat the little warming shack. Woodsmoke rose from its tin chimney. The door swung open. Innes eased from view as Frankie Duff stepped out and shouted to one of the men unloading cargo along the quay.

Leaving the village behind, Innes took the high hill path. Far below, he could see where the walled meadows gave way to the wild open barrens. He could see the ruins of Skarahollow Chapel. A vehicle was parked near where the yew tree lay on its side. He stopped to watch the tiny movement of a man hammering a cold spike at the corner of the tent, the sound arriving a moment later on the wind.

A thin rain began to fall. At the top of the hill sat Kettleskaill House. Innes climbed the narrow path leading to the house, then stopped at the low gate. The tendril of a vine had already coiled around the latch since it was last opened. He pushed into the yard. Near the chicken coop, a bright-orange hen was pecking at worms that had been drawn up by the rain. Innes watched the hen cross the yard. It meandered closer until finally stopping just in front of him, its beak spiking mindlessly at the ground. In a single movement, Innes dove for the chicken, but the hen instantly burst into the air and took a low, clumsy flight across the yard before landing heavily at the corner of the house. It fluffed itself against the cold. Innes got to his feet and wiped the gravel from his hands. Walking to the chicken coop, he lifted the latch. Drifts of feathers were stuck in the wire. Urgent little paw tracks crisscrossed the mud, and broken shells lay scattered all around. At the very top of the nesting box sat four brown eggs. Innes slipped them carefully into his coat pockets, two on each side. After giving the box a last look, he stepped over to the stone barn and stood beneath its eaves. Through the drizzle of rain, he looked across at the old house, its front door hanging on a single hinge, a county notice still nailed to it. The house was abandoned and dark. Behind him, wedged into the walls of the barn, he noticed tiny plastic soldiers hidden here and there among the stones—some crouching, some taking the high ground, some finding cover deep within the cracks. None of them higher than a boy could reach. Innes considered them a moment, then picking the soldiers out of the wall, he set them down in his pockets with the eggs. From the village came the faint echo of a church bell. He turned up his collar, but as he stepped out into the rain, he stopped, sensing movement at the barn door. Sir Winston stood peering out at him, an egg held gently in his mouth. The two stared at each other a moment, then the little dog turned and hurried back into the barn.

* * *

Inside the cave, the fire burned low. Tito sat cross-legged on the ground as Rory carefully trimmed the back of his hair. Ham lay propped against his suitcase, his hands clasped behind his head.

"'*Out from the bending woods they passed,*'" Ham recited. "'*Out 'pon the spit of land.*'" He paused, trying to remember.

"'*The black waves crashing toward them,*'" said Tito. "'*As they leaned across the strand.*'"

"Right, that's right." Ham nodded. "'*As they leaned across the strand.*' And what was the next bit again? Something about a wildwood?"

"OK, you're done," said Rory. As he brushed the hair from Tito's shoulders, he noticed Tito vigorously scratching his head. "Tito, do not tell me you have lice again."

"I do not have lice."

"You're sure?"

"Yes, I'm sure," he said indignantly, and as he tried very hard not to scratch, a sound came from outside the hut. Everyone sat in silence until Innes came ducking through the door.

"Well, you were up early," said Ham.

"Just out walking." Innes went to the back of the cave and set the buckets down. "Passed by your house on the way back though."

Tito looked up at him. "You went to Kettleskaill?"

"Are they still working down by the chapel?" asked Rory.

"Yeah, there were a few men down there." Innes came over to the fire. "Was a little dog in the barn too."

Tito looked up. "Was he gray? With a white underside?"

"Yeah. He looked well fed." Innes drew two eggs from each pocket. "Chicken's laying too."

Tito took the eggs proudly. "I'll bet there's a double yolker in there."

"Here, we'll boil those. They'll last longer." Rory placed the eggs down into a pot of water already steaming on the fire.

Innes reached into his pockets again. "Found these as well." He set a little tangle of toy soldiers near the fire.

"Look, Rory. You remember these?" Tito knelt to them. "Mrs. Renfro gave me these. She gave you some too, Rory, you remember, and it wasn't even your birthday."

Rory quietly watched Tito untangle the men. "They never stood up too good."

Innes stared at the fire a moment, having more to say. "You know, it didn't seem to me like anyone was living there just at the moment." He laid his coat across his pack. Rory didn't look up. "And the front door looks to have been kicked in."

"Did it?" asked Rory.

"It did, yeah. In fact, I'm going to say the house looked to be abandoned."

Tito stole a glance at Rory.

"So how long have you two been living on your own?" Innes asked. "At the house?"

"We're not living on our own."

"How long, Rory?"

Rory thought to lie again. He poked the fire a little. "Four months," he said finally. "Maybe a little more."

Ham sat up. "Four months?"

"And how long have you been living out here?" Innes asked. "You and Tito?

"A few days."

"That part's true," said Tito.

Then a thought came to Ham. "And Mrs. Renfro?" he asked carefully.

Tito kept his eyes down. He smoothed the dirt for a long moment. "She got a cancer," he said quietly, trying to stand one of the little men upright. "In her stomach." He went over to his pack and began arranging and rearranging his belongings deep within it. The cave fell silent except for the sound of the fire.

"Alone all that time." Ham shook his head. "And you never spoke with someone?"

"Like who exactly?" asked Rory. "The constable? He's with the county; it's them that ran us off."

"What about the clinic?" asked Innes. "You could speak with Aggie."

"We already did all that. Not with her, but…" Rory shook his head. "They sent someone out to take us off-island. Said there's nowhere for us right now on Skara Skaill."

"Rory says they could separate us," added Tito. "Since we're only half."

"It doesn't matter anyway because we're not doing that. So just—" Rory tried to end the discussion. "We'll go back to

Kettleskaill when they're done digging down there, and that's it. I'll be finding a job soon anyway, so."

They all stared at the fire. The eggs bumped against each other down in the boiling water. After a while, Rory drew a cloth from his pocket and unfolded it on the ground.

"So I've been working on these." On the cloth lay Innes's green coins. All but a few had been pried loose and separated one from the other. Rory took a little penknife and started etching away at the bits of green crust. "Look, you can just make out the date on this one. You see? 1962."

"So are any of them actually clean enough to spend?" Innes asked.

"No, because you're not going to want to spend these."

"Why not?"

"Because these are from when they were all silver. You're going to want to sell these for weight."

"Sell them?" asked Ham. "To who?"

Tito looked up from his pack. "Not Otis, Rory."

"And who's Otis then?" asked Ham.

"A big dobber is who. And a crook."

"More like a half crook," said Rory.

"And he knows the Duffs," said Tito. "And all the other ones down at the wharf. And you know he'll still be mad about last time, Rory."

"Why? What happened last time?" asked Innes.

"He tried to cheat us is what. So Rory put a rock on the scale."

"He did what?" asked Ham.

"He put a rock on the scale. But only because Otis was gonna cheat us first, like usual."

Ham looked at the boys, and a little smile came over his face. “I believe we’ve got a couple of proper outlaws here, Innes.”

Rory spooned the eggs from the boiling water and set them aside to cool.

“So how much are we talking about here for the coins, would you say?” asked Innes. “Give or take?”

“Oh, hard to say without a scale,” said Rory. “But right now, it’s almost seven quid an ounce for silver.”

“That much?”

“More maybe.”

“But not Otis, Rory,” said Tito again. “He’ll just say we stole them anyway.”

“Well, but it’d be Innes that deals with him though, right?” asked Ham.

Rory shook his head. “Otis won’t deal with anyone he doesn’t know.”

Taking up an egg, Innes thoughtfully rolled it back and forth between his hands to warm them.

XIV

THE FERRYMAN CRANKED THE winch as the ramp slowly lowered onto the dock. Like a draft horse working a well-worn track, he plodded down the ramp into the dark. As the black water lapped at the hull of the ferry, Alastair and Jameson sat in the front seat of the little car, looking through the windshield.

"Are we meant to go, do you think?" asked Jameson.

Alastair craned his neck out the window. "You'd think he'd say something."

From out in the darkness, a flashlight switched on, beckoning them forward. Jameson quickly shifted into drive, but the car didn't move.

"Parking brake," he remembered, and after releasing the handle, the car eased down the gangway and rolled to a stop. Out at the edge of the headlights, a thin road headed off in either direction.

Alastair looked at a map spread across his lap, a penlight in hand. "Was this the most recent map of the islands?" he asked.

"It was the only map of the islands."

Alastair ran his finger across it. "OK, so here we are. Just at the ferry slip. Of which apparently there are two. One here and one in the village. But according to this map, that road just ahead there is either a submerged roadbed, a tidal flat, or some sort of buried cable from the mainland." Seeing the ferryman trudging past, Alastair rolled down the window and raised his eyebrows. "Yes, pardon me, but by any chance might you know the way to the Vat and Fiddle?"

The ferryman stopped, and scratching the back of his head, he began answering in a long series of mumbles, grunts, and yawns.

Jameson started to speak, but Alastair waved him off.

"Ah. Well, perhaps you could be so kind as to point us in the direction we should go?"

Alastair and Jameson drove along in the dark, their headlights casting a cone of yellow light onto the narrow road unspooling before them. From out of the dark, a man on a bike suddenly appeared ghostlike in the headlights while another man listed drunkenly alongside him. Jameson swerved, and as they passed the men, a snatch of the song they were singing came in through the open window.

With a bunnet of ice upon their head,
Nikkity nakkity no no no,
In boots of frost and snow they tread,
Nikkity nakkity no.

The Little Folk sow their seeds below,
Nikkity nakkity no no no,
'Neath the island evermore they hoe,
Nikkity nakkity no.

Jameson glanced in the rearview. "Well, those two certainly look as if they'd know the way to a pub. Should we go back?"

"No need," said Alastair, for just ahead, a little tavern appeared over the rise, its windows lit brightly in the darkness.

The car's headlights swept across the gravel drive, then came to a stop. A sign above the door read *The Vat and Fiddle*.

"Oh, please let the kitchen still be open," said Jameson, stepping out of the car. "I could murder a plate of anything."

"That and a room for the night," said Alastair. But as they approached the inn, the windows suddenly went dark, and the hardware of the big wooden door latched tight. Jameson ran to the door and knocked. He looked up at the darkened building as the sign over the door blinked out.

In the quiet of the car, they sat staring blankly through the windshield.

"Have we any food left?" asked Alastair.

Jameson switched on the cabin light and rummaged through a paper sack at his feet. "A sleeve of crackers and two fingers of peanut butter."

Jameson began assembling little sandwiches of peanut butter crackers. He passed a small stack to Alastair. They sat in silence, chewing.

"Well," Alastair finished his last cracker and swept the crumbs off his lap, "certainly won't be the first time I've had to sleep rough." He wadded his coat into a makeshift pillow.

Jameson sat staring out the side window. "Should we establish an area for the loo, do you think?"

"It'll only be the one night, Jameson. I'm sure anywhere will do." Alastair looked out into the dark. A hard wind blew in from somewhere off the water, buffeting the little car. "You know, it's been too long since I've been in the field," he said quietly, staring out at the tall grass leaning flat in the wind, a sea of stars above. "Much too long." He set his glasses on the dash and lowered his seat back flat. "Goodnight, Jameson."

"G'night, sir." And after readying himself for sleep, Jameson reached up and switched off the light, casting the car into blackness.

* * *

Innes lay against his pack. The fire glowed dim in the darkness while the others slept quietly. Suddenly Innes sat up. At the opening of the cave, a shadow was crouching low to the ground, its eyes shining as it crept inside. Slowly Innes reached for a heavy stick lying near the fire. He shifted onto his knees, and as the shadow inched closer to where the boys lay, he raised the stick overhead. But then he stopped and lowered it again, for edging into the firelight was Sir Winston, mud-spattered and cold. The two stared at each other a moment before Sir Winston hurried over and tucked in tightly against Tito's side, keeping his eyes on Innes all the while. Innes leaned back against his pack as the little dog laid his chin flat upon his paws and let go a long sigh.

* * *

The predawn gray came through the car window. Alastair opened a sleepy eye; the imprint of his wadded tweed jacket was pressed into the side of his face. Groggily he looked out the side window, then lurched back.

"Bloody hell!" he cried, for just outside the window was a black-bearded face pressed hard against the glass.

From the other seat, Jameson opened his eyes. "Scottish Blackface." He yawned as the big sheep bumped its yellow teeth against the window.

Alastair sat up, and looking out, he could see that the car was surrounded on all sides by a large flock of sheep, each of them identical to the one chewing sideways at his window. Out across the drive, a few early risers were making their way into the Vat and Fiddle.

"Inn's open," said Jameson, shoving his arm into his jacket.

More sheep came and pressed against Alastair's window, gaping in at him. "And how exactly are we supposed to get through all that?"

"Ah, you can just push right through them, sir." Jameson forced the door open. "I grew up around the likes of these fellas here." He waded out among the flock.

Alastair set a manilla work folder on the dash and cracked open his door. "Excuse me." He slid his angular frame through the door. "Shoo, shoo there. If you don't mind." And with his hands over his head, Alastair pressed through the flock as the sheep stared mindlessly up at him.

Inside, the inn was low and quiet. Dark hewn beams ran across the ceiling, and the morning light angled in against the white-washed walls. A tiny fire smoked in the hearth. Clutches of local men stood at the bar murmuring in morning voices over steaming mugs. As Alastair and Jameson stepped through the door, a few of the men glanced over, then turned back to their cups. Jameson found a table in the corner. A waitress came up, a pot in each hand.

"Coffee or tea?" she asked.

"Tea, please," said Alastair.

"And will you be wanting breakfast as well?"

"We very much will be, yes," said Jameson, rubbing his hands together as she filled their mugs.

"The full breakfast then?" she asked, pulling silverware and napkins from her apron.

"Two, please." Alastair nodded.

The waitress left, and after a few minutes, she returned again, placing two steaming platters in front of them. Fried eggs, a portion of beans, four link sausages, crisp potato wedges, stewed tomatoes, and two slices of very dark toast.

"Will there be anything else?"

"Actually, miss, there is one other thing," asked Alastair. "Could you possibly tell us where we might find a Miss Ada Coburn?"

The waitress paused and looked them over more carefully than before. "And who may I say is asking?"

"Of course, my apologies. I'm Alastair Clements, and this is my associate, Jameson Hewitt. We're from the Ashenrose Museum." Alastair began digging into his pockets. "I think I may have a card somewhere." He pulled out a bent business card. "We just had a few questions for her, is all. Nothing for her to be concerned about, I can assure you."

The waitress looked at the card, then tucked it into her apron. "Wait here."

Alastair and Jameson unrolled their cutlery. As they went to work on their plates of food, the front door swung open with a clatter. Frankie and Munro Duff stepped into the inn.

Moving evenly across the room, Frankie cast an assessing look at the two strangers eating in the corner. He bellied up to the bar. Munro tapped the counter for service.

The door from the kitchen opened. The waitress again came through it, but this time, she was followed by a young lady to whom she was whispering and pointing toward the table.

Alastair and Jameson quickly scraped back their chairs as Ada arrived.

"May I help you?" she asked as they got to their feet.

"Yes, very sorry to disturb you, Miss Coburn. My name is Alastair Clements. This is my associate, Jameson Hewitt. Perhaps your friend there may have mentioned we were hoping for a moment of your time?"

"She did." Ada studied the two men. "But I've got to think you have the wrong person. I work at the pub here, and, well, that's pretty much it. Actually, that's entirely it."

"Right, of course." Alastair nodded. "And as I said, we're very sorry for intruding unannounced like this, but may I ask, since there are a lot of Coburns on the island, are you the Ada related to a Mr. Norval Coburn?" Ada looked at them more warily now. "If you'll allow me, Miss Coburn." Alastair offered her a chair. "Perhaps I could give you a fuller explanation as to why we're here."

Standing at the bar, Frankie drew a boiled egg from a bowl on the counter and slowly tapped it on the counter, seeming to pay no attention whatsoever to what was happening at the corner table as Ada took a seat.

"Two days ago, my office was in receipt of a letter," said Alastair. "A letter containing information that originated from a Mr. Norval Coburn here on Skara Skaill. In it was a photograph of a coin. Your name was given as its owner."

"Is that what this is about? The coin?"

"So you're familiar with it then?"

"Why? Is it valuable or something?"

"Well, before we get to that, if you could just—well we're very keen to understand anything you might know about it." Alastair said. "Its history with your family, how it came into your possession. That sort of thing."

Ada thought a moment. "Alright. Well, Norval's my uncle. Norval Coburn. He's something of a history buff, I guess you'd say. And when he saw the coin, he said he might try finding out more about it, do some asking around or what have you. I didn't really think much of it. He'd told me he'd sent off a few letters, but that was it really." She looked at them both. "I suppose that's how it made its way to you then?"

"We get a good deal of these sorts of inquiries," said Alastair. "But if you would, could you possibly tell us how the coin came into your possession?"

"Well, alright. It was at the Fhøghar Fair. That would've been, what, almost a week ago now? I was working at the pie stand there; we do one every year. And so this fellow, he comes up." Ada stopped. "Wait, you're not thinking he stole it or anything, are you?"

"Absolutely not," said Alastair. "We have no reason to think so."

"Because I wouldn't want to get anyone in trouble."

"You have my word, Miss Coburn." Alastair nodded for her to continue.

"Alright. Well, so I'd seen him earlier that night, at the stone put. He'd won it, and we do the pies for the prizes, me and another girl from the pub here, so I remembered him well enough. Anyway, he come up to the booth—this would have been later—and he was admiring the pies and what have you.

Was very enthusiastic about them. He was quite nice really, so I thought to give him one, you know, for winning and all. Plus he said something had happened to the other ones."

"The other ones what?" asked Jameson, his pen to his notepad.

"The other pies."

"And what did happen to the other pies?"

"Jameson, could we just—please, go ahead, miss."

"Well, like I said, I wanted to give him an extra pie, and also we were closing up for the night, and we never want to carry anything back if we can help it. But he said, 'No, no, I want to pay for it.' And so he holds his money out, in his hand, counting it out, you know, and so I tell him again I wouldn't take anything for it, but he insists. So just to put an end to it really, I picked out a couple of coins from his hand. It was then that I saw the green one, and I said I thought it looked sorta interesting, you know. So he gave it to me. And, well, I guess that was it really."

Alastair looked at her. "I'm sorry, are you saying he just gave you the coin? To buy a pie?"

Ada nodded. "That's right."

"A pie?" Alastair asked again. "He bought pie with it?"

"He did, yeah."

"And you're sure it was the same coin? The one you showed your uncle?"

"I'm sure." Ada nodded. "Why, would you like to see it?" And before Alastair could say a word, Ada reached to her collar, drew out a silver chain with a green coin dangling from it, and laid it on the table.

At the bar, Frankie stared dead ahead at the mirror, sipping his coffee. Munro nodded at him, then pressed away from the counter and started across to the front door. At the sound of the door closing, Alastair glanced over his shoulder, then putting his glasses on, he bent to the coin.

"Ah, and I see you've drilled a hole in it," he said, clearing his throat. "Right through the middle." The coin was cleaner than in the photo, and Alastair could see a silver hue coming through the green. It was thin, as if it had been punched from sheet metal. He studied it a long moment, then peeled off his glasses. "Miss Coburn, I, well, I very much need to ask you exactly, just exactly what else you can tell us about this gentleman from the fair?"

* * *

The sheep had moved off, and the little car sat alone outside the inn. The morning fog was gone, and as Alastair and Jameson crossed the gravel drive, they could now see their surroundings in the clear light of day. Up the road was the village of Skara Skaill. Out beyond the inn, open fields stretched away toward the cliffs. In the distance, sets of green waves washed in against the rocks below.

Inside the car, the cabin was warm and muffled. Alastair shoved his topcoat into the back seat. He stopped, then searched around the car a moment.

"What is it?" asked Jameson.

"Have you seen the folder?"

"What folder?"

"The folder, the manilla folder, the coin folder with all the papers and the photograph?" Alastair dug through his leather satchel. "I set it right here on the dash."

Jameson looked into the back seat. "Nothing back here."

"Well, it can't have just disappeared, Jameson."

As Alastair and Jameson searched around beneath the seat, Frankie Duff stepped out of the inn and slowly passed the little car as he walked off toward the village, alone.

XV

THE BADGER CLIMBED UP through the hole, a cigarette in his mouth, a line of smoke curling into his eye. He lifted out a bucket of rubble and set it down. But as he started back down the ladder, he saw a black car making its way slowly across the field.

Hurrying off the ladder, he grabbed a folder off the table, stepped out into the rain, and opened the door. Lord Marwick was sitting in the back seat, a wool blanket draped across his lap.

"Go and take some air, driver," said Lord Marwick. The driver stepped out as the Badger climbed into the back seat, closing the door behind him.

Lord Marwick nodded at the folder the Badger held in his hand. "Is that it?" He took the folder and opened it. It was marked *Ashenrose Museum.* Rain pattered gently on the roof as he looked down through his bifocals, slowly turning each page. When he was done, he closed the folder in his lap.

"And this woman from the inn, you've spoken with her?"

"Yes, sir. She says when she counted up the money at the end of the fair, the coin was just there in the money box, mixed in with the rest. She didn't recall anyone in particular giving it to her."

“And you trust that answer?”

“Well, I couldn’t say for certain.”

Lord Marwick sat quietly a moment. “So let me see if I understand correctly. Within a matter of days since uncovering the most promising dig site we’ve found, certainly in my lifetime, a thousand-year-old Byzantium dirham just happens to appear out of the clear blue sky at our local fair? Exchanged for a pie. A coin that in both date and historical record carries the exact provenance that generations of my family have been searching for lo these many years.” Lord Marwick laid his hands gently on the folder. “And this coin, Mr. Croy, are we to believe it has chosen to appear on our island, at this moment, out of thin air?” The Badger said nothing. “Or does it not, in fact, make more sense, albeit strange, that such a coin would come out of, oh, say, a dig site? A site of the very sort lying here beneath our feet? A site that just so happened to have a break-in within the last few days. Or are we to believe these two events are merely a coincidence?”

“It would seem unlikely, sir.”

“It would seem unlikely,” Lord Marwick repeated. “And if that weren’t enough, we now have two interlopers arrived on the island, our island, making inquiries about the very coin in question.” He breathed deeply. “So let us talk plainly now you and I, Mr. Croy, of practical matters, yes? This man who passed this coin, I want him found, whoever he may be. For all we know, he may just be a simpleton, a fool who stumbled upon a single coin and was soon parted from it. To him, a shiny object in the dust, nothing more. Or perhaps he may in fact be the one, or one of a group of men, who broke into the site below and has already absconded with the entirety of what may have been lying beneath this chapel.” Lord Marwick squeezed his eyes closed at the thought. "So listen to me carefully now, Mr. Croy. I want him found. I want him found, and I want those goons of yours to keep their eyes open and their ears to the ground for anything, and I mean anything, out of the ordinary on the island. I want whoever passed that coin—man, woman, or child—to be found, Mr. Croy. Am I clear?"

"Yes, sir."

"Am I indeed? Because somewhere within this island lies my birthright. A birthright my family has long sought to reacquire, and buried with it lies the very story of the Northern Islands, a story lost to the fog of history." Lord Marwick turned and faced the Badger. "Now you get it done, Mr. Croy. Get it done, and I'll make it worth your while. A small share of what's found, eh? Or perhaps one of these properties lying empty of late? Part of the landed gentry, eh, lad? How does that sound to you?"

The Badger stared in silence. "Sir, it sounds…" He paused, the words catching in his throat. "Well, sir, it would be—"

"But if you should fail me, Badger. Or, and I can hardly bring myself to say it, if you should betray me, heaven forbid, you'll find yourself right back in that hole in the ground where I found you, yeah? Which, as we both know, is your birthright. Do we understand each other?"

"Yes, sir."

"There's a good lad." Lord Marwick tapped his ring on the window for the driver. "Because whatever comes out of that hole, Mr. Croy, or to whatever hole it leads, belongs to me."

* * *

The evening sky slowly faded to black. To the east, the faint lights of the village were just blinking on along the horizon. Ham blew on his hands against the cold.

"What time did you say you're meeting him again?"

"Four o'clock," said Rory.

Ham looked up at the darkening sky. "Are you telling me it's not even four yet?"

"Ten 'til," said Tito, putting his watch to his ear.

"I'd forgotten how early it gets dark in these islands." Ham stamped the cold from his feet. "There's something about the dark, you know? Ever notice that? How your thoughts just seem to get sort of, what—"

"Darker?" asked Innes.

"Yeah." Ham turned his back to the wind. "So you really think it's alright for Rory to go alone?"

"He'll be alright," said Innes. "Otis is harmless. It's the ones he works for are the problem."

Rory scanned out into the dark. "Look." He pointed to a low ridge in the distance. "You see them?"

"Is it Otis?" asked Tito. But looking out, they could see the dark silhouettes of the moor ponies. The herd had been shadowing them since they left the cliff huts.

"Don't tell me they're still following us," said Ham. "It's been days now. I think you've cast a spell on them, Innes."

Tito swung his light around to make sure Sir Winston was staying close. The beam of light lit a string of standing stones looming out in the dark. "Why are we meeting him way out here anyway?"

"This is just where he said. At the north road." Rory felt the bag of coins in his pocket. "Alright. I guess I'll head up."

"Look. If you need anything," Innes nodded, "we'll be right here, yeah?"

Rory started away up the path. As he reached the dirt road, the wind picked up, and buttoning his coat to his chin, he waited.

After some time, Rory looked back and shrugged in the direction he knew Innes and the others were waiting. But as he turned again to the road, he saw something odd moving out in the blackness. A tiny orange speck bobbing along in the dark. He kept his eyes fixed on it, and as the speck fell to the ground, he heard the faint crunch of footsteps approaching.

"Where's your car?" Rory asked.

"Back up the road, where you're supposed to be," said Otis, his moonlike face appearing out of the darkness. Rory took a step back as another face suddenly appeared out of the gloom.

"Yeah, back up the road, where you're supposed to be," said Rat, coming alongside.

"You said meet by the Kelvig Stones." Rory gestured back toward the standing stones beyond the road.

"Yeah, but them ain't the Kelvig Stones, now, are they?" said Rat, a toothpick in his mouth.

"They are."

"Wrong. Them's the Tendish Stones, mate." He clicked on a large billy-club flashlight and shined it at the stones, lighting them white against the blackness. "Them's *Paleolific*."

"Neolithic," muttered Rory to himself.

"What's that you said?" asked Rat. "And where's that sprat brother of yours anyway?"

"You two owe me five quid from the other day," said Otis. "I'll be having that money tonight, I can promise you."

Rat shone his light in Rory's face. "Or maybe we should take you down to the wharf and leave you to them fellas down there, eh, boy? And why shouldn't we do that?"

"Because I can make it up to you, that's why." Rory pulled a small pouch from his jacket.

Otis looked at it casually. "Old coins, you said?"

"All silver." Rory rolled down the top of the bag, showing the clutch of coins inside. "No copper, no nickel."

Rat lowered his flashlight down into the pouch of green corroded coins. "And what the hell are those?"

"They're silver underneath. See the edging?" Rory took out a coin and held it in the light.

"They do look old, Otis," Rat said earnestly.

Otis took the coin in his sausagey fingers, scratching it with his thumbnail. Taking the pouch, he brought out a little case from his pocket. Inside was a tiny hanging scale. He clipped the pouch to the scale, noting its weight. Lowering heavily onto one knee, he laid the coins on the ground in rows. From the case, Otis brought out a small dropper-bottle and squeezed a single drop of clear liquid onto each coin. The coins immediately began to sizzle. As the bubbles began to turn blue, Rory turned to Otis.

"Silver. What'd I say."

"Hang on," said Otis. "Let's just wait 'til they're clean."

"It's seven an ounce for silver."

"Hang on, I said. What's your hurry?"

From behind him, Rory heard a match snap to life, and glancing back, he saw Rat light a cigarette before waving the match out with a flourish. From up the road, two yellow headlights suddenly blinked on. Rory stood up.

"Who's that?"

"No one." Otis hoisted himself to his feet. "My ride, is all."

"Your ride?" Rory watched the headlights rolling forward.

"So look here," said Otis, pulling a wad of bills from his pocket. "I can give you five an ounce. That'd be fifty quid. It's a good price. I'll even forget about that fiver you stole from me on that last deal." He held out the money, trying to draw Rory's attention from the car approaching up the road. "It's a good price, fifty."

Rory stared out at the headlights, then suddenly turned to Otis. "I'll take it."

But as Rory grabbed for the bills, Rat stepped over, snatching him hard by the collar.

"What's the rush, boy?"

"Hold on to him, Rat."

In a sudden burst, Rory tried to tear himself free, but as they held on to him, the outer pocket of Rat's leather coat tore loose and dangled down by a thread. Rat looked heartbroken at his tattered coat, then up at Rory, a sad fury in his eyes.

"Why, you little maggot. That cost me sixty quid." He jerked Rory hard by the collar. Then from out of the darkness came a voice.

"I'd take your hands off him if I were you."

Rat wheeled around just as Innes came striding out of the dark, with Ham and Tito right behind.

"Let him go, Rat," said Innes. "Do it now."

Rat backed away. "I told you he was back, Otis. Didn't I tell you I seen him at the clinic?"

"I said let him go, Rat."

"Hang on to him, Rat." Otis glanced back at the approaching headlights.

In a flash, Innes and Ham came rushing forward, and seeing them come, Rat shoved Rory away as he stumbled back.

"Ah, Jesus, Rat," shouted Otis, and they could only stand and watch as Innes hurried Rory and the others away, disappearing into the night.

The car rolled slowly to a stop. Into the headlights stepped Munro Duff. He looked at Otis and Rat standing there alone.

"Why's it only you two? Rat waved the match."

"Yeah, well, we had him. Then Rat here lets the kid go."

"Well, if that big gorilla came running at you."

"What're you talking about?" asked Munro. "What's he talking about, Otis?"

"Like I said. Was that one from the fair; he come running up out of the dark there with Innes."

"Innes?"

"It was Innes, wasn't it, Otis? You seen him."

"What are you on about, Rat? Are you telling me Innes Mackie came running out of the dark just now?"

"Yeah," said Otis. "Was definitely him."

"Just now?"

"With them two little scroungers."

Munro scanned out into the dark. "Jesus. We better get back to Frankie. Badger's gonna want to know about this." He turned to Otis. "So did the kid have any old coins or what?"

"Oh yeah, right." Otis stepped over to where the coins were lying out on the ground. Rat knelt beside him, shining his light on the newly cleaned coins.

"So are they old or what?" asked Munro.

"Well," Rat picked through them, "here's an old one. 1962." He handed the coin up to Munro. "And, alright, we've got a '61, a '64, a '63, another '61. OK, here's a '60." Rat flicked through the other coins. "That looks to be the oldest."

"What, that's it?" asked Munro. "1960? Are you bloody joking me?"

"No, actually that's good," said Otis, clearing his throat. "You see, any of your coins minted in 1964 or earlier, those ones are gonna be silver. Anything minted after 1964 is when they started to introduce other kinds of metals into the—"

"Oh, would you please shut it," said Munro. "The Badger said keep a look out for anything old. Like *old* old. Not 19-bloody-60." He pitched the coin into the dirt. "Bloody hell." He started away for the car, waving them off as he went. "Wasted my whole sodding night out here with you two clots."

Rat watched Munro go, then muttered quietly to Otis, "It's not really fair that. Nobody said *old* old, they just said old. Could be a bit more precise in their communication, if you ask me."

Munro shouted from the car, "Let's go. I got places to be."

"What about the coins?" called Rat, but Otis cut him off.

"It's alright, we'll get them when we'll get them," he called. "Come on, Rat," said Otis overloudly. "Wouldn't want to leave twenty quid worth of silver lying in the dirt now, would we?"

"Yeah, well, hurry it up," shouted Munro as he climbed into the car.

Rat knelt beside Otis. "What do you mean twenty quid? I thought you said they was worth fifty?"

Otis shushed him. "More like eighty actually. But Munro don't know that now, does he?"

Rat smiled. "Christmas come early."

As the two hurriedly filled the bag, a thin blackened coin that had been encrusted to the back of another dropped into the dust.

"Oy, what's this then?" Otis brought the strange little coin into the light. "And what's your story now, eh?"

XVI

OUTSIDE THE CAVE, RORY sat alone at the fire, restitching the torn collar of his coat. Innes stepped out through the opening. In the firelight, he could see the fresh scuffs raked red across Rory's neck.

Innes turned and looked out at the darkness. "Ham go for water?"

"I guess." Rory stayed bent over his work.

Innes watched as Rory drew the needle and thread through, then fed it back around again.

"So before, with Otis and Rat. Is that how you and Tito get by?"

"Is what how we get by?"

"Dealing with the likes of them?"

Rory slipped his coat back on. "Sometimes." From the hem of his pants, he pulled out the stub of a cigarette and took a twig from the fire. "We do alright, me and Tito." He blew on the ember and touched it to his cigarette. "I'll be looking for real work soon, so."

Tito came out of the cave with a roll of heavy tape. "Except not down at the wharf." The sole of his shoe lolled loose with every step. "Rory, can you do it?" Tito handed Rory the tape.

"What's this about the wharf now?" asked Innes.

"They asked Rory to work down there."

"Who? The Badger?"

"And the others ones too. They're always asking him." Tito sat in the dirt and pulled off his shoe. "But he told them no, didn't you, Rory?" Tito glanced at Innes. "He told them no." Tito leaned close watching Rory fix his shoe. "So did you know him then? The Badger?" he asked Innes. "When you were living here?"

"I knew him."

"And did they call him the Badger then?"

"They did, yeah."

"And why did they?"

Innes thought a moment, remembering. "You know the house built into the hillside? It's fallen in now. There on the backside of the village?"

"We know it," said Rory. "Why, did he live there?"

"Him and his brothers." Innes pitched a stick on the fire. "And I mean if anyone ever went passing by it too close, or took even the slightest odd look at the place, they'd be straight out in the yard ready for a fight."

"Like a badger," said Tito.

"Like that."

"So it was just him and his brothers living there then? Just them? And where are they now, his brothers?"

"I'm sure nowhere good."

Rory had been listening closely. "So how is it he went from that, to working up at Marwick Hall?"

"Did he work there?" asked Tito.

"Actually, was me and him both working there for a time."

Rory looked up. "And how'd you manage that then? Getting a job there?"

"My father. He used to deliver his mussels up there, clams, fish, and all that. He knew people in the kitchens down there. They started me off just running little errands for the house, whatever there was. Didn't pay much, but the cook, she'd always make you a little plate, send you home with something."

"And the Badger, he worked there too?"

"He did, yeah," said Innes, and nothing more.

Rory and Tito stared at him, waiting.

"Alright. Well, yeah I'd been there a little while by then when the Badger, he started coming around, you know, asking if there was any kind of work or what have you. Every time they'd tell him the same thing—there was nothing for him outside, and he was too rough for inside work, then they'd send him off. Next morning though, there he is again, before the house was even up, already started in on some little work, stacking wood, sweeping up. No one had said do it, mind you, so off they'd send him again. But the next morning, and the morning after, there he was, same thing, until finally I think they just gave up, asked him if he could do one little job. And that was it."

"And now he's running the wharf." Rory stared thoughtfully into the fire. "I guess he wanted out of that hole in the ground."

Innes nodded. "I guess he did."

Rory considered the fire a moment more, then from his coat he drew out a wad of money.

"Jesus, Rory," whispered Tito. "Where'd that come from?"

"From Otis. I took it off him during the scuffle." Rory held the money out to Innes. "For the coins. It's fifty quid."

Ham came striding in out of the dark, a bucket of water in his hands. "Are those ponies just gonna follow us around wherever we go now or what?" Sir Winston came hurrying along behind. "And Sir Winston needs to stop following me to the bathroom. He just sits there staring." Ham stopped, now seeing the money in Rory's hand. "What's all this then?"

"Rory nicked it. From Otis," said Tito. "While they were scuffling."

"He nicked it?"

"I didn't nick it. He got the coins."

"Fifty quid," said Tito. "But why didn't you say anything before?"

"I don't know. I'm saying it now."

Innes considered the fold of money in Rory's hands. "You know, if I'd known how all that was gonna go—" He paused, then nodding his thanks, he took the bills.

"And if I'm not mistaken," said Ham, "I believe that's the second time you two have gotten the better of that particular fella." He rolled up his sleeves. "It really does appear we're running with a pair of proper outlaws here, Innes." Ham backed up a step and poured the bucket of water over his head.

"He's getting ready for his date," announced Tito.

"Date?" Innes asked.

"With Ada," said Ham, water streaming off his head. "From the fair."

"You asked her on a date right then and there?"

Tito rocked forward on his knees. "She asked him."

"She didn't."

"She did," said Ham, drying his hair with a rag. "And you needn't sound so shocked about it."

"And am I the last to hear about this then?"

"Wasn't keeping it a secret. She just said, 'Would you like to have some tea sometime?' And I said, 'Why, that would be lovely.' And she suggested when and where. And I said, 'That would be lovely.' And then I regretted saying lovely twice in a row like that, but I don't think she noticed."

"For tea?" asked Innes. "You're going for tea?"

"I am. And by 'tea,' I'm hoping she means beer." Ham tried to flatten his beard as he ducked into the cave, whistling as he went. Tito smiled watching him go, and from his pocket, he pulled out a pencil and a scrap of paper, writing as he followed Ham into the cave.

"What's he always writing down like that anyway?" asked Innes.

"I don't know," said Rory. "Just things he wants to remember."

From the fold of money, Innes counted off a few bills. "Here." He held them out to Rory. "Go on. I told you I would."

Rory took the bills and tucked them into his coat.

Ham came back outside, coat on, hat in hand.

Innes counted out a few more bills. "And here Ham, these are for you."

"And what's that for then?"

"Because I owe you. For getting me to the clinic, for one thing."

"Nope," said Ham, tucking in his shirt. "No need."

"What, so you'll just show up for your tea empty-handed?"

"First off, I'll not be showing up empty-handed." Ham took a little clutch of wildflowers from his coat. "And second, I've still got a few bob tucked away for emergencies. And yes, if you're wondering, this qualifies as an emergency. And I'll not be taking money for helping out a mate. No."

Innes paused at that. "Yeah, well, I was a stranger to you then, so."

"Well, I know you now, so you can just put that away." Ham patted the dust off his pants.

Innes turned to Tito coming out of the cave. "Here Tito, I've got a few quid for you as well. For helping me out with everything. Also, I have a favor to ask you."

"What kind of favor?"

"I'm going to need you to take a bit of money to Miss Aggie for me. Whenever you see her again, OK?"

"Miss Aggie? Why don't you just give it to her yourself?"

"My thoughts exactly," said Ham, slipping on his coat. "Should make a point of it."

"Well, in case I don't see her."

"What do you mean? You'll see her," said Tito.

"Actually." Innes paused. "Now that I have the money for the crossing." Tito immediately looked up at him. "I mean, the ferry's not for a couple days yet, but—"

"Oh. Yeah, I know that." Tito averted his eyes. "I know."

Rory studied Tito a moment, then took Tito's money from Innes.

"We'll do your favor for you." Rory stuffed the bills into his pocket, flicked his cigarette into the fire, and stood up.

As Ham readied himself to go, Sir Winston stood bolt upright, growling into the darkness. A huge brown mass suddenly came barreling past them and stopped in a cloud of dust at the edge of the firelight. It was Eustice, his big rump facing them as he gazed out in the direction of the moor ponies.

"Not again," said Rory as the big mule whinnied forlornly out toward the herd.

"Well, Ham," Innes got to his feet, "looks like your ride's here."

"What, me? I'm late as it is."

"Drop him on the way back then? I'm sure Mr. Begbie won't notice."

Rory took Eustice by the bridle.

"I suppose I've done enough walking for one day." Ham looked into the mule's big brown eyes. "You and me must be cut from the same cloth, eh, big fella? Looking for love and all that." He eased himself nervously onto Eustice's back and sat a moment, gripping the reins. "Not much of a horseman really." Tito handed up the clutch of wildflowers. "Thanks, mate. How do I look?"

"And what do I know about it?" said Tito, backing away as Eustice shifted his giant hooves.

"Alright, well, wish me luck, boys." Ham pulled his cap from his pocket and flopped it on his head.

"You're not wearing that old flat cap on a date?" asked Tito. "Only the old-timers wear those."

"I don't know, I like it up there." Then giving the reins a little twitch, Ham and Eustice started plodding forward, and quicker than you'd think, the two faded into the night.

* * *

Frankie Duff sat alone in the darkened car, a stale cup of coffee on the dash. He lit a cigarette, watching as an old man stooped slowly across the drive, then disappeared into the Vat and Fiddle. Exhaling a stream of smoke through the crack in the window, Frankie sat back and crossed his arms, his leather jacket strained against the vinyl seats. A car pulled up behind him and stopped. Its yellow headlights blinked out. Eyeing the side mirror, Frankie saw three figures approaching the car, as Munro, Otis, and Rat opened the doors and climbed in.

"So?" Frankie asked.

"Twenty quid worth of coins. Twenty," said Munro, landing in the front seat. "Bloody waste of time." He leaned forward and took Frankie's cigarette pack from the dash. "One of them looked like it maybe could be old, but that was it. Otis has it." Frankie looked in the rearview.

"Well, come on then, let's have it."

"Yeah, OK, but Munro said he'd tell the Badger it was me that found it." Otis reached into his pocket. "And if it's worth anything I get my cut?"

"Yeah, yeah, would you come on with it?" Otis passed the thin coin forward. It was tiny in Frankie's hand. "Is that it? How much silver could that even be?"

"Actually, it's more likely electrum than silver."

"What the hell's electrum?"

"Electrum? Oh." Otis cleared his throat. "Well, electrum would be one of your naturally occurring alloys. Was often used in ancient times for making jewelry say, or coinage, of course, or sometimes even—"

"Oh, will you please shut it?" Frankie slipped the coin into his pocket and glanced in the rearview at Rat, who was looking quite disheveled, his jacket torn. "And what happened to you?"

"The sodding kid tore it, is what," muttered Rat.

"What do you mean, he tore it?"

"Apparently, Rat got into it with the kid," said Munro.

"Finally found someone your own size to scrap with, eh, Rat?"

"Yeah, well, I was trying to hang on to him when Innes come up out of nowhere."

"Innes?" Frankie turned to Munro. "What the hell's he talking about, Munro?"

"Yeah, and that big one from the fair again too," added Rat.

"Jesus Christ, Munro, were you not gonna say anything?"

"Well, I was getting to it."

"You were getting to it? Innes bloody Mackie shows up out of nowhere during a transaction such as that, what with all that's going on around the island, and you were *getting to it*?" Frankie rubbed his forehead. "Was it just that one from the fair that was with him?"

"Just him. And them two scroungers."

"And you're sure? That was it?"

"That was it. Innes doesn't have a new crew, Frankie."

Frankie closed his eyes, trying to think. "Alright. Well, we're gonna have to tell the Badger. But if he says one bloody thing to me about it, I swear to God."

Frankie stuck a cigarette in his mouth. Rat reached forward with his lighter, flicking it open with a little flourish. But as Frankie bent to the flame, Rat suddenly narrowed his eyes at the front windshield.

"What the hell?" For there, walking in off the moors, appeared a massive gray mule, a rider on his back. "Oy. Oy, that's him. That's him right there." They watched as Ham crossed the gravel drive, then dismounted at the front of the inn. "And that's Begbie's mule he's on too. I seen him in the square with it from before."

"What do you think, Frankie? Should we go say hello?" Munro cracked open the door.

"Would you shut that?" snapped Frankie as he watched Ham tie Eustice to a post. "The Badger has me watching this place all day for them two from the museum, and you want to make a scene right here in the driveway?"

"Well, what then?"

Munro clicked the car door closed as Ham opened the front door of the inn. Light and sound came pouring out into the night, then was gone again as the door closed behind him.

"What should we do, Frankie?"

"I don't know. Just shut up and let me think a minute." Frankie stared a long moment at the light coming through the windows of the inn, then he turned to Munro.

* * *

Inside the Vat and Fiddle, the hearth washed the low ceiling in an orange glow. In the corner, a trio played for a few dancers as the light from the fire fractured golden across the glasses and the silvered mirror behind the bar. Clusters of patrons leaned in to hear or leaned back to laugh as a story rolled along. Just inside the threshold, Ham stopped, hat in hand, the cold of the moors still leaving his coat. Some of the regulars took notice of him as other men do when a large man appears among them. In the thin light, Ham searched the room. From out of the kitchen, he saw Ada appear, balancing a tray as she worked from table to table, person to person, and then looking up, she saw him standing there. He gave her a little wave, and she pointed him toward a table near the fire. Ham moved gingerly through the crowd, nodding polite how-do-you-dos as he made his way across the floor. He hung his overcoat on the back of a chair, dropped his hat on the table, then sat down and took in the room. Ada disappeared into the kitchen, but before the door stopped swinging, she was out again, apron off.

As she arrived at the table, Ham stood quickly to greet her. But as he did, the table rose up with him and began to turn over until he caught the table leg with one hand and the lit candle with the other. With the only greeting left available to him, he bowed his head to her in a courtly manner. Ada smiled at the sight of him, table in one hand, candle in the other.

"Ah, but you didn't have to bring me anything," she laughed, then seeing the hot candle wax running down his thumb, she hurried over with a dish towel. "Here, let me," she said, and Ham was all too happy to sit still for her as she cleaned his hand. Ada gave him his hand back and relit the candle. "There." She set the candle between them.

Ham tried to think of what to say first. "Oh." He pulled the little bundle of flowers from his overcoat. "These are what I had meant to give you."

"They're lovely, Ham. Thank you." The other waitress stopped at the table carrying a tray of beers. Ada looked at Ham. "Shall we have something then?"

"Of course. And it was tea you were thinking?" asked Ham. "You'd mentioned tea before."

"Well, there is tea, but we also make a very nice ale here at the inn. It draws right up from the cellar."

"Oh, well, I mean, if you're having one."

"A pint for the gentleman, and I will have a half, please, Jo."

As the waitress placed two glasses in front of them, Ham felt for his money.

"You're with Ada," said the waitress. "It's on the house." Then she set down a glass of water. "For the flowers." With an approving nod she smiled a little wink at Ada and headed away.

Ada arranged the flowers in the center of the table, then picked up her glass. "Well, cheers."

"Cheers it is," said Ham, and despite trying very much not to, he slaked off a third of the beer with a single sip. "Well, now that is a humming ale," he said, taking an admiring look at the glass. They sat awkwardly a moment, smiling at each other. Ham noticed a little dish of sugar cubes on the next table over. He reached across and took a few.

"Would you have rather had tea then?" asked Ada.

"Tea? Oh, no, these are for my mule. Well, I mean he's not mine exactly; I'm dropping him home on the way back. He's just out front there." Ham thumbed toward the door. "Oh, and before I forget, I wanted to make sure and tell you that the pie you gave me at the fair, it was the best I've ever had. It really was."

"Ah you were probably just overhungry." Ada smiled, then a thought came across her face. She leaned forward quietly. "So I have to say, now that you mention the pie."

"What about it?"

"Well, you remember the coin? The one you gave me for it?"

"See, now you've beaten me to it," said Ham, quickly patting his pockets for money. "I know you said you'd wanted to give me that pie, but I really—"

"No. No, it's not that," she said, lowering her voice to a whisper. "What I was going to say was—well as it turns out, the coin is old." She nodded. "Quite old."

"Is it?" whispered Ham, not sure why they were whispering. "I suppose it did look a little worse for wear."

"Right. And so just by chance really, I happened to show it to my uncle. He's quite keen on that sort of thing and—" Ada paused.

"What? What is it?"

She leaned closer. "Well, there were a couple of men in here this morning asking questions about it. About the coin. And they—well they said they wanted to talk with you as well."

"With me?"

"They'd only just arrived off the ferry. Hang on, they gave me their card." Ada searched her pockets. "Apparently, they're some sort of authorities on this type of matter."

"And what sort of matter would that be, I wonder?" asked Ham, taking a concerned sip of his beer. "The kind that brings you across on the ferry, I suppose."

"The thing is"—Ada leaned in closer still—"they're still here."

"What, here in the pub?"

She tilted her head toward the corner of the room. Ham sat a moment, then casually glanced over his shoulder. At a table in the far corner sat Alastair and Jameson, looking everywhere except at Ham.

"I'm sorry," said Ada. "I didn't know how to put them off."

"Ah no, what else could you do." He looked over again, and this time, Alastair and Jameson gave him a little wave. "I suppose we'll have to ask them over?"

"I suppose so."

Ham nodded at them, and immediately they began making their way through the crowd.

"We are so very sorry to bother you both," said Alastair, arriving at the table. "We feel terribly about all this cloak-and-dagger business. If I might introduce myself. Alastair Clements, Antiquities Fellow at the Ashenrose Museum. This is my assistant, Jameson Hewitt. Might we possibly take just a moment of your time?" Ham gestured to a chair. Alastair sat down and nodded politely to Ada. "I suppose Miss Coburn here has told you we have a few questions we'd like to ask, if that would be alright? Again, I do apologize for the intrusion. And I'm sorry, it's Ham, yes?"

"That's right. Hamish."

"Hamish," repeated Jameson, pulling out his pad. "And is there a last name?"

Ada slid aside the flowers. "Now you said you're certain he'd done nothing wrong."

"Well, I know *I'm* certain of it," said Ham.

The waitress approached the table with another tray of glasses.

"Can I get you anything, Ada, love? she asked, cutting her eyes in annoyance at Alastair and Jameson. "At your table for *two*?"

"Ham?" Ada asked.

"Well, I'm willing if you are."

Jo set two fresh glasses in front of them and moved off.

"Miss Coburn's quite right," said Alastair. "There's certainly no need for last names at this point if that's something you're not comfortable with—"

"It's Little," said Ham. "Hamish Little. And I've not got a thing to hide."

"Again, Mr. Little, my apologies if we've given you the wrong impression, but, well, it's just we'd be very curious to know anything you can tell us about the coin. Anything at all. How it came into your possession. That sort of thing?"

They waited as Ham took a sip of beer. "Well, alright. Not that I can see how this is any of your concern really. No disrespect intended, you understand." He mulled over his answer. "It was a friend who gave it to me."

"A friend? And so it was his coin, your friend?"

"It was, yes. Well, his father's actually."

"His father's," repeated Jameson, writing in his pad.

"Yes, but he's deceased now, so I suppose just put it down as my friend's coin." Ham took another quick sip. "But like I said, my friend, he gave it to me, which I suppose technically makes it my coin." He picked his beer up, then set it down again. "Except that I gave it to Ada, which would make it hers, of course, so I guess just mark it down as Ada's coin." Ham thought again. "Unless that makes any kind of a problem for her, and in that case, just put it down as mine."

Jameson had long since stopped taking notes.

"Perhaps," said Alastair, "perhaps it would be easier if you just gave us the name of your friend?"

"The one who gave me the coin?"

"Him, yes."

"Um." Ham thought a moment. "No."

"No? And may I ask why not?"

"Because—well no particular reason really. It's just he's been keeping to himself at the moment."

"Has he?" said Jameson, shooting a glance at Alastair.

"Alright, well perhaps we can come back to that one," suggested Alastair. "So your friend, he gives you the coin, and then while at the fair, you proceed to spend it? Do I have that right?"

"That's right."

"So would I be right in assuming you knew nothing about the coin? I mean, having spent it on, as I understand it, pie."

Jameson leaned to Ada. "Although I'm sure it was a very nice pie, miss."

"The coin was in my possession all of an hour. Look, can I ask what this is all about? Is the coin valuable or something?"

"On its own it's of moderate value. In truth it's the coin's historical value we're after. Potentially quite a significant historical value."

"What, like for Skara Skaill, you mean?" asked Ada.

"For Skara Skaill, yes. And beyond even. Possibly far beyond." Alastair turned to Ham. "So I ask you again, Mr. Little, this friend of yours, I feel certain if he knew just how important, how potentially vitally important—"

"Sorry, answer's no. It's like I said, he's a bit on the private side just at the moment."

A graveness came over Alastair now. "Mr. Little, please, I implore you. I've spent my entire life on this type of—"

"Alright." Ham held up his hand, wax still on his thumb. "Alright, I'll ask him for you. I'll ask him, but only to meet you here at the inn, yeah? I'll ask him, and I'll get word back to you here in the morning. But that's it, I'll not do any more than that. And to be honest, I wouldn't get my hopes up if I were you." Then hearing the band starting up again, he turned to Ada. "Well, then, Miss Coburn, what say you?" He nodded to the dance floor. "Shall we?"

"Why, I'd be delighted, Mr. Little."

Alastair jumped to his feet. "Mr. Little. Mr. Little, wait," he called as Ham and Ada started away. "You simply cannot just walk away and leave us here on the off chance he'll agree to meet us. Please, if we could just have a name, or where to find him?"

"Now look," said Ham, "I've told you what I've told you. And I've told you what I'll do. And as for me walking away"—he offered Ada his arm—"I'm not walking, Mr. Clements. I'm dancing." And after glancing over to see if she appreciated his clever line, Ham led Ada out among the crowd onto the dance floor.

* * *

Outside the Vat and Fiddle, Munro Duff immediately turned from the window and hurried along the side wall. As he made the corner, he clipped his shoulder at the edge of the stone building. "Son of a—"

The wind met him head-on as he hustled across the gravel drive. Reaching the car, he opened the door and wedged himself in, wind-blasted and panting.

Frankie looked at him. "Well? What did you see?"

Munro held up a finger, trying hard to catch his breath.

XVII

THE BADGER WORKED ALONE in the hole, powdered white with rock dust, knee-deep in the chamber floor like a ghost digging his own grave. His pickax rose and fell, rose and fell, until finally he slowed, letting the handle fall to the ground. Wearily he stepped from the hole. The chamber was mostly cleared now of the rubble that had filled it days before. Across the stone floor, holes were dug in a grid, small piles of earth next to each one. He lit a cigarette. As he stood quietly considering the empty room, he looked up at the symbol carved high on the back wall. Three circles made from a single continuous line. Lowering his gaze, his eyes came to rest upon the row of faded paintings all around the walls; one-dimensional, crude, carefully made. Their simple scenes immemorial, familiar. Sheep across a sweep of open meadow. A heron in the mud. Squares of tilled fields. Farmers bent to their work. A new gray chapel, its ancient ruins sitting up above him now in the open air. As he stepped along the row, the Badger stopped at one of the paintings. A single stone crag resembling a crooked old man stood sentinel like a watchman, high on the hill above a shoreline. It was familiar to him. He had seen it as a child, once from the water and once from the land on the far side of the island. He knew its features well, unaltered across time. At the sight of it, he drifted closer. But as he did, he saw something in the picture he hadn't noticed before. Deep within its faded landscape, out beyond the stone crag, ran a string of little caves painted high along a ridge. Within one of the caves, bent in prayer, knelt a tiny monk, his face a daub of white, barely visible within the blackened pigment. The Badger studied the tilting face a moment. From there, his eyes moved through the painting and down the sweep of ridgeline to the flats along the shore, ending in a thick shadow of aged pigment, bottle-dark. The Badger struck a match and bent close. The flicker of light reached deeper into the painted shadow, and from its depths, emerging out of the receding darkness, faint traces slowly took shape.

A stand of trees. A dark wood.

A wildwood.

And beyond it, a spit of land reaching into the sea and a black ship rocking at anchor.

The Badger's eyes stayed fixed upon it, and bending closer still, he stopped and slowly sank to his knees.

* * *

The fire had burned itself down to embers, and the band played its last note. As the barman dried the glasses and the musicians laid their instruments in their cases, Ham and Ada stepped apart, smiling, and bid each other goodnight.

Outside the air was cold and clear, and the last of the stragglers headed off into the night. Ham stood alone beneath the inn's wooden sign. He could smell the thrill of woodsmoke in the air.

"Thank you for that," he said, tipping his tweed cap to the heavens. Looking up, he saw the comet hanging amid the great wash of stars sprayed across the northern sky. He turned to Eustice, standing quietly at the post. "And look what I have for you." He pulled the sugar cubes from his pocket, but as he did, the big mule's eyes widened and his ears lay flat back as he startled in fear and yanked away.

* * *

Inside the inn, sitting in the furthermost corner, Alastair and Jameson quickly stood up and set off down the narrow hall leading out the back door.

Outside, they hurried along the wall of the inn. They stopped at the front corner and peered slowly around.

"Do you see him?" whispered Jameson.

"No." But as Alastair leaned out to get a fuller view, he stopped, then straightened up.

"What is it?" And leaning around, Jameson saw it too. It was Eustice at the front of the inn, running wildly in broad circles across the gravel, his reins dragging along behind. Alastair and Jameson hurried from the corner, but as the big mule saw them, he lurched and bolted toward the road. Clattering and skittering over the pavement, he ran to the grassy ditch and in a single leap, disappeared out onto the moors.

Alastair ran to the road and looked out into the blackness. Seeing nothing, he turned back to the inn in time to see Jameson picking something out of the gravel. A worn tweed cap, run over flat and covered in dust.

* * *

Leaning against his pack, Tito lay staring up at the night sky. The white smear of light hung high among the stars, its tail trailing away behind.

"And you're sure it's moving?" he asked.

"It's moving," said Rory.

"Because it looks like it's sitting still."

"It's not."

"So where is it going then? Just off to nowhere?"

"It goes around the sun, then way out to where there's almost nothing. Then the sun pulls it back again."

"The sun does it?" Tito considered that. "So just round and round then?"

"Just round and round." Rory reached into Tito's pack and pulled out the leather purse. "Look, I'm putting your money in here, see?" He opened the flap, showing Tito the money Innes had given him. "You can do with it what you want." He placed the money inside, pausing a moment to notice the faded designs and pigments down within the lining of the purse.

Innes came walking up out of the dark. "Herd's still out there." As he set a bundle of sticks near the fire, he noticed Tito looking up at the comet. "Looks like it's just sitting there, doesn't it?"

"See, that's what I said."

Innes stoked the fire. "Used to be they thought comets were a sign of something."

"A sign of what?" asked Tito.

"I don't know. Like something coming."

"It's not a sign of anything," said Rory, lighting the stub of a cigarette. "It's just dust and ice."

"So what makes it shine like that then?" Tito asked.

"It's just how the light catches it."

Tito stared up at the comet. "Pretty good ice."

Innes sat down in the firelight, watching as Rory smoked. "Aren't you a little young for that?" he asked, pulling off his boots.

"What are you, my father?"

Innes held up his palms as Rory took another drag.

Tito looked out toward the darkness. "Has anyone seen Sir Winston?" He attempted a thin whistle.

But hearing something, Rory put his finger to his lips. Then Innes heard it too. A single footfall. Then another. Then from out of the dark came Sir Winston, and right behind him, exhausted and mud-spattered, trudged Eustice, his reins trailing along the ground.

Tito jumped to his feet. "Where's Ham?"

Innes walked to the edge of the firelight and scanned out. "I'm sure he's fine. Eustice probably just ran off after the ponies again."

"But what if Eustice threw him off?" asked Tito. "What if he hit his head or something? He said he's not the best horseman."

Innes looked at Tito, and at Rory holding the riderless Eustice by the bridle, then turning, he stared out beyond the firelight in the direction the mule had come.

* * *

The Badger drove headlong through the dark. As he came over the last rise, he saw Marwick Hall dead ahead out in the blackness.

Passing through the main gate, he continued around to the service entrance. As he went, he could see the front of the manor. Shining cars glittered black in the lamplight; the gentlemen and ladies of the Ancient Order of Albion had arrived on the island. Continuing past, he turned and drove along the back of the manor, slowing a little where a dark-green TV truck and a few cars were parked, *The Times* stenciled on one of the doors. A group of men stood smoking and talking together in the dark. Radio news came quietly from a car window. At the very back of the house, the Badger got out and hurried toward the light above the service entrance.

* * *

Innes slid down off Eustice and walked to the front of the Vat and Fiddle. The inn was pitch dark. He tried the handle. Rory and Tito waited atop the big mule as Sir Winston circled near the front door.

"Maybe we missed him along the way?" called Tito as he and Rory dropped to the ground. Innes looked up at the darkened windows.

"You don't think he could be asleep in there, do you?" asked Rory. But as he led Eustice to the front of the inn, he stopped. "Innes." He pointed at a scattering of massive mule prints all around the ground. "I guess they made it this far at least."

In the moonlight, Innes followed the wide arc of the hoof tracks across the gravel drive until finally he stopped at a broad boot print in the dust.

"That's Ham's," said Tito.

"And how can you know that?" Rory asked.

"I've walked behind him enough." Tito set his foot into the huge print.

Slowly they followed the prints out to the middle of the driveway. Sir Winston meandered ahead, nose to the ground.

"They end here. See?" said Rory. "With all these others."

Tito squatted down. "How can they just disappear like that? Out here in the middle?"

Suddenly Innes turned and hurried out to the center of the road, staring into the distance.

"What is it?" Rory called. Then looking at the ground around him, he saw it too. Two tire tracks, the gravel spray shooting back and away from the very spot the prints had vanished.

* * *

Alastair and Jameson sat in their car at a dead stop. Through the front windshield, fixed squarely in the headlights, stood a behemoth, shaggy and block-headed, its horns wider than a man's outstretched arms. The bull stared blankly into the headlights, chewing its cud, puffs of breath pumping from its wet nostrils. Alastair stared at the bull, then reached over and honked a long blast on the horn. At the sound, the big bull lowered his head menacingly, and to clear up any doubt about his mood, he dropped an angry plop of manure on the road for good measure.

"He seems out of sorts," said Jameson, staring through the windshield. After a few moments, a strange sound could be heard approaching from somewhere behind them. "Sir? Do you hear something? Is that a horse?"

Coming alongside the car, Eustice's long face appeared at the window. Innes, Rory, and Tito looked down from his back.

"Excuse me," said Alastair, looking up at them. "You wouldn't happen to know who that fellow there belongs to, would you?" He nodded at the bull. "We've been trying to pass for quite some time now."

"He doesn't belong to anyone," said Rory. "That one does whatever he likes."

"And he likes standing in the road," added Tito.

"I can see that."

Innes looked down into the back seat, and seeing nothing, he turned to Alastair. "You wouldn't happen to have seen another car pass this way, would you?"

"A car, you say?" Alastair cast a sidelong glance at Jameson. "And why do you ask?"

"Not meaning to be rude, but did you see a car or didn't you? We're in a bit of a hurry."

"As are we, if we could ever get this road cleared."

As they all assessed each other a moment, Tito saw Sir Winston trotting straight out toward the bull. Without breaking stride, the little dog continued past him up the road, nose to the pavement. Innes took one last glance into the car, then urged Eustice forward.

"Wait, sir?" called Alastair as Jameson stuck his head out the window.

"Hold on, excuse me?" But as the big mule stepped into the headlights, Jameson saw Eustice clearly for the first time. "Sir, isn't that the same mule we saw at the inn?" And as Eustice gave a wide berth off the side of the road, the big bull stared straight into the headlights, chewing its cud.

XVIII

THE BADGER HURRIED DOWN the corridor, tiled in white. As he reached the end of the hall, he looked left toward the frenzy of the kitchens. He waited there until a stout man in a black dinner jacket made his way over, clipboard in hand.

"I need to see the earl," said the Badger.

"Dinner's already being served," the man said flatly.

"It can't wait. He'll want to know."

The man eyed the Badger, covered in rock dust, an urgency about him, then without a word, he led him down the passage toward the back stairs.

The Badger stood alone in the small anteroom. A steady ticking came from the clock in the corner, muted sounds of music came through the walls. There was a small desk at one end and two stiff-backed chairs at the other. Between them, a high casement window with heavy velvet curtains that hung to the floor. The Badger went to sit down, but remembering his filthy clothes, he stayed standing and waited.

* * *

Eustice's hooves clopped along in the perfect darkness. Tito could feel the animal's wide back shifting with every step. After some time, the ground began rising beneath them, and reaching the top of the rise, they saw Marwick Hall lit up like an ocean liner out in the blackness. Innes reined Eustice to a stop. For a moment, they stared at the lights in the distance, the smell of salt air coming in from somewhere off the water. Innes urged Eustice off the road and into the ghostly whiteness of the sandy ground, stopping in a patch of low bushes.

"What are we doing?" asked Rory. "You're not thinking someone took him in there?"

"If I'm honest, I don't have a clue where he is. But the manor's the only thing even out this way." Innes dismounted, and at a low wall looked out at the lights of Marwick Hall. "For all we know, he's probably back at the cave hut wondering where we've run off to."

Rory tied Eustice's reins to a heavy stone, and stepping through the tumbledown wall, they picked their way across the stony ground as Sir Winston circled ahead in the moonlight. Keeping the manor at a distance, they could see the gravel drive at the front of the house and the dark reflections of cars glinting in the gaslight. The faintest sounds of music came carrying in on the wind, and as they moved along quietly, they saw shadows of gentlemen and ladies passing across the lit upper windows.

They came around the back of the house. A single light could be seen just ahead. Hurrying closer, they knelt low behind a tall hedge of hawthorns, and through its gaps, they could see a service entrance.

"That's the kitchens through there," whispered Innes. Crates and boxes were stacked nearby, and jutting away from the entrance was a tall stone abutment covered in thick ivy. Along the length of it ran a wall of split firewood stacked as tightly as bricks. Far down the drive sat a green van. Several cars were parked just beyond it.

"We should start down there," whispered Innes.

But as they stood to go, Rory turned to Tito. "Nope. You stay here."

"What? No, I'm coming."

"No you're not." Rory nodded at Sir Winston. "What if they have dogs? You think he's gonna stay quiet?"

"They most definitely have dogs," said Innes. "And someone should keep an eye on that door there anyway."

"Fine." Tito nodded, and as Innes and Rory started away behind the hawthorns, Tito squatted down with Sir Winston, low within the hedge.

* * *

The Badger stared at the high-polished door, waiting. The fire burned low, glowing weakly on the brass bin next to the hearth. A swell of muted laughter came through the walls, and as it died away, a gear on the clock clicked once, releasing a single chime marking the half hour. The Badger set his watch to it. On the table by the door sat a small silver bowl full of red candies. He took one, straightened the bowl, then walked over to the casement window. The moon emerged from behind the clouds, and in the silvered light, he saw the hawthorn hedge and the service vehicles parked at the far corner of the house. Then something below caught his eye. He leaned to the window.

"Bloody hell." He glanced up at the clock, and as another rise of laughter came through the walls, he turned and hurried for the door.

* * *

Tito lay low and still. In the night air, he could smell the damp earth. His hands lay flat on the smooth dirt beneath the hedge. As he watched the door, a few ants began climbing over the backs of his hands. Tito watched their black silhouettes moving clumsily about, bumbling through the tiny hairs on his hand. Suddenly Sir Winston stood up, his attention drawn to something moving in the shadows at the back of the manor. As Tito squinted into the darkness, the service door swung open. A servant, followed by a great grizzled wolfhound, came out and scraped a platter of gristle and bones onto the ground. Leaving the wolfhound to his meal, the servant returned through the service door, but immediately it burst open again, and this time the Badger himself came striding through it. Tito lowered flat, watching as he marched out of the light and toward the dark movement along the wall.

The Badger stopped where Frankie, Munro, Otis, and Rat stood in the dark.

"What have I told you about coming here?" he hissed at Frankie. "What have I told you? And didn't I say for you to watch them two at the pub?"

"I did."

"He did." Munro nodded. "Go on, Frankie. Tell him the rest."

Tito could hear the low tones of the shadows speaking along the wall. Backing away, he looked down the hedgerow for any sign of Innes and Rory returning. Seeing nothing, he turned to Sir Winston, but where the little dog had been, there was now only a warm place in the dirt. Tito looked up to see Sir Winston walking in plain view across the gravel drive, inching ever closer to the big dog working the scraps. A low growl now came from the hound, and his great paw slowly curled around the bone he was grinding. Sir Winston stopped in front of him. The wolfhound's eyes ticked upward, then in a din of gnashing teeth, it snapped up the pile of scraps, cantered back across the gravel drive, and disappeared through the swinging door. Tito slumped in relief, but only for a moment, for Sir Winston, too, now hurried to the service door, nosed it open, and pushed inside.

Looking toward the men in the shadows, Tito turned and hurried low along the back of the hedge. He squatted down. Straight across from him was the stone abutment, its wall of firewood only a few feet beyond the hedge where he knelt. Tito took a last look toward the shadows, then in one quick movement, he pushed through the hedge and tucked behind the wall. Taking up an armful of firewood, he hurried across to the service door and slipped inside.

* * *

Innes and Rory moved low and quiet, stopping where the hedge ended and the wild gorse began.

"So where now?" whispered Rory, catching his breath.

"I don't know, but I swear to God, if he's sitting back at the cave airing his feet out…" The muffled boom and hiss of the ocean came in on the wind. They stood a moment, looking back at the cars parked behind the manor. Then from somewhere behind them came a faint *thunk* out in the dark. They looked but could see nothing. Slowly they started forward. At their feet appeared the sandy whiteness of a two-track path.

Rory stopped. "Can you see it?"

At first Innes saw nothing, but as his eyes squinted into the darkness, he now saw the dull silhouette of a sedan sitting in the path up ahead.

Rory leaned close. "That's Frankie Duff's car."

Signaling for Rory to stay back, Innes started forward, step by careful step. Suddenly from somewhere nearby a rush of chaos exploded out of the dark, and Innes found himself sprawling sideways through the air and landing in a heap. Above him, a massive figure circled wildly around, and as Innes tried to scramble away, a rock came sailing in, and then another, thumping off the man's broad back as he turned and bellowed blindly, a bag over his head.

"How about you take these ropes off and fight me like a man?"

The smothered voice coming through the bag was one that Innes knew.

"Ham?"

The man stopped. "Innes?" he asked as another rock came whistling in and bounced off his head. "Bloody hell!"

"Rory! Stop, it's Ham." Innes scrambled to his feet and lifted the bag from Ham's head.

"Oh, thank God above," gasped Ham as he gulped in the night air, his hair sweated flat, his hands tied behind his back.

"Are you alright?" asked Innes. "What happened?"

"Those two brothers is what happened. And I'm happy to chat all about it, but first I'm very much going to need you to untie me." Ham quickly turned his back, offering his hands. "They didn't give me a single bathroom break."

"Oh, right, hang on." Innes fumbled with the ropes.

"Quick as you can, please."

"There. Done."

Ham rushed desperately into the bushes, and after an astonishingly long time, he hurried back. "Ready." He nodded. "Where's Tito?"

"This way, come on." As they turned to go, the wind off the water changed directions, and a low murmur of voices could now be heard approaching from somewhere out in the dark.

"It's them," whispered Ham. He picked up a rock at his feet. "I'll not be going back in that bag again, I can promise you that."

As Ham readied himself, Rory leaned close. "Frankie carries a gun."

"A gun?"

Rory nodded. "Always."

Ham slowly lowered the rock as Innes pulled them away into the dark. As they hurried through the low bushes, the wind started picking up and carried with it the snap of salt air as the voices faded again to silence. After a little distance, Innes stopped, for here the ground dropped sharply down to the water below. They stood a moment, listening hard into the wind. After a moment, the voices came again, calling to each other out in the dark. Rory could see that the cliff dropped down to a broad ledge that ran along the cliff face. Innes pointed them down to it, but as he and Rory began lowering themselves down, they looked up to see Ham still standing above them.

"Come on," whispered Innes.

"If I'm honest, I'm not particularly good with heights."

"Oh no? And how are you with guns?"

Glancing once more behind him, Ham slid himself slowly down the ledge until his feet touched solid earth again.

"OK. Good." He exhaled. "This is good."

The three stood tight against the cliff wall, listening. The waves washed steadily below. Then from out of the wind the voices came again, more urgently now, approaching from above.

"What is it with those two?" whispered Ham.

"Sounds like more than just two now."

"Come on, this way." Innes started along the ledge.

Where the ledge curved out of view, a trickle of water flowed from the rock face. As they approached it, they could see an open seam in the cliffside, wide enough for a man to duck through. Just inside the opening was a wrought-iron gate, slick in the salt air. A bright copper lock bolted it closed.

Innes felt all around the opening. "There was a key," he said, running his hands along the rocks, finding nothing. "There was always a key."

"What was it you said your job here was again?" asked Ham.

A thin shower of pebbles sprinkled from above as a beam of light began sweeping along the ledge. Innes and Rory backed tight against the wall, when from behind them there came a wet wrenching sound, and turning, they saw Ham pulling the entire gate loose from the stone.

"That mortar could use a bit of a freshen up."

* * *

Inside the manor house, Tito found himself in the long corridor tiled in white, the load of firewood in his arms. Across the far end of the hall, he saw two servants pass by, loaded trays in hand. As he started up the corridor, tight against the wall, he immediately came to an open door. Inside was a dark cloakroom, boots and coats and umbrellas lined along the wall.

"Winston?" he whispered. Hearing nothing, he continued on, and approaching the end of the corridor, he heard voices. He peered low around the corner. To the left was a massive butcher-block table with kitchen staff bustling around it, to the right a backstair and two swinging doors. From down the corridor came a loud bang as the Badger came striding through the door. Tito stepped quickly around the corner. A stream of servants carrying platters of food hurried past him and pushed through the double doors at the back staircase. Before the doors had stopped swinging, a tall waiter came shouldering through with a tray of dishes, and right behind him, sniffing the air, was the massive wolfhound eyeing the scraps. Sir Winston was nowhere to be seen. Tito tried to tuck out of the way, but as the tall waiter hurried past, he spoke without looking down.

"Firewood. Second floor," he said, snapping his fingers toward the stairs.

For a moment Tito didn't move. But with one last look toward the kitchens for Sir Winston, he started for the service stairs and through the swinging doors.

With the load of wood in his arms, Tito labored up the steps. Reaching the top, he carefully pushed through the double doors, finding himself alone in an oak-paneled landing the size of a small room. Across the muffled carpet were two high mahogany doors. Music came from somewhere through the walls. The door on the left swung open as a waiter hurried through it, and rebalancing a tray at his shoulder, he half glanced at Tito standing there, arms full of wood. Reaching over with his free hand, the waiter looped his finger into a brass ring that was set flush into the wall. As he pulled the ring, a half door invisible in the paneling eased open with a sigh.

"In there," the waiter nodded, before pushing through the swinging doors and starting down the stairs. But as the doors settled to a close, Tito saw the Badger on the staircase below, making his way up. Tito stepped to the hidden door and pulled it closed behind him.

Inside was complete darkness. Through the door, Tito heard the Badger cross the landing and pass through the mahogany doors. Then all was quiet. Carefully Tito set the firewood down. He touched the place where their edges had dug creases into his arms, then he felt for the door. He patted all around it, but found no knob and no latch. He gave it a little push. It didn't budge. Setting his feet, he pushed against it with all he had, once, and again, then he backed away. As he stood in the blackness, listening to his own breathing, a cold finger of air came brushing across the back of his neck. He wheeled around, and looking blindly into the dark, he began to sense something strange. An openness. An emptiness. Slowly his eyes adjusted to see a speck of orange light, and he realized what he thought had been the back of the closet was in fact a long void receding away. Tito stared as the tiny orange glow breathed brighter, then faded again into darkness. From the door, he took a single step, and then another, and continuing slowly forward, he could feel the wall change from wood to stone beneath his hand. A muffled murmur of music came faintly through the walls. Deeper into the passage he went, until finally he could see that the glowing light was in fact seeping through the seams of a little hatch, half again as small as the hidden door. He stepped to it and knelt down. It was barely big enough for a child to crawl through.

On the ground beneath him, he could feel scattered scraps of bark and kindling. Along the hatch's frame, names and initials were etched all around, visible in the thin light.

Brother Poley. H.L.H. 1710.
Tanny Boy '36. Bertsie. The Badger.

He stared a moment at the sight of the Badger's name. Feeling around the hatch, his hand passed over the traces of other names, long since faded away. His hand bumped into a small egg-shaped knob. Rising on his knees, he turned the knob and slowly opened the hatch. A sudden wash of golden light came angling into the opening as the clamor of voices rose above the tinkling of glasses and laughter and music. Quickly Tito backed into the dark. The little hatch had opened directly into a tall brass bin full of firewood, shielding Tito from view. Up beyond the rim of the firebox, firelight flickered against the burnished molding of the great room, and Tito could see the top of a towering Christmas tree glittering in the corner. Another swell of laughter rose up, and as the sound of voices came closer, Tito quickly backed away, closing the hatch behind him. Deeper down the long passage he saw nothing but blackness, and from the direction he had come, a line of light shone at the base of the hidden door. He sat a moment, and a hard fear settled over him, and pressing his eyes with the heels of his hands, he slumped against the wall. Opening his eyes again, he realized something hard was jutting into his back. Another egg-shaped knob. And there in the wall behind him he saw the very dimmest outline of a second hatch, identical to the first. He put his ear to it, then slowly turned the knob. This hatch also opened into a large firebox, but the hearth was almost cold, and the ceiling above was dim. Tito crawled low through the hatch.

Looking up, he could see bookshelves to the ceiling. The room was silent except for the faint ticking of a clock. He readied himself to climb out, but out of the silence, a voice came striding into the room. A voice he had heard many times before, coming over the radio at Christmastime, booming across the village square. Tito stayed low like a rabbit, deathly still, for this was the voice of Lord Marwick, a few feet from him now.

"So that's your urgent news then, is it? That you've found not a single sign of the hoard, but rather a painting of, what was it, a little monk kneeling in a cave? That's what you've interrupted my dinner to tell me?"

"Well, yes, sir, but... Well, it's not so much what's painted *in* the cave. But what's painted near it," came a second voice, and Tito knew it to be the Badger's.

"And what would that be, pray tell?" Tito could smell the smoke from Lord Marwick's cigar.

"Well, it looks to be a small wood, sir."

"A wood?"

"Yes, sir. And a spit of land."

"Oh, and a spit of land besides?" mocked Lord Marwick. "'*Out from the bending woods they passed, out 'pon the spit of land.*' Yes, Mr. Croy, very dramatic. Look, even if this painting of yours was somehow depicting the last known site of the Harald Hoard, what exactly would you have me do with that, eh? It's still just a picture of a spit of land and a wood that's now many centuries gone. Not exactly a map now, is it? In fact, what you've got there, Mr. Croy, is a description of basically every shoreline on Skara Skaill."

"No, sir." The Badger hesitated. "It isn't."

"Oh no? And why is that exactly?"

Tito heard footsteps on the carpet, and a cigar stub landed in the ashes next to him. Quickly he backed away through the opening, and as he closed the hatch, the Badger's words came to him broken and faint.

"...the painting—on the hill above the wood—the old man standing—overlooking it all."

* * *

Innes led them along through the dark, water dripping down the walls. Up ahead, a glint of light reflected in the blackness. As they continued deeper in, the trickle of water at their feet narrowed into a stone gutter, and they could see a reflection of light up ahead at the end of the passage. Reaching it, they stopped at a little squat archway, barely big enough for a man to squeeze through. Inside it, a set of narrow stairs disappeared straight up through solid rock.

Ham turned to Innes. "Not really great with tight spaces."

"You have a better plan then, do you?"

Ham looked back at the far end of the passage as lights began sweeping around at the opening. "What is it with these two brothers?"

Rory ducked through the arch.

"You should go next," said Ham. "In case I get stuck."

"Go on," said Innes. "I'll push from the back."

Ham stooped into the archway, but as he squeezed his way up the stairs, he saw Rory stopped just ahead at a low, heavy door.

"It's locked." Rory glanced back. "What do we do?"

By way of an answer, Ham immediately booted open the door. "Really not good with tight spaces."

Peering through the little door, they looked out into an enormous high-ceilinged gallery. At the far end of the silent hall stood two gigantic doors. Moonlight angled down through their transoms.

"Have you brought us out through the bloody manor, Innes?"

"Just go."

Stepping out into the gallery, they started for the doors, their heels echoing as they went. All around, pillars rose up to the ceiling like burnished trees in a shadowy wood. Along the walls hung lustrous paintings of earls past sitting astride finely rigged horses, an easy patrimony on their faces, heavy staffs in their hands. Innes slowed at the sight of them, but only for a moment, before Ham opened the towering doors, and they all slipped silently through.

* * *

The only sound in the room now was the steady ticking of the grandfather clock. Tito peered slowly over the firebox, and seeing no one, he climbed out and hurried to the open door. As he passed the bowl of red candies on the table, he slipped a fistful into his pocket, then started across the landing and down the stairs.

Passing the bustle of the kitchens, he kept his head down and his eyes up, looking for Sir Winston as he passed. As he made the corner and headed down the long hall, Tito again stopped at the cloakroom. "Sir Winston," he whispered. He skidded a few of the candies into the closet and listened. Hearing nothing, he started again down the corridor, dropping candies as he went. At the service door, he stopped and cast his eyes back once more. "Winston," he whispered, and then again, almost to himself,

"Winston." But as he stood there, the stout man with the clipboard appeared at the top of the hall. Tito let one last candy slip from his hand, then turned to the door and pushed through.

After hurrying across the gravel, he dove headlong into the hedges and quickly rummaged a piece of bread from his pack. He knelt down and whistled thinly into the darkness, once, then again. From behind him, he heard something fast approaching as Rory, Innes, and Ham came rushing into view.

"Ham, they found you!"

"They found me alright." Ham nodded, catching his breath.

"Come on, Tito, we've gotta go," said Rory. "Where's Sir Winston?"

Tito paused, then nodded toward the manor. "I tried to find him, but—"

"Find him? You're not telling me you went in there?"

"Well what was I supposed to do, Rory?"

"Gotta go, boys," said Innes, scanning out into the dark. "Right now."

Tito turned again to the service door. "One minute."

"We don't have a minute, Tito." Rory grabbed up Tito's pack.

Tito's eye stayed on the back door. "Don't ask me to leave him, Rory. Please don't ask me that." Glancing back, Tito could see they were all staring at him, waiting, and after taking one last look at the door, he took his pack off Rory's shoulder and put it on his own. Without another word he started silently past them as they all turned into the darkness together, leaving the lights of Marwick Hall behind.

XIX

ALASTAIR'S HEAD RESTED ON the dashboard. Out in the headlights, the big bull stood unconcerned. Suddenly Jameson sat bolt upright.

"Sir?"

Alastair lifted his head in time to see Eustice clatter across the road before disappearing again out onto the moors, his muddied reins trailing behind him. Hearing the mule galloping past, the bull looked back, then placing one hoof delicately over the other, he turned and wandered slowly away into the dark.

"Sir, wasn't that the same mule again?" Stepping out of the car, they hurried up the road. As Alastair reached the crest of the hill, he could now see the lights of Marwick Hall in the distance. Then something else caught his eye—two sets of headlights moving slowly through the fields and a line of flashlights sweeping the darkness in front of them.

"What do you think all that is?" asked Jameson.

"If I had to guess, I'd say that's a search party."

As they stood watching, the group of lights slowed, stopped, then circled back together.

"Sir, what with all that's going on, I'm wondering if perhaps we shouldn't—?"

"Douse the lights?" Alastair nodded. "I couldn't agree more."

Out in the darkness, the two sets of headlights started moving again, and as they bumped onto the narrow road, they turned and headed straight to where Alastair and Jameson stood. The first vehicle approached without stopping, and as it sped past, they could see several silhouettes sitting inside. As it disappeared over the rise, the second vehicle, a white Rover, came to a stop directly in front of them, its diesel engine thrumming. Alastair and Jameson squinted into the headlights as the Badger climbed out of the car.

"Evening, gentlemen," he said, and striding straight past them, he began searching all around their car.

"Excuse me? May we help you with something?" asked Alastair.

"Nothing for you to worry yourself about, Mr. Clements." The Badger tapped the trunk, listening.

"I'm sorry, have we met? I'm afraid you have the advantage of me, sir."

"I do at that," said the Badger, circling the vehicle, glancing into the windows. "So what brings you two gentlemen out onto the heath so late at night?"

Jameson stepped forward. "You'll forgive me, but I can't see how that's any of your concern."

"Well, but I'm afraid it is." The Badger turned to them. "You see, all this land, this all belongs to Lord Marwick, you understand. So when I saw your headlights there, I thought perhaps I should pay a visit. See if maybe you weren't lost."

"No, we're quite alright, thank you," said Jameson. "And last I checked, this is a public road."

"It's alright, Jameson." Alastair turned to the Badger. "Thank you, we do appreciate your concern, but no, not lost. Just getting the lay of the land is all really."

"Right." The Badger nodded, his eyes down. "And I don't suppose either of you gents happened to see anything out of the ordinary tonight, eh? While you were getting the lay of the land?"

"No, nothing out of the ordinary," said Alastair. "Nothing besides a very large bull blocking the road."

"And that was it then?"

"It was, yes."

"And you're sure of that then, are you?"

"I believe he's said so," said Jameson. "And tell me, did your search party there find what it was looking for?"

"Jameson."

The Badger took a fuller measure of them now. "Was probably just a couple of drunks wandering around in the fog, is all. Now and again a body gets pulled out of the bogs out here. And we certainly wouldn't want that." He tilted his eyes back at their car once more. "Well, I suppose I should be on my way then. But here's a bit of free advice, gentlemen. I'd keep to the roads if I were you. Being strangers to the island and all. Not exactly safe to wander around out here after dark."

"Oh no?" asked Jameson. "And why would that be exactly?"

The Badger smiled a little. "Because if the moors don't get you, the Little People will."

"Right, well, we'll take that under advisement."

"Fair warning." The Badger shrugged, and touching the place where a cap would've been, he turned and started for his car. "And a good Fhøghartide to you, gentlemen."

Alastair and Jameson stood and watched as the Badger climbed in and circled his vehicle off the road, then headed straight out across the moors.

"And just who does he think he is?" asked Jameson. "I'd say a liar, is what. Out looking for drunks. I mean, a man may have been taken for all we know." He turned to Alastair. "Shouldn't we speak with the local authorities, sir? I mean really, at this point?"

"Jameson," said Alastair, watching the Rover's taillights disappear into the blackness, "I've got a funny feeling we just did."

* * *

One by one they splashed across the stream, blurring the moon's reflection down within it. Ham labored up the bank shaking his head.

"That bloody mule."

"I tied him good," said Rory. "And don't even say it, Tito."

"Alright, we should be good here." Innes looked back in the direction they'd come. "OK, Tito, start again. And you're sure it was them, yeah? The Badger and Lord Marwick?"

"It was them."

"But if you couldn't see them?"

"He knows," said Rory.

"Alright, so just from the beginning. They said what exactly? That they had Ham in the car?"

Tito nodded. "Because the Duffs had seen him at the inn."

"With the two men who'd been asking about the coin, yes?"

"That sodding coin," said Ham.

"What else, Tito? What else did they say?"

"Well, I couldn't hear so good from down in the bin there, but they were talking about the dig site at the chapel and all that's going on down there. It sounded maybe like they think the coin came from there, like Ham nicked it or something during the break-in."

"Break-in?" asked Ham. "And what break-in is that now?"

"Yeah, OK, it wasn't a break-in exactly," said Rory. "Me and Tito, we just went in and had a look around, was all. There were a couple of little things we found, but no coins, nothing like that."

"Well, isn't that lovely. I'm a wanted man for a coin I didn't steal and a break-in I didn't do."

Rory could see something in Tito's eyes.

"What, Tito?"

"Well, it isn't just Ham they're after now, Rory. They said they'd found a second coin."

"A second coin? What do you mean a second?"

"It was in with those ones you sold to Otis and Rat. And now they're thinking all of us are in on it somehow. Like maybe we came across more of them down there." Tito turned to Innes. "And he's got the Badger working on it now, I heard him. And his crew."

"That means the constable," added Rory.

"The constable?" Ham turned to Innes. "Are we saying the constable's looking for us now too? Innes, what the hell's going on?"

"I don't know." Innes paused. "But—so about the constable."

"Oh, what now?"

"Well, so it's possible—actually more than possible—that he's got a warrant out on me. From a while back. You should probably know."

"Well, isn't this just a fine mess."

Tito turned close to Rory. "I just want to go home, Rory. I just want to go home to Kettleskaill."

Above them, the clouds were darkening, and the wind had turned from the north.

Rory looked at Innes. "At least they won't know about the cliff huts. For now."

Innes nodded. He studied the boys a moment, then glancing out into the darkness, his eyes fell upon something strange along the horizon line—a blood-red glow at the far end of the valley, pulsing ever higher into the night sky.

* * *

A black column of smoke rose high above them as they scrambled over the rise. Down in the swale sat Mr. Begbie's farmhouse, burning hot in the blackness. Smoke rolled from its windows and seethed through its thatched roof as Innes reached the front door. He kicked at it, and as it broke open, a tongue of thick smoke flowed heavily out.

"Mr. Begbie?" Innes shouted. He tried to step through the door, but the heat and smoke drove him back. "Mr. Begbie!"

From out at the edge of the firelight Rory called out. "Here! He's over here!" They ran to Rory as Mr. Begbie came walking slowly out of the darkness, his pigs trailing along behind.

"Are you alright?" asked Ham. "Are you alright, sir?"

Mr. Begbie stared up at them, his eyes like two disks in a mask of soot.

"Have you seen Eustice?" he asked, confusion on his face. "We'd just been about to go out and unhitch him."

"I'm sure he's only run off after the ponies again." Tito nodded.

"We'd just putten a bell on him, so we could hear when he runs off. You don't hear anything, do you?"

Innes could see that Mr. Begbie's hands were trembling. "Perhaps we should sit down a moment, alright? Just here?"

Mr. Begbie nodded. "If maybe I could take someone's hand?"

Taking him by the hand, Innes guided Mr. Begbie over, gently sitting him on the wall. Tito pulled a canteen from his pack.

"You should try and drink," said Innes. Mr. Begbie looked up at him, only now seeming to recognize them all. He brought the canteen shakily to his lips. "Do you think maybe you could tell us what happened?" Innes asked.

Mr. Begbie collected himself. "Well, we were just in the house there, having our supper, when the pigs ran to the door like they do when someone's coming up." He took another sip of water. "But it was odd, that."

"What was odd?"

"Callers, that time of night. So we blew out the candle and sat very still in the dark. But they knocked harder then, calling for us to come out. Said they needed a word. It was then we decided to step out the back door and climb up to our spot there." Mr. Begbie gestured to the dark hill behind the house. "They started shouting then and pounding on the door. That went on for some time." He paused. "Then we heard the glass breaking. And the fire went up. And we could see their faces then."

"And who was it?" asked Innes.

"Was those two brothers. From the village."

"Again with those two," said Ham.

"But what could they have wanted with you?" Innes asked.

"See, now there's what's strange." Mr. Begbie looked at Innes. "It weren't me they were calling for. It was you lot."

"Oh, I told you, Rory. Didn't I tell you?"

"And what would them brothers be wanting with you?"

“To be honest, we’re not exactly sure what’s happened,” said Innes. “We think it may be the Badger that’s put them onto us.”

“The Badger?” said Mr. Begbie. “Well, that’s not the kind of trouble you want. And I do just wonder, what would make them come looking for you out here at my place?”

Rory quickly looked at Innes. “The mule.”

“The mule?” asked Ham.”

“They would’ve seen Ham with him at the Vat and Fiddle. Everyone knows who Eustice belongs to. They must’ve figured Mr. Begbie knew us.”

Innes nodded. “Or knew where to find us.”

“But Rory, didn’t Rat see us with Eustice in the square too?” Tito asked, staring wide-eyed at Rory, then at Innes. “When we took Innes to the clinic?”

“The clinic,” Rory whispered, but Innes was already on his feet, and as a coldness shot straight through him, he turned and looked out across the moors toward the village.

* * *

The village sat silent in the predawn. From the far end of the square, a Rover rolled evenly to a stop. Its headlights blinked out. In the front seat, Frankie and Munro sat looking out over the square as a weather report squelched quietly over the wireless. In the far back of the vehicle, Otis and Rat sat facing each other in the jump seats. Newly loaded picks and shovels lay on the floor at their feet.

“Why’ve we stopped here?” asked Rat.

“We’ve got an errand to do first.” Frankie clicked open the door and stepped outside. “You two stay here. And keep quiet.”

Walking across the square, Munro hurried ahead to the back alley as Frankie crossed the street to the front steps. The clinic was dark. Glancing over his shoulder, Frankie drew a ring of keys from his pocket and opened the door.

At the far end of the hall, Frankie saw Munro's silhouette already easing open the back door. Silently they moved down the dim hall past a bin of cast-off clothes. Aggie's hazelwood walking stick leaned in the corner. A line of light shone beneath her bedroom door. Frankie put his finger to his lips, and closing his fist around the knob, he threw the door open. The room was partially lit from a bulb dangling in the closet. The bedclothes were in disarray. On the night table, a radio played low. As Munro searched the closet, Frankie lifted the corner of the bed and scanned the empty room.

"Bloody hell," he said, dropping the bed to the ground. Taking one last look around, he waved Munro out, and they hurried back into the hall and out the front door.

* * *

A gray mist lay below as Innes hurried them down the long slope from the village. When they had reached the bottom, Aggie grabbed him by the arm.

"OK, now tell me what's happened. What do you mean they've burned it down?"

"He's fine, Mr. Begbie's alright. Tito's with him."

"Was that a Rover back there, Innes?" asked Rory as he and Ham caught up.

"Innes, we've got to go," said Ham. "We need to get to Ada."

"Ada?" asked Aggie. "Ada's gone. She took the mail boat last night."

“And you’re sure?” asked Ham. “You’re certain of it?”

“Yeah, she said she wanted to beat this storm that’s coming. But what do you mean you need to get her? Get her from what? Can someone please tell me what’s going on?”

“I’ll tell you everything we know, but if we could just—” Innes tried to get everyone moving again. “If we could just talk about it on the way?”

“On the way to where? Innes, tell me what’s happened.”

“Alright.” Innes glanced back up the hill. “Alright, well, that’s just it. We don’t exactly know, but last night, a few of the Badger’s men tried to take Ham.”

“They did more than just try,” said Ham.

“What do you mean, take him?”

“And now with Mr. Begbie’s farm. Like I said, we don’t know exactly, but we think they may be going after anyone that might know how to find us.”

Aggie paused. “And that’s why you’ve come for me?”

“And now we very much need to go.”

Aggie tied her hair back as they started quickly away. “And so we’ll be going for the constable then, yeah?”

“Yeah, about that,” said Ham.

Innes glanced at her. “I’m thinking you might need to have a look at Mr. Begbie first.”

“And Tito’s with him, you said?” Aggie tried to read Innes’s face. “At Kettleskaill?”

“No, miss,” said Rory, picking up the pace. “Not exactly.”

XX

THE FIRST DROPS OF rain dotted the windshield as Jameson steered through the cobbled streets of the village.

"There," said Alastair, pointing to the phone booth at the corner as Jameson pulled the car to the curb.

The wind pounded them as they crossed the street and crammed inside the booth. Alastair closed the folding door behind them and took up the receiver. He clicked the flapper a few times.

"No dial tone."

Through the glass, they could see an old man leaning into the wind, slowly making his way up the sidewalk. Jameson opened the door.

"Excuse me, would you happen to know if there's a working telephone nearby?"

The man looked up at them. "Well, that all depends."

"Depends on what?"

"On whether that phone there is making a crackling type noise or no noise at all?"

"A crackling type noise," said Alastair.

"Ah, well, in that case, there'll be no working phones on the island at present. It's the undersea cable. It gets dragged about when the waves start kicking up."

"For how long?"

"For as long as there's weather." The man squinted up at the darkening sky. "And it looks like we're in for a good one." The man started again up the lane.

They stood in the tiny booth, the rain pattering against the roof.

"So, what now?" asked Jameson.

As Alastair stared through the glass, thinking, something odd caught his eye. Pushing through the door, he walked across the street to the wall and stopped at the slope leading down from the village. He stood looking out, and as Jameson came alongside, he saw it too: a white pillar of smoke steaming upward at the far end of the valley.

"What's that, do you suppose?" asked Jameson. "A wildfire?"

"In the rain?" Alastair turned to Jameson. "Where was it Miss Coburn said our friend Ham was living again?"

"She didn't say. She just said out on the moors." Jameson paused. "You're not thinking that fire has something to do with all of this?"

Alastair stared out at the smoke spreading across the horizon.

"Frankly, Jameson, I'm not sure what to think anymore."

* * *

As Rory hurried along at the front, a wall of wind gusted past them. Across the path, a line of ants was disappearing quickly beneath the ground as the first drops of rain struck the dust around them. A thin sound carried in on the wind, once, then again.

"It's Tito," Rory called back to the others.

As Ham and Rory hurried ahead, Aggie slowed a little at the sight of the tiny figure waving at them in the distance, the line of caves at his back.

"So you've all been staying here then?" She stared out at the cold hollows along the base of the rise. "And Mr. Begbie, he's in there as well?" she asked.

"I know," said Innes. "It's just we didn't have anywhere else to take him."

Aggie considered the caves a moment. Her thoughts went to Mr. Begbie, trying to recall his medicines. "It'll be alright." Then looping her scarf around her, she started off again as they began passing through the broad field of boulders fanning out in front of them. "Should've brought my walking stick."

"Well, we did rush you out the door."

Aggie found a little smile for him, and as they stepped carefully down through a tangle of rocks, tight knots of wildflowers were tucked low in the stoney ground around them.

"I can't see how they grow in the rocks like that."

"That's stitchwort there," said Innes, finding their way through.

"Which, the white ones?"

He nodded. "And that's wood sage. That's bog pimpernel there next to it."

"So you know them then?"

"I know them." He stepped higher onto the rocks. "Those ones there are thyme."

"I'm envious that you know that," she said as they passed a clutch of tiny blue blossoms vibrating low in the wind. "And those?"

"Not sure. My dad, he'd have just called them volunteers."

Aggie stepped down through shoulder-high rocks, then out again. "And what was he like, your father?"

Innes was slow to answer. "He was a lot of ways, I guess." They passed over a little gap. "But as far as that sort of thing, he certainly believed in the magic of this place, I'll say that."

A hard gust came pounding past them, pressing their clothes flat. "I'm sorry about all this," he called back to her through the wind.

"Innes, you needn't apologize." Aggie held her scarf close.

"I just mean for getting you into the middle of whatever this is."

"Well, there's no need. Really, it's hardly more than a house call. Anyway it's not me that's had the hardship. In fact, I feel like it's me who should be thanking you."

"Me? For what?"

"For watching out for those boys all this time, for one. And Mr. Begbie," she said. "Well, and for this morning. And while I'm at it, for a very large bucket of mussels for the clinic. And my walking stick, of course."

"Well, like I said, I owed you."

"You know, I've never met someone quite so determined to pay their way at a free clinic."

"It was nothing. Hardly a payment."

"But you see, it wasn't nothing." Aggie stopped, then crossed over. "Sometimes I've felt quite alone with it all, you know. With the clinic. With being new to the island and that. It was very much more than nothing, Innes."

"Yeah, well, we haven't always had someone like you on the island. A doctor, I mean. Living out here. I think I'd said." Innes paused. "And we should've had."

Aggie heard something new in his voice now.

"Yes," she nodded. "You should've had."

Innes slowed to make sure he stayed with her. "There was a doctor who'd come across on the mail boat, but that was just once a week. They said there was no budget for anything more. So everyone would queue up in the alley or back in the yard there. They'd pay with whatever they had. A chicken, or eggs maybe. A load of peat or what have you."

"Or mussels," said Aggie.

"Or mussels."

"Well, people can't be expected to give more than they have."

"No." He stopped and looked back at her, and as he watched her pick her way through the rocks, the wind spinning up her hair, he knew things would be different now.

He watched her a moment before starting off again.

"You asked about my father," he said, "what he was like." Innes kept his eyes on the path as they made their way through. "I was to have a sister," he said finally. "I don't think I'd said."

"No." Aggie slowed, glancing at him. "You didn't say."

His eyes stayed on the ground as they stepped through the rocks.

Wood sage.

"It was winter. Fhøghartide," he said. "And the weather was bad."

Aggie's eyes were on him now.

"And the labor came early."

Stitchwort.

"And my mother. She was having seizures."

She watched him as he tried to find the words.

"But the ferry couldn't run. So the clinic was empty that morning."

Bindweed.

"And they couldn't stop them. The seizures."

Thyme.

"They couldn't make them stop."

Aggie came alongside him, studying the side of his face.

"You asked about my father," he said again. "Well, he and I, we—" He paused, nodding to himself. "Well, that was that."

They stood together among the rocks.

"Innes." She met his eyes as the wind shifted across them.

"So that's why I wanted to help, you know, if I could. However little." He looked up at her as cold drops of rain began pattering around them. "Because the island needs you, Aggie."

"Well, I'm not going anywhere, Innes," she said, nodding, making sure he knew. "I'll not be going anywhere."

Carrying in on the wind came a faint cry, and turning toward the caves, they could see Tito and Rory waving urgently for them to come.

"You know, Innes, I'm starting to believe this island needs you too."

* * *

Keeping the column of smoke centered in the windshield, Jameson wrestled the steering wheel as the little car rattled across the moor.

"There, do you see it?" Alastair pointed, but as the car crested over the rise, the steering wheel jerked hard, and the car tipped forward, coming to a hard stop. Jameson ground the gears, but the car didn't move. He opened the door and walked to the front of the car.

"We've high-centered," he called. The car's undercarriage rested firmly on a rocky knob as the wheels spun slowly to a stop.

"Oh, well, that's just lovely," said Alastair, stepping out.

Jameson looked up at the column of smoke. "At least we found the fire."

Where the house used to be, only the walls and chimney remained. Blackened beams lay smoldering in the rain. A blanket of ash covered the floor. At the front door, Alastair leaned inside, and as the rain came harder, everything the fire had been unable to burn away began to slowly emerge out of the ash. Alastair stepped through the rubble and stopped at a line of small objects at the base of the wall.

Squatting next to him, Jameson picked up one of the objects. "Bloody hell!" He instantly snatched back his hand.

Alastair took a handkerchief from his pocket and picked up the steaming object, still cooling in the rain. It was an iron ax-head.

"A nice piece." Alastair studied it a moment. "Very nice. Pict." But as he set the ax-head down, another object caught his eye. From the ashes, he lifted the stone figure of a boy and held it beneath a trickle of water, watching as the three conjoined circles etched there were washed clean. Alastair stared at it a moment, then lifting his eyes, he looked again at the shell of the burned-out house, and at the ax-head, and at the stone boy in his hands. "Jameson?" he asked. "Did I ever tell you what it was that called me to this line of work? As a young man? As a boy?" Alastair turned to him. "Just exactly what it was."

* * *

"The Harald Hoard? What are you on about, Tito?" said Ham as they ducked in out of the rain.

"Well, it wasn't me that said it." Tito nodded toward Mr. Begbie.

"Tito, I'm thinking Mr. Begbie has had a hard night," said Innes, watching as Aggie went over and tended to Mr. Begbie, who was lying beneath a blanket. He could see that the old man was paper white and seemingly smaller than before.

Aggie spoke quietly over her shoulder. "If we could get that fire built up, please?"

Tito followed Innes quickly to the fire. "You think he'll be alright?"

"I'm sure he just needs to rest."

"Go on, Tito. Tell him the rest," said Rory as Innes stoked the fire. "Tell him what you told me."

"Alright," Tito began. "Well, on the walk out here, Mr. Begbie was saying how he felt quite dizzy." Ham waved for Tito to keep his voice low.

"He said he felt quite dizzy," whispered Tito. "And he said it might help if I kept talking to him, you know, while we were walking."

"You did good with all that, Tito." Ham set a few cans of beans into the embers.

"I kept trying to think of what else I could say to him. So I told him about the Badger and the earl and all that. And while I was telling it, some of the other things they'd been saying came back to me."

"What other things?" asked Ham.

"Well, like things from down in the dig site. Like how the Badger was saying how on the walls down there, there was a hill, and a spit of land painted, and a ship in the picture out beyond it at anchor." Tito stopped.

"Go on, Tito." Rory nodded.

Tito glanced at him. "You say it, Rory."

"Tito said they were also talking about a wood."

"A wood?" asked Ham. "What do you mean, a wood?"

"A wildwood. He heard the Badger say there was a wildwood in the picture."

"And beyond it a spit of land," said Tito again. "And a ship at anchor."

"OK, Tito, listen to me," said Innes. "I want you to listen, both of you. People have been digging holes for a thousand years looking for that hoard. All over these islands. And the only thing they ever got for their trouble was older. It's just talk, alright? That's all it is."

"But they weren't just talking about it. They're on to it. They're heading out to it."

"Oh, they're on to it are they? And where would they be heading out to exactly?"

"I don't know. To the place with the spit of land and the hill rising above it and all that."

"OK Tito, you just described every stretch of shoreline on this island."

"Well, and what about the wildwood?"

"And what about it?" asked Innes. "There hasn't been a stand of trees on Skara Skaill for hundreds of years. There's hardly so much as a wooden fencepost left on these islands by way of a marker."

"Well, I heard them. And they're on to it."

"And the best of luck to them," said Innes, turning to his pack.

"It *is* a good story though," said Ham.

"Yeah, and that's all it is."

"Well, I believe it," said Tito. "And so does Rory, but he won't say so because of you. Because he knows you don't."

"Shut up, Tito."

"Look." Innes lowered his voice. "You can all believe in whatever you want, it's fine by me. But let me tell you another story. And this one you can definitely believe in. This island never gave up nothing to no one. Ever. That's the real story of this place".

"I like Tito's story better," said Ham.

Tito stared at Innes a moment, then with nothing left to say, he knelt quietly at the fire.

Innes handed Ham a few more cans of beans. "Here, and there's more food in the back if anyone needs anything." Innes stood up and began buttoning his coat.

"And where are you going?" Ham asked.

"To find the Badger."

"What?" Ham got to his feet.

"This has all gone too far. I'm going to sort it out."

"Not alone you're bloody not."

Aggie glanced back at them. "If there's anything ready, I'd like Mr. Begbie to try and eat."

"I'm not hungry, love." He nodded weakly. "But if there was another blanket?"

Rory took a blanket over as Ham spoke quietly to Innes. "And where are you going to go anyway, eh? You said it yourself, there's no telling where they've headed."

As Tito knelt by the fire, a thought seemed to come over him. "What about the old man?" he asked, almost to himself.

"He said he wasn't hungry," said Ham. "But it's not really too polite for you to call him that, Tito."

"No. The Badger said there was an old man." Tito looked up from the fire. "In the painting."

"What are you talking about, an old man?" asked Rory.

"On the wall, down in the dig site, he said there was an old man in the painting."

"Sorry, say that again?" Innes asked.

"What, that there was an old man in the painting? Well, that's what he said. An old man near the wood."

"Near the wood?" asked Innes. "He said near the wood?"

"Yeah. Why? Do you think maybe that's something?"

"Tito." Innes turned squarely to him now. "Can you remember, did he say *an* old man or *the* old man?"

Tito thought a moment. "The old man."

"And you're sure? You're sure of it?"

"Yeah. *The* old man. Definitely." Tito nodded. "Why? Does it make a difference?"

Innes fell silent, and as a thought came over him, Mr. Begbie's voice came weakly from the back of the cave. "It makes all the difference in the world, lad," he said, trying to lift his head. "All the difference that there is in the world."

XXI

INNES LED THEM UP the spine of the ridge. As they crested over the rise, the wind and rain became frozen sleet, pelting sideways across them. They hunched low, battening down their hats and coats as Tito crouched in close.

"We've never been to this part of the island, have we, Rory? To the Barrens."

"Tito, I told you if you're coming with us, you have to keep up."

"You brought your pack with you?" asked Ham over the wind.

"He never leaves it."

"I've got our trowels in there." Tito nodded. "For the hoard."

"Tito." Innes started, then stopped. "Well, come on then, if we're going."

Climbing higher, they were narrowed into a single file until finally Innes began leading them down the other side. As they started lower, the wind whistled above them into the heights, and in the new stillness, they continued along the leeward ridge as if inside a cloud. Stony crags jutted into view all around them. Water ran slick between the lichen stone and moss at their feet. Innes came to a stop.

"Are we lost?" Tito asked.

Innes scanned out across the heights, trying to get his bearings. "There's a pass somewhere along here that leads the way down, but—"

Suddenly out of the fog there came a piercing cry. They all stood deathly still, listening into the wind.

"Can you see him, Rory?" whispered Innes. Then the sound came again, echoing off the veiled heights above.

"There." Rory pointed lower along the ridge, and as the cloud thinned away, a huge bull elk slowly emerged out of the fog. They squatted low. From this distance, they could see the plumes of the elk's breath in the cold air. The fur on his massive shoulders shifted in the wind; icy rain dripped from his antlers. Stretching its throat, the elk let forth a long, whistling bugle that echoed into the emptiness before slowly dying away in chuffing cries. No one moved. After silent minutes, the elk finally turned and strode regally away, descending lower beneath the ridge before disappearing again into the mist.

Ham looked at Innes. "I don't know about you, but that looks to be the way down."

* * *

"One. Two. Three!" Alastair and Jameson pushed against the car's bumper with all they had. "I'm afraid she's good and stuck, sir."

Alastair stepped away from the car. As he looked back across the rolling moorlands, a gust of wind tried to snatch his hat away.

"On foot it's got to be, what, an hour back to the village?"

"At least," said Jameson. "And with no sun for direction it all starts to look the same."

"Well, we can't stay here. The weather's only getting worse."

And so, gathering their belongings, they started out across the moors, unsure of their heading, leaving the little car behind.

After walking along for some time, Jameson slowed, then stopped.

"Did you hear something, sir?"

As they stood listening, a faint metallic sound came in on the wind. Slowly they began moving in the direction the sound had come. The ground became uneven and began to slope steeply away, and as the sound came again, they could now see a dark mass down in the ravine below.

"Do you see it, sir?" whispered Jameson. As the mist slowly thinned, an old truck frame came into view, and harnessed to it stood a massive gray mule. Eustice.

Carefully they started down. As they approached the mule, they could see that the cart's back tires were wedged tightly into a snarl of slick rocks. In the back, coils of rope and rusted odds and ends sat in the rain. There was no sign of a driver. Moving closer, Jameson saw that the mule's hide was spotted with fresh singe marks, and its eyes were wild and white as it looked sidelong at the two men. Jameson slowly reached out his hand.

"Whoa now. Easy." But as he went to stroke the mule's neck, it jerked its head, snapping its yellow teeth at him.

"Careful," said Alastair.

"Ahh, it's fine, sir, I know his type." Jameson reached out again. "Alright now, we've got no quarrel, you and I." Eustice heaved hard in his harness, his eyes fixed straight ahead. "Shall we see if we can't get him loose, sir?"

Alastair walked to the other side of the cart. Rainwater ran through the rocks. He knelt down at the back wheel, and one by one, he rolled the rocks away. Slowly the cart's tires began to turn, then suddenly lurched as Eustice stumbled forward. And as the big mule found his footing, he began clattering haltingly out onto the flats with Jameson and Alastair jogging alongside.

"Sir, what with the circumstances and all—"

"Jameson, I couldn't agree more." And grabbing ahold of the cart, they quickly clambered aboard.

Immediately Jameson began looking around the cart. "I'll just need the reins," he said, searching beneath the seat. After a moment he popped up again.

"No reins."

"What?"

"They appear to be chewed off, sir."

"Are you sure?"

Jameson glanced again. "Quite sure." As Eustice began picking up speed, they clung tightly to the sideboard. "He certainly seems to have a mind of his own, doesn't he, sir?" shouted Jameson through the clamor, and as the cart bounced violently along, the big mule set a due course deeper into the fog.

* * *

The sky darkened as Innes led them steadily downward. At their backs, the barren heights disappeared into the mists above. But as they reached the flats at the bottom, the path somehow continued lower still, down into the very ground itself. As the earth rose up around them, they found themselves deep inside a harrowed path, the moor grasses looking down at them, the wind passing over their heads.

Ham looked warily at the earthen walls on either side of them. "What is this place?"

"It's a *hola weg*," said Rory.

Tito nodded. "The Little People made them."

"They did not," said Rory. "They're old sheep paths. It's the rainwater washing through that makes them."

They continued moving through the dark hollow. Tito stayed close at Rory's back, a mist of sea air beading lightly on Rory's woolen coat. On either side of them, stones were locked tight within the earth at differing depths of time.

Up ahead, they could see the end of the path. As they came out onto level ground, the sky had darkened further, and the wind brought with it the faint boom of waves and the snap of salt air.

After a little farther on, Innes slowed, then stopped, listening into the wind. Ham came alongside and began to sense something just ahead of them, something solid, immovable, standing darkly in the mist.

"Innes?"

But Innes continued forward, and as the dark mass rose higher above them, a lone crag slowly emerged from the fog, cold rain running down its rock face.

"So is that him then?" whispered Ham as they all stopped. "The Old Man?"

Innes nodded.

"Was it put here?" asked Tito. "Or is it part of here?"

"Part of here," said Rory.

They all stood staring up at the ancient stone looming above them, keeping watch, forever facing the sound of the waves crashing and receding and crashing again somewhere out in the gloom.

"Come on," said Innes. "We'll want to be quiet from here on."

As they made their way down, the grass became thinner and sandier, and the sounds of waves came in heavy off the water.

The shoreline lay before them, arcing out into a long headland that flattened away into a low rocky plane ending in the sea.

Suddenly Innes stopped in the tall grass, for out in the darkness, high along the headland, a white light moved carefully through a warren of caves, dimming and brightening as it went. "Well, that's certainly where I would have started."

They stood watching the light when, from behind them, there came a footfall. Then another, then something was there, and moving out in the darkness, they could now see the gray mass of the moor ponies passing ghostlike across the hillside above them.

"Bloody hell," exhaled Ham. "Those horses are gonna be the end of me." He turned again to the caves along the ridge. "So what now? What's our next move, would you think?"

"Not sure we exactly have a next move really," said Innes. "I mean, they're already out here."

"Wait, what?"

"Well, what would you have us do, Ham? Climb up there and ask them to budge over?"

"So, that's it then? We came all this way just to see how well they're getting on?"

"OK, you do recall I wasn't too keen on all this nonsense to begin with?"

A wall of cold rain suddenly came sweeping in off the water. High above the headlands, silent flashes of lighting began illuminating the upper reaches of the towering clouds. As the lightning pulsed across the black water below, Innes could see sets of waves assembling, strange and malformed, roiling with disorder before reversing in on themselves and running back out to sea.

Then in the lowering tide, he saw them. As he drifted forward, the others saw them too, breaking the surface, hundreds of them, slick and glistening, their rounded heads emerging out of the water, their black stubs rising up as the tide lowered down around them.

"Innes?" whispered Ham. "You're seeing this, right?"

The mass of dark heads rose everywhere in the pulsing light.

Tito pressed close to Rory. "Little People," he whispered.

"Innes, what's happening? What the hell are they?" But Innes only stared in silence, blinking away the rain. Then slowly he turned to the others.

"Tree stumps," he answered.

"What?"

"They're tree stumps." At the water's edge, Innes stood and stared in remembrance. "I'd forgotten. My father told me he'd seen this once." As they stood gaping out at the ancient ruin of trees, brined and petrified, a sandbar began rising up, slowly following the stumps through the surface of the water. Then out beyond it all, emerging from the tide, a mass, low and dark, broadened out into a solid shoal—a spit of land—the sandbar bridging out to it, then back again, back through the primeval wildwood, back to them now, standing on the shore.

XXII

THE BADGER SWUNG HIS flashlight back and forth within the depths of the caves. His metal detector gave no reading. He dropped a shiny new coin at his feet, but the metal detector made no sound.

"Bloody hell." Taking his walkie-talkie from his coat, he switched it on.

"Frankie." Only static poured through it. "Frankie, pick up."

Stepping out in the rain, he made his way along the ledge and up the narrow path to the level ground above.

Parked near the cliffs sat the two Rovers. Frankie and Munro stood with Otis and Rat beneath an open hatch, smoking quietly out of the rain. The Badger came striding in from the dark.

"Did you not hear me calling you just now?"

"Were you calling us?" asked Munro. "I think maybe the radios aren't working."

The Badger stared at them all standing there. "You enjoying yourselves?"

"You said to stay with the vehicles," said Rat.

"Yeah, and now I'm saying something different, unless you don't care about getting paid for all this?"

"We care, boss."

"Then get down there and pick up a bloody shovel. We're doing it by hand."

Dropping their cigarettes, they quickly moved off. All except Frankie, who took a leisurely draw from his cigarette before slowly following the others down the cliff path. The Badger watched him go, then walking to the driver's door, he reached in and clicked on the wireless. Empty static came from it too, and looking up into the night sky, he considered the electrical storm high among the clouds.

Beneath the hatch, the Badger pulled out a cigarette and lit it. He stared through the rain at the silent throbs of lightning illuminating the water. But as he looked out, something strange caught his eye. In the distance, a tiny speck of light blinked on, moving far out in the darkness. He stared a moment, then reaching back, he switched off the cabin light. As his eyes adjusted to the dark and distance, it seemed that the speck of light was somehow, impossibly, moving across the surface of the water itself. Stepping from beneath the hatch, he drifted to the cliff's edge, and as he stared into the blackness, the rain pummeled heavily down, dousing the dead cigarette in his hand as the tiny light blinked off.

* * *

For good measure, Tito pounded the butt of his darkened flashlight once more. As they hurried across the sandbar, Ham looked warily at the black water churning through the stumps all around them. "Never been much for water," he said.

"Didn't you used to work on a fishing boat?" asked Tito, hurrying alongside.

As they reached the bank, they clambered out onto a flat shoal the size of a small churchyard. From out of the blackness, the sky suddenly flashed white, illuminating the newborn shoal like an empty tabletop.

"Fhøghar tides," Innes shouted through the wind. "Lowest of the year."

"OK, well, now that we've seen it, who's for getting back?" said Ham, eyeing the water all around.

"What do mean, back?" called Tito. "We've only just got here."

"Well, what's there to see?" said Ham, scanning the featureless sweep of sand and pebbles. "No reason to stay out on this little patch, not unless you're a peat digger."

"Peat?" Rory studied the shoal. "What, out here in the water?"

"Well, and it wasn't always water now, was it?" Ham nodded back at the ancient tree stumps bridging across to the land. And as if to prove his point, he gouged his heel deep into the sand and drew out a lump of smooth black earth from beneath it. "I was a decent digger in my day. Not great, but I could find it alright."

Innes watched as the peat in Ham's hand ran dark in the rain.

"So the shoal—are you saying we're standing on an old bog right here?"

"Yeah, would've been." Ham wiped the peat from his hands. "Before it dried up and got sanded over."

Innes considered the shoal a moment. "So all this, this whole thing you're saying?"

"The whole thing, yeah. Which I'd very much like to get off of if you don't mind."

But as Ham started to go, Innes turned and faced the shoal once more.

A thought came over him then, a quite impossible thought. And turning back, he saw Rory already nodding at him.

"A bog," repeated Rory through the rain.

"No." Innes shook his head. "Can't be that. Can't be."

"What are you on about?" asked Ham. "Can't be what?"

Innes turned to him. "Ham, how old would you say this bog would've been?"

"What do you mean, how old?"

"Just if you had to say."

"Yeah, OK, this definitely seems like something we could talk about back on dry land."

"How old, Ham?"

"Well, I don't know. Old. Really old." But as Ham paused to consider a better answer, Tito had already begun digging the trowels out of his pack. "What're you doing, Tito?"

Then Ham stopped, and slowly turning, he looked anew at the shoal of peat beneath their feet, while back across the shoreline, high upon the hill, the Old Man stood in the darkness overlooking it all as flashes of light danced silently among the clouds.

XXIII

DEEP WITHIN THE SHOAL'S embankment, Ham shoveled urgently with a trowel, cutting away slabs of peat with each stroke. Innes and Rory scooped back the earth as Tito knelt at the mouth of the shaft, shining his light. Every few feet, Rory hauled in a length of driftwood to joist the earthen roof above their heads. Deeper into the embankment they went, carving out the wall, plowing out the peat, their faces dirt-smeared in the thin light.

Suddenly Ham called back, "Tito, the light?"

Squeezing through, Tito shined his flashlight where Ham knelt at the front wall. In the weak circle of light, something was embedded in the peat.

"What is that, a root?" Tito asked.

As Ham dug around it, a mummified foreleg and hoof slowly came into view, its desiccated hide shrunk tightly around the bone.

"Is it a moor pony?" asked Rory, but as Ham continued digging, a flat forehead and curved oxhorn appeared in the earthen wall.

Above the horn, a perfectly preserved strip of harness twisted away through the packed earth, and a faint smell of leather came into the shaft. Ham tugged the reins a little as a cascade of peat broke free and tumbled into his lap. Where before there had been only earth, a tight cluster of objects now appeared in the dirt wall. The arced edge of an iron-clad wheel, the metal brackets of a wood-plank cart, and at the very base of it, just emerging from the peat, was the crushed corner of an oaken chest, no bigger than a toolbox. And there, out from a split in its wood, ran a dull vein of coins disappearing into the primordial bog.

Ham glanced wordlessly at Innes, then reaching forward, he drew one of the coins from the wall. He gazed at it a moment, then handed it to Innes, who held it in his palm for Tito to shine his light. They all bent reverently over the little coin, ancient and dark.

"Rory?" whispered Tito, but Rory's gaze stayed fixed on the coin. "Rory, have we found it?"

Rory slowly raised his eyes. "I don't know, Tito," he whispered, staring in stunned disbelief at the coins in the wall.

"But it's something, right?" Tito asked. "It's something?"

"It's bloody madness, is what it is," said Ham, lowering his voice. "That's not the Harald Hoard right there, is it, Innes? Is that what that is, the Harald Hoard, right there in front of us?" And getting no reply, he turned to them all. "Could someone please say something because I don't know what!"

Suddenly another slab of earth crumbled loose, and the corners of several more boxes now appeared in the peat.

"It appears we've got our answer," said Innes as the muted boom of the waves filled the deadened void.

"So what do we do now?" whispered Ham. "I mean, what do we even do, Innes?"

"I don't know." Innes stared silently at the wall. "I mean, I never thought we'd actually find the bloody thing."

"So, what, do we just haul it out then? I mean, are there more in there do you think? There's probably more in there, wouldn't you think, Innes?"

"Ham, I really don't know. You do realize this is my first hoard, yeah?"

Tito stared quietly at Rory.

"What is it, Tito?" But Tito only shook his head. "What is it?" he asked again.

Tito leaned to him. "Do you think maybe we—" He looked up at Rory, his eyes blinking back tears. "Do you think maybe we could live at Kettleskaill again now, Rory?" he whispered. "Do you think this would be enough?"

The light from Tito's flashlight suddenly blinked out, and the shaft went dark.

"Hang on." In the darkness, they could hear Tito smacking the end of the flashlight when suddenly a blinding beam of white light snapped on, filling the shaft.

Then a voice came from down the passage.

"And how's that then? Bright enough for you?" Shielding their eyes, they saw a silhouette crouched at the opening. "And I wouldn't worry yourself too much about how to carry all that out of there."

"Who's there?" called Ham. But this was a voice Innes knew well.

"What say everyone come on out, and we'll have ourselves a little chat," said the Badger. No one moved. "Or we could drag you out feet first, if you'd rather." He showed his gun. "I'll not ask again."

Slowly they crawled out of the shaft, and as they stood up, Frankie and Munro instantly appeared out of the blinding light, pulling Tito and Rory away.

"You'll take your hands off them," shouted Ham, but as he started forward, the Badger raised his gun.

"Let's have none of that," he said, gesturing casually with the barrel. "We'll have no heroes today." The Badger turned his light on Innes's face, keeping it there a moment as the rain cut sideways through the beam. "Innes." He nodded. "Been a while." The Badger smirked at Innes, filthy from head to toe. "Looks like you've been doing alright for yourself out in the world though." He waved the light at Ham. "And who's this then, eh? Your new crew?"

"What are we doing, Badger?" said Innes, a flatness in his voice.

"You know, Innes, I might ask you the very same. But first you can drop that trowel you've got there." Innes stood a moment, then from behind his back a trowel fell to the sand. "So. Innes. What brings you back to Skara Skaill, eh?"

"I won't be staying, if that's what's on your mind."

"Come back to take what's mine, have you?"

"Just let them go, Badger."

"Ah, but you see, it's not you that calls the shots around here anymore now, is it?" The Badger started over to the shaft in the embankment, his eyes on Innes as he went. "You and your crew there have been quite a thorn in my side of late, you know that?" He bent to the opening and shined his light, studying the inside. "But you do good work, I'll give you that." He straightened up. "Funny that it's you and me again, eh, Innes? After all this time." He looked over at the boys. "You know, it was Innes here who got me started down at the wharf. Big step up after the kitchens, am I right, Innes? Working for scraps we were back then." The Badger saw the look in Rory's eyes. "Oh yeah, we were his crew. He used to run all that down at the wharf, or didn't he say? He was Lord Marwick's man back then, isn't that right, Innes?" The seawater rinsed through the rocks behind the Badger. "Until you lost your focus." He turned again to the opening, and tucking his gun into his belt, he looked back at Frankie. "If he moves, shoot him." Then crouching low, he disappeared into the shaft.

Without a word, Frankie moved his jacket aside to display the pistol at his waist. From the corner of his eye, Innes saw Otis and Rat standing above him on the shoal.

The Badger reemerged from the hole, dusting the sand from his hands. He looked at all of them now, as if they were pieces on a chess board.

"Right. So this is how it's going to go from here." He turned to Innes and Ham. "You two are going back in that hole and are going to keep digging until I say stop. And while you're in there, them two"—he pointed his flashlight at Rory and Tito—"they'll be locked up in the Rover across the way waiting for you. So let's not have any messing about, yeah? Clear enough?" The Badger turned to Frankie. "Frisk them. And turn out their pockets. If a single one of them coins turns up somewhere else, the earl, well, he'll—" The Badger watched Frankie pat them down. When Frankie was done, the Badger waved them all away.

Innes and Ham stood their ground, unmoving.

"Well, now." The Badger smiled. "And what's all this then?"

"Let them go, Badger," said Innes.

"Oh I see. You two feeling big then, are you? Is that it?" The Badger touched his hand to his belt. "Well, I'm afraid the gun says different."

Innes looked at the gun, then turned calmly to the boys. "Just do whatever they say, alright? It'll be OK."

Frankie shoved Innes and Ham toward the shaft. He stood over them as they got down on their hands and knees and crawled inside.

The Badger looked up at Otis and Rat on the shoal. "You two get in there with them. Make yourselves useful for once." The two men hurried down the embankment, and as Munro started the boys across the shoal, the Badger waved Frankie over. "I want you right there at the opening. Whatever comes out, you bring it to me. I'll mark it down, then you take it across and get it loaded onto the Rover. My Rover. Then come straight back to me, are we clear? I say who sees it, touches it, or even bloody knows about it. You understand me?"

With barely a nod, Frankie started casually for the opening.

"Oy," called the Badger. "Yeah, I'm afraid I'm gonna need a verbal on that, Frankie."

Frankie slowly came to a stop. "Yeah, boss. I hear you."

"Good. And, Frankie—" The Badger reached out his hand. "Leave the gun."

For an instant, Frankie's hand hung motionless at his side. "You know. We never really sorted out who'll be getting what. Our cuts, I mean. Never quite got around to discussing that."

"Did we not?" The Badger cocked his head. "And what, you're figuring now would be a good time then, yeah? That how you see it?"

Frankie considered the Badger a moment more, then taking the gun from his waist, he handed it over, butt end first.

"I suppose it can keep," he said, and stepping to the opening, he bent down on one knee and waited.

* * *

Faces filthy with sweat, Innes and Ham dug away at the corner of yet another oaken box appearing out of the dirt. They pried it loose and set it heavily on the ground.

"Come on, let's have it," called Rat, waving his light. Innes passed the box back to Rat, who inched it toward Otis, who crawled it the last few feet to the mouth of the tunnel where Frankie lifted it away. Innes watched Frankie's every movement as the rain came harder across the opening.

Ham started in digging again but then suddenly lurched back. "Bloody hell," he shouted as a shower of dirt cascaded down. Innes turned to see, and as the dust thinned away, his breath caught fast in his chest. For buried there in the wall, something came slowly into view. A human face, its profile embedded in the earth.

"What've you got there?" asked Rat, crawling closer to see.

The Badger shouted up the tunnel, "What the hell's going on in there?"

"We've found a body, boss," called Rat. "An old dried-up one. Like a mummy."

The Badger thought a moment. "Well, dig around it."

"You heard the man. Dig around it."

Innes and Ham turned back to the wall. The peat had preserved the face a reddish-brown ocher. Its skin was drawn tightly against the bones of its smooth cheek. Its eyes were closed and its hair plaited, a faint redness remained in it.

"Do you think he was one of the soldiers?" whispered Ham as he started tentatively digging around it. "That was hauling the hoard away?" A narrow shoulder emerged from the peat, and the side of a leg, and then a bare foot drawn up close like a child asleep.

"That's no soldier," said Innes. A string tied a small leather cap to the boy's head. As they brushed away the peat, the thin bones of the back of the boy's hand appeared. And just beneath it, contorted at a hard angle, a man's hand came into view, holding the boy's hand tight, bound to him at the wrist and lashed to an oxcart handle.

Innes stared at the coarseness of the man's plain clothes, at the little bone buttons of the boy's coat, carefully sewn, at the two peat-stained hands, one clutching the other, entombed in the ground, as if fashioned from Skara Skaill itself.

"Innes?" whispered Ham. "Is that? I mean, you don't think that's—"

The sound of the wind and water came to them muffled and deep.

"Ham." Innes slowly lifted his eyes. "I think it's time we were up out of this hole."

From out of the silence, Rat called out, "What're you doing up there? C'mon, let's hurry it up." As Rat waved his light at them, Otis began muttering to himself.

"Bit of water coming in here, Rat," he said, looking at a dark puddle slowly broadening around him. As Rat turned, one of the joists in the mud sagged a little. Otis glanced up at it just as the joist lurched hard to one side and a heavy load of earth collapsed into the tunnel. Otis sat buried to his waist.

"I'm alright," he said, sweeping dirt from his hair. "I'm alright."

"Oy. What's happening in there?" the Badger called into the opening.

"We've had a bit of a cave-in," said Otis. "I'm thinking maybe we should come out now."

"Bloody hell," exhaled the Badger. "Alright. Are there any other boxes ready to come out? That's eight, for now."

"Not seeing any more, boss," called Rat.

"Alright, hang on." The Badger disappeared.

Outside, the Badger waved for Frankie who was returning across the shoal.

"OK we're gonna stop for now," he said, the rain coming harder. "But this is how it's gonna go. I'll start back with the first Rover. You and Munro get them out of there then close up the hole, but good and tight, yeah, until we can get out here with more equipment. Then get everybody loaded and get back to the village. But hurry it up; I'm gonna need you and Munro both."

"And what exactly are we supposed to do with them two back at the village?" asked Frankie. "And with them boys?"

"That's nothing for you to worry about. We can give Innes to the constable, as a present. Just get them all to the wharf and keep them there. I'll deal with all that later." The Badger turned to go. "But hurry it up."

"That's a lot of loose ends down in that hole, don't you think?" said Frankie. "You sure that's how you want to play it?"

The Badger turned back to Frankie. "How I want to play it? Sorry, have we got a problem here, Frankie? Is it you running the show now is it?"

"No, boss. It's your show."

"You're bloody right it is. Because it seems to me like your memory might be failing you of late. Now you get them loaded like I told you. And hurry it the hell up." The Badger eyed Frankie a moment more, then stepped up the bank and headed across the shoal.

Innes saw Frankie's boots stop at the opening.

Frankie squatted down, shovel in hand. "Anything else to bring out?" He peered in, the rain slanting hard across the mouth of the passage.

"Nope, that's everything," said Rat.

"Right." Frankie nodded, assessing the shaft a long moment.

From the back of the shaft, Innes saw as Frankie's eyes turned black, but his words of warning came too late. For Frankie was already drawing the shovel back and ramming it forward, jarring the last remaining joist as a load of wet earth collapsed into the passage, burying Otis and Rat neck deep.

"Go, Ham!" shouted Innes. "Go now!" And as they began crawling up the shaft, Frankie again drew back the shovel, and again hammered the joist down, this time shattering it in two as Ham suddenly disappeared from view, the pummeling weight of the earth pounding down around him. Then everything went black.

From the silence around him, Innes knew he was buried in a small void. "Ham!" he shouted blindly into the dark. "Ham, can you hear me?" he called, gouging desperately at the wall of mud. Innes stopped and listened hard before starting again. From somewhere deep within the mound he felt movement, and as he dug toward it, the ground surged upward and something large heaved clear, clutching at him in the blackness.

"Ham?" shouted Innes. "Is that you?"

"Oh, good Jesus," came Ham's voice, coughing for air. "Those other two," he shouted. "I could feel them in there." He began clawing at the dirt but was immediately blocked by the driftwood joist buried across the shaft. "Hang on." As he hauled the joist free, the mound suddenly shifted and slid away, and feeling a hand flailing out of the earth, the two pulled together as a body came sliding from the mud. Immediately plunging in again, Innes found a bent elbow, and he and Ham hauled the second man out of the earth like a breeched foal.

"Are you alright?" shouted Innes. "Is everyone alright?"

Otis and Rat gasped for air. Suddenly a flashlight clicked on, and the four found themselves staring at each other, buried to their waists, all but the whites of their eyes covered in mud, as Rat somehow still held on to his flashlight.

"Otis?" said Rat, retching out black dirt. "Did Frankie just try to kill us? I think Frankie might've just tried to kill us."

"Oh, you think?" said Ham.

"I thought I was a dead man," said Otis, staring in shock.

"Well, you might still be right about that," said Innes, for in the light, they could now see they were half buried in a low void, and all around them, a thin seep of seawater trickled through the loosened earth. Instantly Ham turned and began digging wildly at the wall of mud.

Innes squeezed in alongside him and called back to the others, "You two just keep raking back the dirt."

Immediately Rat spoke up. "Coming in pretty good back here, fellas. How long do you think it'll be?"

"How long? We've only just started."

"Well, it's coming in pretty good," said Rat again as Otis sat hyperventilating in the icy water.

"How about you shut up and keep working," shouted Ham. "And tell your friend there to stop hogging up all the air like that."

Innes stole a glance back. A slurry of dark seawater was already pooling in the back of the shaft.

"OK, Ham, we've got to dig, lad! We've really got to dig." As they tore desperately at the wall, Innes again glanced over his shoulder. But at the sight of the icy water rising rapidly up the walls, he began to slow.

"Come on, Innes, let's go! What're you doing?"

Innes stared at the black water. "Ham." But Ham kept digging. "Ham, it isn't working."

"Well, not if you bloody sit there, it isn't."

"Are we gonna die down here?" whimpered Rat. "Is that what's happening? Are we gonna die?"

"Ham. It's no good."

"I can do it," said Ham, clawing at the mud. "And could someone please shut him up?" But taking a glance back, Ham, too, now saw the icy water rising quickly above Otis's chest. Ham slowly stopped digging as Rat began to pray.

"Dear Lord, if you get us outta here, I promise to mend my ways. Church every day and all that if you could just this once answer a single bloody prayer of mine." But as Rat crossed himself, heavy clods of earth from the top of the shaft began splashing into the water.

"Prayer answered," said Otis. "God says no."

As the clods fell heavier all around them, Ham's breathing came fast and shallow.

"Innes, I'm sure I've mentioned this, but—"

"You don't care for tight spaces, I know." Innes watched as the black water rose steadily around them. "Not so good with them myself, just at the moment." But no sooner had he said it than through the mud ceiling, the point of a shovel suddenly appeared.

"Innes!" shouted Ham as the shovel jabbed through again.

"Hey! Hello! Hey!" Innes fought his way through the water. "Hey, we're here! We're down here!"

Shouting and calling out, they bunched together, looking up through the hole like a stovepipe through a mud ceiling, and there at the top of it, ringed with sky, was a face, Jameson's face, looking down at them.

"Hello in the hole," he called down as an eruption of shouts and cries flew up from below. "No time for pleasantries, rope coming down. Tug when ready."

"Right," Innes shouted back, and as a knotted rope came lowering through the hole, Rat grabbed it, gave a tug, and immediately began slipping through the opening. A moment later, the rope came through again.

Innes looked over at Otis, shivering hard in the icy water. "Alright, I suppose you next."

Otis stared at Innes, then at the rope. "I don't think I can do it."

"Go on, you'll make it."

"I can't do it," he said, terror in his eyes, the water at his chin.

"Oh, would you grab the rope, you great tub," said Ham. "We've got no time for that." Ham shoved him to the opening, and as Otis took hold, the rope immediately snapped taut. With Ham and Innes forcing him upward, Otis slowly began squeezing through the hole.

As the rope dropped through a third time, Innes and Ham looked at each other, their cheeks pressed against the mud ceiling as the shaft squeezed closed with water.

"Go on then." Innes nodded.

"No." Ham pushed Innes to the rope. "They'll just have to pull us both—" he said as the last slip of air left the shaft.

Outside, rain pounded across the shoal as Alastair and Jameson and Otis and Rat heaved on the rope, pulling with all they had. An instant later, Innes came sliding out onto solid ground like a newborn infant born from the shoal itself, with Ham flopping out right behind.

"Is anyone else still down there?" shouted Alastair, running over.

"No, no one," gasped Ham.

Jameson helped them to their feet. "Are you alright?"

"Yeah," said Ham, looking at Innes, realizing it was true. "We're alright." And reaching across, he hugged Innes in with one huge arm, his eyes shining at him, and as a wide smile spread across Ham's mud-covered face, he saw Rat and Otis standing there watching them. "Oh, and why not?" he said, pulling them in too, and they did not resist.

Catching his breath, Innes turned to Alastair and Jameson. "But how did you find us?"

"Wasn't us that found you," said Jameson, pointing to the shore. "Was him." Looking across, they saw Eustice, still attached to his cart, standing happily among the herd of moor ponies grazing on the hill. "He led us right to the herd there. Then we saw all this." Jameson nodded at the dug-out shaft of the embankment.

"Oh, I could kiss that mule right now," said Ham. "Smack on the lips."

Jameson drew a flat woolen cap from his pocket and handed it to Ham. "We've been looking all over for you, Mr. Little."

"So what was all this then?" asked Alastair. "What's happened?"

Ham looked at Innes. "I think we can trust them, Innes. I mean, who else have we got?"

"Me, I make it a practice of trusting no one," muttered Rat.

"Trust us with what?" asked Alastair.

"What we need to do is find the boys, Ham. And right now." Innes looked toward the shore. "When you got here, did you see anyone at all?"

"No. No one," said Alastair. "But what's happened? Trust us with what?"

"Innes, you don't think they'd hurt them, do you?" asked Ham.

"Well..." Rat paused. "I mean, they did just try and bury us alive over it."

"Jesus. But where would they have taken them, Innes?"

"Taken who?" asked Alastair. "Can someone please tell us what's happened?"

"Actually—" Rat glanced at Otis, "we might have an idea where they've gone."

Otis nodded. "But could we maybe get across to the land first?" he said, shivering, as a surge of black seawater belched up out of the hole and began spreading quickly across the shoal.

* * *

Ham splashed across the sandbar, with Alastair hurrying alongside.

"I ask again, Mr. Little, trust us with what? Can you at least tell us if it's something to do with the coin?" But suddenly Alastair stopped, and as the lightning pulsed high above him, he saw again, as if for the first time, the spit of shoal slowly sinking in the tide and the stumps of the ancient wildwood leading across to the shore. "My God," he whispered as the Fhøghartide waters dragged heavily against his feet. "Is this a bloody poem we're standing in the middle of?"

XXIV

FIGHTING THE STEERING WHEEL with one hand, the Badger worked the wireless with the other. Empty static poured from it. Leaning forward, he tapped the compass, its needle swinging aimlessly. "Is nothing bloody working out here?" he shouted to himself, squinting through the windshield. At the back hatch, still smelling of damp earth and peat, the oaken boxes were stacked beneath a tarp as the Rover bucked its way across the moors, the storm closing in.

Far behind, in the second Rover, Tito and Rory sat slumped in the jump seats, caked in mud. Munro sat across from them, his arms folded against his chest, his eyes closed. Frankie drove along in silence. The air in the cabin was heavy and close, and the windows were foggy from the men's breathing. Frankie took a rag and wiped a circle in the windshield. Through it, the red taillights of the first Rover slowly appeared ahead in the rain. As they came along behind, Rory could see the Badger at the wheel of the empty Rover.

"Are they not in there?" Tito whispered to Rory.

Munro opened a slack eye. "Don't worry yourself. They're in there."

As Munro's eye slowly closed again, Tito leaned close to Rory.

"Can you see them, Rory?" he whispered again, his eyes wide. "I mean, if they're not in there?"

"Oy." Munro sat up. "What did I just say? You keep your eyes in the bloody car. I told you they're in there."

Frankie glanced in the rearview. "You know, Munro, for some reason I don't think he believes you."

Munro glared hard at Rory. "Your brother had best keep his mouth shut, or I'll shut it for him. You understand me?"

"Actually," Frankie said, turning his anvil head, "it's alright, Munro. Go on, lad, speak your mind. I'm sure you've got plenty to say on the matter, don't you, boy?"

Rory gave Tito a grave look, quietly shaking his head.

"Go ahead. Don't be shy." Frankie smiled darkly into the rearview. "He knows plenty. He's a talker, this one, Munro." Frankie watched Tito a moment more, then lowering his eyes to the windshield, he stared dead ahead. "Got plenty to say, this one does."

The cabin fell quiet again as the rain hammered on the metal roof. Looking out, Tito stole one last glance at the Rover, moving empty through the dark pall of rain.

* * *

The Badger squinted through the windshield, barely able to see beyond the hood. From out of the wireless came a thin voice, emerging like a ghost through the static.

"Badger. Do you read? Are you there, Badger?"

The Badger snatched up the radio. "Badger here."

"Hang on, Badger. Sir? I have him." In the background came the sound of glasses and plates and hurried preparation. Lord Marwick's voice came through the receiver.

"Where the bloody hell have you been? Didn't I say to keep this channel open?"

"Yes, sir, it has been. It's this storm; none of the electronics seem to be working. But we're heading back to you now—"

"To me? No, the closing ceremony starts in an hour. No you stay where you are. I don't give a damn about the storm; you just keep looking, you understand me?"

The Badger waited until Lord Marwick had finished. Then he raised the handset again.

* * *

In every corner of the square, the villagers stood in the rain beneath umbrellas and awnings and eaves. At the front of the square sat the high-arched entrance to the old carriage house, and there within it, a stage had been set. Along the side of the square, a center-pole tent had been raised, and beneath it, the members of the Ancient Order and their guests milled about in a hum of small talk. A quartet played in the corner of the tent, its tune competing against the wind. Lined along the curbs beyond the square, drivers stood at their cars and waited beneath umbrellas, ready to carry the members away to the ferries and to their holidays once the ceremony was over and the storm had passed. A group of reporters were gathered near the foot of the stage, and at the center of the square, parked by the statue, a cameraman stood on the roof of a green TV truck, holding his tripod steady against the wind.

On the dais, a microphone sat at the ready.

Backstage, Lord Marwick stood looking out through a gap in the curtain as the stout man from the manor, clipboard in hand, stepped forward and cleared his throat.

"The additional tables per your request, sir." The man gestured to two long tables being arranged just off the foot of the stage.

"Good. And I've got a last-minute change to the program as well. Nothing for you to worry about. Just a little surprise addition." Lord Marwick took a sip of champagne. "And what do we know about the power?"

"Still out, I'm afraid, sir. Telephones as well. But we've sent for a generator."

Lord Marwick looked out at the darkened TV truck in the square. "I want to be told the very moment the power is back on, you understand?"

"Very good, sir."

The Rover hissed along the lane. Rain swept across the pavement in sheets. The Badger could see the village just ahead, its cobbled lanes choked with people. He stopped at a side alley and stepped out. The second Rover stopped just behind.

Through the windshield, Rory could see the Badger and the Duffs talking out in the rain. He glanced at Tito looking cold and wet and pale in the corner.

"Tito," he whispered, but before Tito could answer, the back door of the Rover swung open and Munro leaned in.

"Out."

Rory and Tito stepped out into the rain. Tito stood in the alley shivering as the Badger eased the empty Rover away through the crowd. Suddenly Tito stooped over and threw up a splatter of vomit onto the cobbles, his thin shoulders heaving. Without a word, he straightened up and wiped his sleeve across his mouth.

"Let's go," said Munro, starting the boys down the lane. "I guess you should've taken that job down at the wharf when you had the chance, eh, boy?"

Frankie watched as the Badger's Rover disappeared into the crowd, and taking a last draw from his cigarette, he flicked it away into the streaming gutter.

The Badger drove slowly up the lane, the crowd parting around him. To his right, he had an open view of the square and could see the TV truck by the statue, and the dignitaries beneath the tent, and the throng of villagers standing in the rain. Reaching the alley, he drove halfway down to a wooden gate. Upon seeing the Rover, a man quickly swung open the gate and waved him through.

Massive and mud-spattered, the Rover idled to a stop backstage, its engine pinging as it cooled. All around, sparkling glasses and plates of food were being carried past the stage and out to the tent in the square. As the Badger climbed down, Lord Marwick came hurrying over.

"Everyone out. Take it to the tent." He waved. "Everything to the tent." The waitstaff picked up platters of food and trays of champagne as they hurried through the curtain.

The backstage was silent. The Badger went to the Rover, and pulling open the cargo doors, he slipped off the muddy tarp and backed away. For a moment, Lord Marwick kept his distance. Then slowly stepping forward, his eyes moved over the hardwood chests, blackened and brined and strange. The Badger watched him a moment before hurrying to the side door.

From the floorboard, he lifted out a metal bin and brought it around, setting it on the back hatch.

"This one was damaged when we found it." Down in the bin was the first of the oaken chests, its corner crushed in. A cluster of loose coins sat dull within a bed of peat. "They're all there." The Badger nodded. "Every one."

As Lord Marwick took up one of the coins, the Badger could see the slightest tremor in his hand. Lord Marwick touched the thin coin in his palm, then turned to the wooden chest and slowly raised the lid. He gazed wordlessly inside, then closed it again. And laying his hand gently on the chest, he closed his eyes as the music from the square came carrying in.

"Unload them," he said finally. "But only you. No one else. I want no one else touching them until I've made the announcement. The tables are at the front, already in place."

"Yes, sir."

Lord Marwick took a calming breath. "And send for Constable Tulloch. I want him front and center."

The Badger nodded and turned to go.

"Oh, and Badger?"

"Yes, sir?"

"Actually, I was going to wait on this bit of business, but—well, given the circumstances." The earl stepped to him solemnly. "I haven't forgotten." From inside his breast pocket, Lord Marwick drew out a stiff cardboard envelope, its flap tied with a string. "A member of the landed gentry. Doesn't sound too bad, eh, squire?" The earl tapped the corner of the envelope, then placed it in the Badger's hand. "Two hundred acres. With a proper farmhouse on it as well, as discussed." The Badger stared in silence at the envelope in his hand. "You know, Mr. Croy, it almost seems like you care more about that jot of land there than you do the little piece of the hoard I promised you." Lord Marwick looked evenly at him. "You've come a long way from that hole in the ground, Badger. Now let's make sure we finish the job."

* * *

Far below, Eustice stood grazing in the rain as Innes led them up the village path.

Alastair hurried alongside Ham. "So if it was in a bog, they must've been perfectly preserved then?"

"Come on, Ham," Innes called back. "We haven't got time for all that."

"Can you describe them at least? Were their lids flat or were they curved?"

"That's what you want to know about? The lids?" asked Ham.

The thin sound of music came carrying in from the village, and as they stepped over the wall, Innes stopped at the sight of the crowds.

"So the wharf then? You think that's where they've got them?"

"I'd think so, yeah." Otis nodded.

"You think or you know?" asked Ham.

"Well, I couldn't say for certain. We only work with them fellas now and then."

"They'll be there," said Rat. "There'll be a boat down there. You'll see it, it'll be tied at the dock."

"A boat? What, you're not saying they'd take them off the island?"

"C'mon, Ham," said Innes, already backing away. "Nothing will have left the island yet, not in this weather."

"It'll be tied at the dock," called Rat. "Just the one."

Watching them go, Alastair started for the square. "Alright, Jameson, I'll go through this way. You come in around back. We'll meet at the statue in the middle of the square."

"At the statue," repeated Jameson, but as he turned to go, he noticed Otis and Rat still standing there.

"Well," Rat said, nodding, "I suppose we'll be off too then. Places to be and all that." He paused. "But, well, thanks for saving our lives back there and all."

"Actually," said Otis, "was them other two they were saving, Rat."

"Right. Well, buy one get one free, I suppose, eh? But like I said, it was just—well." Rat stuck out his hand.

"Of course, yeah, absolutely," said Jameson, and shaking Rat's hand, he noticed Otis still shivering and colorless in the rain. "Hey, is he going to be alright?"

"Him? Oh, sure. I'll just get him inside. Turn up the stove."

"Without running into the Duff brothers, I suppose?"

"Oh, no need to worry about them. We're good there."

"You're good? But—well didn't Frankie just—"

"We're good," said Rat again. "And actually, if you're looking for the best way to the back of the square." He stepped off the curb. "That's gonna be down that way there. Actually, c'mon, we'll show you. We're heading that way ourselves." And helping Otis off the curb, the three started across the street together, with Rat chatting all the way.

* * *

Lord Marwick took a sip of champagne and stared through the gap in the curtains. The man with the clipboard came hurrying up again.

"Sorry to interrupt, sir. I'm afraid the weather report's in fact saying we can be expecting worse within the hour. Temperature's dropping as well." Lord Marwick closed his eyes in irritation. "And as for the power, well, sir, it could be another half an hour before they'll have it hooked up. It's being trucked over now."

"Bloody hell." Lord Marwick stared out at the darkened TV truck. "Please tell me there's nothing else?"

"Well, actually, sir—it appears that in the event of any worsening weather, the press corps, and the membership as well, have said they will be unable to remain for the duration of the ceremony."

"What? You can't be serious."

"I'm afraid so, sir."

Lord Marwick looked through the curtain at the darkening clouds, and out at the press corps waiting, and at the members' tent being whipped by the wind.

"But I was thinking, sir, well, perhaps given the limited timing, might I suggest—" From behind his back, he produced a bullhorn. "At least until we've gotten the power back on?"

Lord Marwick considered the bullhorn, then glanced over at the Badger setting the last wooden chest into place.

"Fine. Yes. Let's just get started then. But I want that bloody power back on."

The man bowed, and pushing out through the curtains, he brought the bullhorn to his lips.

"Ladies and gentlemen. Our apologies for the weather, and for the delay, but if you'll be so kind, we will be beginning our program in just a few minutes."

* * *

Fastening his foul-weather overcoat, Constable Tulloch came walking out of the crowd. Two of his men had already taken up positions at the foot of the stage.

"And where have you been?" asked the Badger.

"Making the rounds." The constable nodded toward the curtain. "So is that where you've got them then?"

"What the hell are you talking about?" He considered the constable a moment. "And what do you think you know?"

"What, you think you're the only one with people?" asked the constable. "So, the earl wants me front and center then, does he? The Duffs too unsightly for the occasion?"

"You're just for show, that's all," said the Badger, then climbing the stage stairs, he stationed himself behind the curtain.

From here, the Badger could see the long tables tucked behind the curtains, a white canvas enshrouding what lay beneath. Turning to the square, he looked out and saw Frankie and Munro in the crowd, staring straight at him through the gap in the curtain. The Badger nodded at them, then rotated his finger in a small circle, and without a flicker of reply, the two brothers began patrolling through the square.

XXV

THE SQUELCH OF THE bullhorn came on. Lord Marwick approached the dais.

* * *

At the edge of the village, Aggie scrambled over the low wall and pressed her way into the square. Moving low, she made her way quickly toward the cobbled lane at the far corner, her head covered, her eyes down. As she pushed through the crowd, she could hear the earl's amplified voice ringing out over the square.

> *"May I first say to all the members of the Ancient Order who have made the journey to our fair isles, thank you. And may it not be another hundred years before Skara Skaill is again named the host of this august gathering."*

Reaching the far side of the square, Aggie crossed to the corner, hurried down the alley, and slipped in through the clinic gate.

* * *

Rain hissed across the empty boatyard. Above the wharf, Innes and Ham stayed low behind a mound of moldering planking. Woodsmoke rose from the warming shack. A sad string of Christmas lights had been tacked across it.

On the slope above the shack sat the Duffs' long copper sedan. Two boats rocked nose-to-nose along the quay, a flock of gulls perched along their railings.

"Rat said there'd only be the one?" asked Ham.

Suddenly the two boats rose on a swell, and their hulls banged hard against the pilings. As one, the flock of gulls rose into the air, batting in place against the wind before settling down again, the entire flock coming to roost upon the railings of the boat on the right. Ham turned to Innes.

"I know, I know," said Innes. "The one on the right."

As they stepped out into the open, something caught Innes's eye. He quickly pulled Ham back. At first Ham saw nothing, then in the half-light, two figures appeared crossing the deck. Swaying in unison, they came down the gangway, hurried across the boatyard, and disappeared into the warming shack. An instant later, the shack's door burst open as a man swept a cat out into the rain with his boot, then closed the door again.

"You know, I quite like cats," said Ham, glaring at the shack.

The boatyard was silent. Innes and Ham rose and were out on the path again, and reaching the bottom, they broke into a low run across the yard before crouching behind two pilings along the wharf. The pilings smelled of tar. The boats pressed hard against them. Innes peered over the rusted railing, and seeing nothing, he and Ham hurried up the ramp and across the deck, stopping at an open hatch. Leaning into it, they listened a moment, then stepped onto the welded rungs and climbed down in.

Inside the well, they could hear the hollow drumming of the storm against the hull of the ship. On either side of the ladder were two metal doors. The door on the left was slightly ajar, and inside it, lit by the dim light of the gauges, they could see the greased mechanicals of the cramped engine room. They turned to the other door, listening. Slowly Innes slid the bolt and eased the door open. Inside, a weak blue light cast a haze over the room. Innes and Ham stepped over the threshold and stooped beneath a stained pipe running low over their heads. The room was small. Around the walls, stacks of crates and boxes and burlap sacks deadened the sound within the hold. Innes stepped farther in, scanning the room. He looked back at Ham and shook his head. Taking a last look, Innes began slowly backing toward the door. But as Ham turned and ducked beneath the pipe, a long gray rat streaked across it, skittering past him at eye level.

"Oop," Ham blurted out, too late to stifle himself. They paused a moment, but as they started again for the door, the faintest slip of movement came from somewhere behind them. Innes stopped and looked back, and there in the dim light, leaning out from behind the stacks, stood Rory.

"Rory," cried Innes, and as he and Ham ran to him, Tito leaned out too.

"Oh, thank God," said Ham. "Thank bloody God."

"Are you alright?" asked Innes, looking from one to the other. But as Tito stepped into the open, he looked up at Ham, and at Innes, and at Ham again, then broke into hard tears, hiding his face in his hands.

"Oh, Tito, did they hurt you?" asked Ham. "If they so much as laid a finger on either of you…"

Tito shook his head.

"It's not that," said Rory, waiting for Tito.

"What then?" asked Ham.

Tito tried to look up. "Well we didn't know—" His voice choked as he rubbed the back of his hand across his eyes. "We—well we didn't know what had happened to you."

"Ahh, Tito, no, we're alright. We're *all* alright." Ham knelt to him. "See." He patted his middle. "Fat as ever." Tito blinked up at him. "You're all heart, you are, Tito, do you know that?" Ham's eyes shined at him.

Innes looked over at Rory, standing quietly, caked in mud, a deep exhaustion on his face.

"And you, Rory?" he asked. "And you're alright as well?" Rory started to answer, but could only nod in reply.

"And to think it was you two worried about us," said Ham, looking at them both. "After all you've been through."

At the bottom of the ladder, cold rain fell into the hatch. They waited quietly for Innes to wave them up.

"Oh, Tito, look here," whispered Ham. "I'd almost forgot." He pulled Tito's pack off his own back. "We found it. Was back on the shore there, by the shoal." Tito took hold of it in disbelief.

Climbing out onto the deck, they hurried down the ramp and tucked in tightly at the pilings along the dock. A swell of laughter came from within the warming shack. The yard was empty. As they readied themselves to go, the iron hull of the boat surged hard against the wooden pilings. The flock of gulls rose again into the air, and looking up, Rory turned and without a word lifted the boat's thick loop of rope off the piling, dumping it into the water below. Before they had even noticed, Tito was halfway down the quay lifting off the bowline, heaving it too down into the black water. He ran back and squatted close to Rory as the big boat began to slowly rock itself away.

Ham shook his head with pride. "Proper bloody outlaws."

After checking the warming shack once more, Innes started them quickly across the yard and up toward the lane. But as they gathered at the top, Ham was no longer with them. Across the yard, they saw him passing the Duffs' sedan parked on the slope, and without breaking stride, he kicked free the wheel chock nested beneath its rear tire. Ham arrived alongside Innes as the sedan slowly began to move, crunching gravel, then gathering speed as it rolled through the boatyard and bounded past the warming shack before finally gonging squarely into the hull of the untethered boat at the quay. The sedan teetered a moment over the widening gap, then pitched forward into the water below.

* * *

In the open square, Alastair squeezed through the crowd, head down, collar up, nodding apologetically as he went. Edging along the rope of the members' tent, he heard the low hum of conversation and smelled the damp woolens and cigar smoke hanging in the air beneath the canvas. At the front of the square, Lord Marwick stood at the dais, bullhorn in hand. The man with the clipboard held a large umbrella above him as he spoke.

"And may I also extend our sincerest best wishes to Lord Sutherland, by whom next year's event will be hosted. Lord Sutherland." The earl gestured toward a man nodding politely from the tent. Alastair stayed back within the crowd, and as Lord Marwick began again, he noticed a slight gap in the curtain at the side of the stage. In the darkness behind the opening, he saw the Badger's face, scanning the square. Glancing to his right, Alastair caught sight of Munro Duff patrolling slowly through the crowd, like an icebreaker through pack ice. Alastair eased back against the rope, his eyes fixed on Munro, cold rain streaming off the tent. From behind him, a voice suddenly rang out like a brass bell.

"Is that Alastair Clements?"

Alastair turned to see a gray-haired gentleman standing among a group of men and ladies beneath the tent. "Lord Atlee?"

"Well, I thought as much. What are you doing out there, man?" Lord Atlee stepped to the rope, his ruddy face welcoming Alastair in. "Can we have him in here, please?" He gestured to one of the waiters, and the rope was raised. "Come in, man, let's get you out of the weather." Glancing back toward the square, Alastair saw Munro staring in at him as he turned and stooped beneath the rope.

"Everyone, may I introduce Professor Alastair Clements," announced Lord Atlee. "He, among a great many other things, is the antiquities chair at the Ashenrose." Alastair nodded distractedly, one eye still on the square. "You should also know that this is the man who wrote the definitive works on pre-Christian Britannia. In fact—" Lord Atlee held up his hand as a pledge. "I'll freely admit here before you all that his latest book inspired me to reread the treaty between Alfred the Great and Guthrum the Dane in its original Latin." Lord Atlee now noticed Alastair was caked in wet sand from his boots to his waist. "Don't tell me we've caught you in the middle of a dig of some sort?" he asked, excitedly plucking a glass from a passing tray and handing it to Alastair.

* * *

Inside the darkened clinic, the muted sounds from the square could be heard low and distant. Aggie opened the refrigerator and stared into the whiteness. Taking two medicine bottles from the shelf, she placed them into the bottom of her sack and quickly headed up the hall. She stopped at a bin of cast-off clothes, her hazelwood staff leaning against the rack. Peeling off her rain-soaked coat, she dug deeply into the bin and drew out a man's overcoat. She put it on, but as she belted it tight, she noticed the sounds from the square coming more clearly than before, and turning, she saw the anvil head of Frankie Duff ducking low through the kitchen door.

Aggie stood silently in the darkened hallway as Frankie wiped his boots.

"Some weather out there, eh?"

For a moment, Aggie said nothing, before calling as evenly as she could

"I'm afraid the clinic's closed."

"Closed, is it?" said Frankie, looking up from the mat. "You know, I just can't seem to get that right somehow." He tilted his head toward the dark hall. "Stopped by the other night as well. Me and Munro did. Must've just missed you."

"Well, like I said, clinic's closed," said Aggie, trying to keep her voice steady. "And I'm just on my way out at the moment."

"Are you now?" A sheet of rain blew in across the threshold. Frankie closed the door behind him, as the noises from the square died away. "Seems as if I'm always showing up at the wrong time." He took a step into the kitchen, bringing the smell of cigarettes and wet leather with him. "And where might we be off to in this weather?"

Aggie watched him from up the hall, the front door only a few steps behind where she stood.

"A house call," she said. "And I'm just heading back there now."

"Is that right? And when we stopped by the other night?" Frankie opened the refrigerator and looked in. "Another house call, was it?"

"I'm sure I couldn't say." Aggie watched as he pulled a pack of cigarettes from his pocket and tapped one out. "But I'm already quite late, so." Suddenly she wheeled and started for the front door. Frankie lit his cigarette as he casually passed through the kitchen, his voice following her up the hall.

"Oh, and I almost forgot. You know, we came across your new friend there. Innes. And the other one. And them two little vagrants as well." Aggie slowed a step, before starting again. "Them four had become quite a thorn in the Badger's side." Frankie took a long pull from his cigarette. "But we've taken care of that little matter for him now."

Aggie turned. "And what exactly is that supposed to mean?"

"Take it however you like." He shrugged, continuing slowly up the hall. "But they'd been quite busy of late though, hadn't they? Trespassing. Thieving around."

"And I know that to be a lie."

"Do you now?"

"I do. Yes."

"Well, I can't help but wonder what else you might know about all that. As friendly as you were with them, I mean."

"If you've harmed them in any way, I swear to God…"

"You'll what? Report me to the authorities?" Frankie slowly closed the distance toward her, his bulk filling the narrow hall. "Frankly, miss, you might want to reconsider your tone, seeing that you're without a champion on this island now."

Aggie backed away, and in a flash, she turned and ran for the front door, but as she flung it open, Munro Duff was standing on the top step.

"Close the door, Munro," said Frankie, a deadness in his voice now. Munro closed the door behind him as Aggie backed into the hall. "To be honest—" Frankie tapped his ashes on the floor, "the Badger was gonna hold off on these last bits of unpleasantness for a few days, him being in such a cheerful mood and all. But when I seen you in the square there, and well I'm sorry to say it, but those friends of yours have gotten you good and tangled up in all this now."

"I don't have the slightest idea what you're talking about."

"Oh, but you see, I think you do."

As Frankie came steadily closer, Aggie saw behind him, at the far end of the hall, the back door begin to open, as Tito and Rory stepped quietly through.

"Take whatever food you can find," whispered Rory. "I don't know if we'll be coming back to the village again." As the two crept carefully into the kitchen, Innes and Ham stepped in right behind.

The Duffs stared dumbstruck, as if two ghosts had come passing through the door.

"Frankie?" whispered Munro, but Frankie was already drawing his gun.

"And you can stop it right there," he called, pointing his gun down the hall. The four froze where they stood. "Close the door behind you. Quick now." Slowly they stepped into the kitchen, and as Innes's eyes adjusted to the darkness, Aggie saw him see her.

"I'm alright, Innes. I'm alright."

"Wrong," said Frankie. "In fact, none of you are alright, and if you don't close that door, you'll find out just exactly what I mean." Ham reached back and shut the door. "Now then." Frankie held his gun straight ahead. "I don't know how you all managed to get out of that little trouble from before. But you've certainly found it again right quick, haven't you?"

Innes eased around in front of Tito and Rory, his hands raised. "We got no problem here, Frankie."

Frankie spoke over his shoulder. "You got her back there, Munro?"

"I got her." Munro gripped Aggie hard by the arm.

Innes took a quick step forward, and Frankie cocked the gun.

"Well, come on if you're coming?" Frankie looked past Innes into the kitchen. "Oy." He nodded the gun at Ham. "And you get your hands up where I can see 'em."

"Hands are up, Frankie," said Innes calmly. "Hands are up. But maybe let's lower the gun, yeah? She's got nothing to do with all this." Innes kept one eye on Aggie. "Look, the Badger's got the hoard. You've got us. How about you just let her go, and these boys too? What good can they possibly do you? It's me the Badger wants."

"Sorry, mate, that ship's long sailed. Too many witnesses to too many things."

"Yeah, but see, they don't know anything about that," said Innes just to Frankie. "How things ended down in that hole." He nodded. "What do you say we just let them go, yeah?"

Frankie squeezed the gun tighter. "I'm gonna need you to stop talking now." His eyes were fixed on Innes. "Munro, get down to the wharf, get our car, and bring it around to the alley."

Munro leaned in close. "But shouldn't we tell the Badger first?"

"Just do what I bloody tell ya," hissed Frankie. "This little payday we got coming to us might be the only real money we're ever gonna see, and I'm damn sure not leaving this lot to the Badger."

Innes held his hands higher. "So what are you gonna do then, Frankie? You just gonna shoot us all? You gonna shoot these boys, gonna shoot her? Is that it?"

"Haven't really decided about her just yet. But you four, you don't really think anyone's gonna miss the likes of you now, do you? When you turn up missing? And me and Munro, we'll be long gone by then anyway, off to somewhere nice and warm with our little piece of money. Maybe we'll just bring her along for the ride, eh, love? Either way, it'll be her word against the earl's, won't it? And the constable's. Tulloch's always been looking for something to pin on the Badger anyway. Actually works out real nice now, doesn't it?" Frankie glanced over his shoulder. "Alright, Munro, get the car."

"What do you want me to do with her?"

"Yeah bring her up front here. I want everyone where I can see them. Actually—" Frankie looked at the others. "Strip off your coats, all of you. And turn out your pockets. Hurry it up."

"What, are you gonna rob us too while you're at it?" asked Ham.

"Shut it." Frankie leveled the gun. "We can always put another bag on your head, if you like?"

Slowly they all began taking off their coats, but as they did, Frankie noticed Tito hiding his pack behind his back.

"The bag too. Toss it forward." Tito didn't move. "The bag too, I said."

"Give him the bag, Tito," whispered Rory. But Tito kept his eyes down as if he hadn't heard.

"Oy, and what's all this then?" asked Frankie. "Got something in the bag there, do ya?"

"Just my things."

"Or maybe a few coins that went astray out there, eh?"

"Just give it to him, Tito," whispered Rory.

"I'd listen to your brother there, boy," said Frankie. But still Tito didn't move.

Suddenly Innes turned to Tito.

"Oh, for God's sake, will you just give him the bloody bag?" He snatched the pack from Tito's shoulder, and with a single motion, he tossed it to Frankie. But as the bag hung in the air between them, Innes flashed forward, following it as it flew. The gun twitched in Frankie's hand just as Innes forced the muzzle up and away, the shot echoing flatly in the kitchen, plaster crumbling around them. As Innes's blows came raining down on Frankie, Ham rushed past him and collided with Munro barreling forward, all four men crashing together.

"Go, Aggie!" shouted Innes out of the chaos, for now the hallway was clear straight to the front door. Rory and Tito ran up the hall, stopping where Aggie stood. "Go now!" shouted Innes again. Aggie began pulling the boys away toward the door as the four men smashed around the room, the kitchen tearing apart around them. But as Ham and Munro crashed to the floor, Frankie pulled his gun hand free.

"Let him go! Now!" shouted Frankie, pointing the gun at Ham. "You let him go right now or I will blow your bloody—" But Frankie's voice suddenly broke into a groaning cry as he doubled over in pain, the gun dangling from his shattered hand as it dropped to the floor. Aggie stood behind him, her eyes wide with fear, her hazelwood staff already cocked for another blow. With his good hand, Frankie slammed Aggie against the wall, and as he lunged again for the gun, Innes kicked it skittering away. He and Ham turned and started up the hall, sweeping Aggie and Rory ahead of them, while Tito flew through the front door, hoisting his pack onto his shoulders as he went.

Out on the street, the rain hit them head-on. Up the cobbled lane to the square, they pushed in low among the crowd.

Innes immediately turned to Aggie. "I'm fine, Innes. Really, I'm fine. Is everyone else alright?" But Tito was nodding her toward Ham, his hands on his knees, blood running from a split above his eye. Ham waved it off. All the while Rory kept his eyes fixed behind them.

"We've got to get back to the caves, Innes," said Aggie. "Mr. Begbie's not at all well." She looked knowingly at him. "You understand what I'm telling you?"

Suddenly Rory pointed, for down the lane, Frankie and Munro were pouring out onto the sidewalk as the rest of the Badger's crew barreled up the lane from the wharf.

XXVI

THROUGH THE CROWD, RORY and Tito ran like rabbits through briar as the earl's amplified voice came in fragments above their heads.

> *"…nine centuries ago…my forefather, having been sent out in the service of his liege lord…*
>
> *…did make landfall upon these shores…"*

Glancing back, Innes could see the Duffs and their men fanning out, shouldering their way through the square.

> *"…and in appreciation for his loyalty and good works he would come to be named the first earl of these, our fair islands…"*

As Rory and Tito dodged low beneath the umbrellas, a murmur began spreading through the crowd.

> *"…But upon returning to his ship with men and rightful tariff…ox and cart were lost…and have remained so, lo these many centuries, vanished in the fog of history…"*

Innes and Aggie followed the others deeper into the square while all around them onlookers began moving closer toward the stage.

> *"...but now the very history of these, our beloved isles, having been long silent, speaks to us anew..."*

Weaving through the crowd, Tito was knocked to the pavement. But in an instant, he was up again as Ham toted him like a satchel in hand as they all tucked in tightly where Rory waited, the statue of the first Earl of Skara Skaill looming on one side, the TV truck on the other.

> *"...so today I stand before you, before our esteemed guests, before the people of Skara Skaill and the Northern Islands and beyond...it is my profoundest honor..."*

Huddled low together, they stared wordlessly into each other's faces as the earl's voice came clearly to them now, carrying out to every corner of the square.

> *"...to present to you..."*

The members in the tent pressed forward as the last of the earl's words were drowned out by the upwelling din that rose across the square. Alastair and Lord Atlee stepped against the ropes, staring in silence at the eight blackened boxes opened near the stage, sitting upon the stark white cloth.

A hush fell over the square.

Packed within the coal-black wood were silver pieces from Byzantium and countless coins of the darkest gold. There were hilt fittings, inlaid with garnet. Pommel caps encrusted with gems. Heavy altar crosses twisted and smoldering in red gold. There were candlesticks, and silver cups, and rings of lustrous yellow.

For a long moment, the crowd in the square stood unmoving. Suddenly the silence was broken as the press rushed forward, their cameras flashing, shouting out questions as they squeezed in tight against the ropes.

"Please. Gentlemen, ladies, please—" Lord Marwick waved his hands. "Let me assure you every inch of this find will of course be fully verified. But until such time, I can say with complete confidence that all evidence suggests that what we have here before us is exactly what we believe it to be. The Harald Hoard." The earl looked out as a cacophony of questions were again shouted out from the press.

"How can you be certain, sir?"

"Again, we will of course welcome the fullest scrutiny." Lord Marwick smiled.

"But to make the claim without verification?"

"Yes and how was it found, sir?"

The slightest hint of annoyance now betrayed the earl's face, when from within the members' tent, a voice rang out like a brass bell.

"Lord Marwick? If I may?" called Lord Atlee. "If I may, sir. As luck would have it, we happen to have one of the world's leading authorities on the matter right here in our midst," he said, gesturing to Alastair.

Alastair stood unmoving as all eyes turned to him.

"Is it the hoard, sir?" shouted a voice from the press corps. "Yes, can you verify it?" came another as the reporters strained to see into the tent. Alastair stared out at them, and at the earl standing at the dais, and at the Badger behind the gap in the curtain.

"Well, I—" He paused, glancing at Lord Atlee. "Well I couldn't possibly begin to hazard a guess as to the—I mean, I would of course need a closer look before I was able to make any sort of actual—" Before Alastair could finish, the press was already turning and calling back to the earl.

"Shall he have a look then, sir?"

"Yes, what say you, sir, shall he come forward?"

Lord Marwick looked out at the crowd, and at the press, and at the members in the tent, all anxiously awaiting the news, his news. Suddenly the sound of a sputtering generator could be heard as the lights in the square began to flicker on. The PA crackled to life, and the man on top of the TV truck bent forward, his camera rolling.

"Well, then. It appears the island has given us her answer," said Lord Marwick, gesturing magnanimously for Alastair to come forward.

Alastair glanced once more at Lord Atlee, and as the members stepped aside for him, he ducked beneath the rope.

From behind the curtain, the Badger watched Alastair step carefully through the crowd. But farther out in the square, something else caught his eye. The Badger's gaze narrowed at the sight of his crew and the Duffs searching frantically among the villagers. Quickly he scanned above the crowd for any sign of trouble, while somewhere unseen down within it, Innes and the others crouched low in perfect stillness and watched as the men closed in.

Alastair stood silently at the tables. He stared at the chests there before him, squat and ancient, as if they had emerged through time and come to rest here on the bone-white cloth. Lord

Marwick stepped down from the stage as Alastair approached the first chest. His eyes moved across the brine-black wood, the intricate traces of its carvings. From his pocket, he took out his wire-frame glasses, and reaching into the chest, he drew out a single golden coin. He studied it, but only for a moment, before again turning his attention to the construction of the chest: its hinges and joints, the workings of its lock, the simple beauty of its latch.

"A fortune in gold and he's more interested in the boxes it came in," said Lord Marwick, smiling out at the crowd.

Alastair moved slowly down the line to the next chest, and the next, and upon reaching the fourth, he stopped and leaned in close. In the very corner of the lid, hidden within a swirling pattern of thorns, was the tiny spiral of three conjoined circles carved from a single unbroken line. Gently he touched the lid, inspecting the inner workmanship of the chest itself. With both hands, he felt its wooden joints, running his fingers carefully within the curved lid like a doctor feeling for trouble beneath the skin. A thin veneer of wood began to loosen and sag down, and taking the wooden panel in both hands, he worked it loose and laid it carefully on the cloth.

"And what's that you've got there?" asked Lord Marwick. As he came around the table, he saw, affixed within the smooth curvature of the lid, a large parchment, peat-stained and darkened and damaged with age.

Alastair squinted in close, then looked up at Lord Marwick. "We'll be needing a light."

From the stage, a light was quickly brought down and angled in toward the chest. The microphone from the dais was set on the table as Lord Marwick stood watching Alastair inspect the document. A corner of the parchment had crumbled away in flakes, and across its middle a large swath was blurred and water-stained, its blue-black ink fading away into the velum.

"Well," Lord Marwick stepped closer, "what is it?"

"It's quite damaged," said Alastair. "But I'd say its most likely a letter of provenance. A document of ownership of some sort, which would have been common in such an instance. Quite common actually, with something this valuable." He scanned slowly along the parchment. Around its margins were conjoined circles and swirls of illuminated script, ornately wrought in faded pigments of gold and purple and blue. "Magnificent," he said breathlessly. "But almost certainly a copy. In fact, there looks to be more than one copy here." He leaned close where the parchment had crumbled away in layers. "It's in Latin of course, a document like this. With traces of the vulgate, which would also be right, Skara Skaill having been this remote. And, I believe we may have a date here." Alastair leaned closer, straining to read the words. "In the year of our Lord…" He paused a moment, then looked squarely at the earl. "Nine hundred and eighty one. Most certainly the right timeframe for the hoard itself."

Lord Marwick turned toward the members in the tent as an upwelling of elation came over him. The press surged tighter against the ropes.

"And what does it say, the document?" they called. "Yes, can you read it, sir?"

"Well, and who among us ever bothered with their Latin in school?" said Lord Marwick, playing to the crowd.

Alastair glanced at him over his glasses.

"I did."

* * *

Tito crouched low at the base of the statue. He could smell the grease and rubber of the TV truck parked at his shoulder, the rain dripping from it. Through the gap in its sliding door, he noticed a small screen, flickering black and white. Emerging slowly out of the static came the long table at the foot of the stage, and the line of wooden boxes lying across it, and Alastair's angular frame bent over the parchment. Tito tapped Rory on the shoulder and pointed at the monitor.

Innes glanced back at the boys. "Everyone be ready." He paused a moment at the impossible sight of Alastair there on the screen, before turning and scanning hard through the crowd.

"Be ready, Tito." Rory nodded, but Tito kept his eyes on the monitor, and as the camera slowly closed in, Rory could now clearly see the parchment within the lid and the hoard on full display. "Yeah, well, I suppose it's theirs now, isn't it."

Suddenly Tito turned from the monitor and began rummaging in his pack.

"What're you doing, Tito? Close that." But as Rory took Tito's pack and slung it over his shoulder, he saw in Tito's hand the square purse they had found beneath Skarahollow Chapel.

* * *

Alastair slowly scanned the parchment, studying its blue-black inscriptions laid out in rows of meticulously handwritten lines. "It's hard to make out, as damaged as it is. But I'd say it looks to be a *factum domini* of some sort."

"A what?" someone shouted out from the crowd. "We can't hear you, sir."

"Yes, a what?" asked the earl.

Alastair gave no answer. Carefully he moved his finger along the fading script as it disappeared ghostlike into the crumbled parchment. He stopped, then retraced the script once more.

He stood up suddenly and turned to the earl, his mind working. Without a word, he looked out toward the tent where Lord Atlee's eyes were already on him. Alastair lingered a moment more, then turned again to the earl.

"My apologies, sir, I was mistaken. I'm afraid I will be needing some assistance with the Latin after all." And without waiting for an answer, he leaned to the microphone. "Lord Atlee?"

For a moment, Lord Atlee stood beneath the tent, unmoving. Then Alastair bent to the microphone once more.

"John?"

* * *

Tito stared transfixed inside the purse, trying to see deeper down within it.

"Here, give me that," whispered Rory, grabbing at it, but as Tito stretched the purse wider, its half-rotted laces began to break loose and powder away.

"Look, Rory. Do you see?" Tito pried the purse wider still. "I knew I'd seen it," he said as the purse's stiff front suddenly tumbled open and what was once a leather square now unfolded into a rectangle of three connected panels, its blue-black inscriptions laid out in neat rows of meticulously handwritten lines, its margins framed in illuminated designs of gold and purple and blue.

From the front, Innes glanced back again, only half seeing what Tito held in his hands. But as his eyes settled on it, Innes now saw, stitched tightly into the leather lining, a stiff parchment, its deep seams unfolded. And there, just beyond Tito's shoulder, flickering on the little screen, was its perfect twin, lining the inner curve of the chest.

Slowly Tito raised his eyes. "What is this?" he whispered.

Innes looked from the purse to the screen then back again, watching as Alastair and the earl stooped carefully over its identical match beneath the lid, while Constable Tulloch stood guard over it all, front and center.

"Whatever it is, they are most definitely going to want it."

At that, Rory reached over and lowered the purse from view. "We'll not be caught with that, Tito. The one thing we actually did steal." And refolding it quickly, Rory wedged the purse down into the cobbles at the base of the statue. Then remembering the little carved elk, he pulled it too from his coat and wedged it alongside the purse as Ham and Aggie kept their eyes on the crowd.

"So we'll go for the wall, yeah?" asked Ham.

Innes gauged the distance to the far wall beyond the square. "I don't see how we make that."

"What about the tent then? Gotta be someone in there we could talk to." But the center of the square was crawling with the Badger's men.

"Innes, this is madness," said Aggie. "Can't we just walk out and say something to someone, anyone? We need to get to Mr. Begbie."

"That would only bring the constable, miss," said Rory. "Which means the Badger, which means the Duffs."

"Well, whatever we're gonna do, we'd better do it," said Ham, pointing at two men moving nearby while a third searched closer from the back of the square.

From behind him, Innes felt a tap on his arm. Rory and Tito were staring wordlessly at him. For a moment, Rory said nothing, then slowly he lifted something solid from his coat pocket. In his hand was the black grip of Frankie Duff's gun.

Innes turned to him. "No."

"But you know what they'll do."

"No," he said again, and with his back to the others, Innes took the gun from Rory. "I mean it's not a job for you."

Innes slipped the gun into his own pocket and looked once more at the wall at the far end of the square. And at the men patrolling closer through the crowd. And at the Badger, and the constable keeping steady watch. Then he looked at the boys. Tito in his oversized clothes. Rory filthy and spent, shouldering Tito's pack.

In a sudden hiss, the rain turned to sleet, bouncing off the umbrellas in a cacophony of sound all around the square.

"Alright." Innes nodded. "Alright, we'll go for the wall. Rory and Tito, you'll lead us out. But stay low until you're clear of the crowd, alright? When you reach the wall, go hard for the moors. Tito, you stay right with Rory, alright? And don't look back."

Glancing again at the little screen, Innes saw Lord Atlee join Alastair and the earl leaning intently over the parchment. He considered them one last time, then turned again to the others, looking quietly at them all. At Ham. At Rory. At Tito. And at Aggie. At Aggie. And his eyes stayed with hers.

"What?" she asked. "What is it?"

"Nothing." He nodded. "It'll be alright," he said, finding a smile for her, while down in his pocket his hand closed tight around the gun.

Rory started them forward. As Innes rose up, he drew the pistol out of his coat and wedged it within the cobbles that were filling with frozen rain at the foot of the statue. Then grabbing up the purse, he began moving low and steady through the crowd.

Tito held tight to Rory's coattail. He could feel Ham's hand squarely on his back as Aggie stepped quickly at his side, and as the crowd began to thin away, Tito let go of Rory's coat and was running, darting between the widening gaps with Rory appearing and disappearing just ahead of him. Suddenly he was out, out in the open air.

"Run, Tito," came Ham's voice. And Tito ran, his heels clipping over the cobbles with Aggie flying at his side, her coattails flapping behind her as they raced for the wall. But as he scrambled up the stones, Tito saw that Rory was staring back toward the village, back toward Ham, who was standing at the edge of the square searching above the crowd.

"Where's Innes?" asked Tito. But there was no sign of him. "Where is he, Rory?"

Then Aggie saw him. Alone. Running, pressing his way through the crowd, but instead of running toward them, toward the wall, he was running away, away to the very front of the square, away toward the constable, toward the earl, toward the Badger. And from behind him in every direction came the Duffs and their men, quickly closing the gap. Aggie held Tito back as Rory bolted back toward the square. But as he crossed the lane, one of the Duffs' men came elbowing out of the crowd, swinging wildly at Ham and staggering him back.

"Ham!" warned Rory as a second man stepped into the clear. Ham grabbed ahold of the first man and bulled him into the second, and all three went crashing to the ground within the crowd.

Ham lay face down on the cold cobbles, his face bloodied, shoes trampling all around him. But in an instant, he was up again, lifted from all directions as a circle of villagers brought him to his feet. Reaching through the crowd, Rory pulled Ham into the clear.

"He's still in there," Ham shouted. "Can you see him?" But as they looked back, the two men were already up again, pushing their way through the crowd as another of the Badger's men shouldered toward them.

"Come on, Ham!" shouted Rory.

Ham searched desperately above the crowd.

"Come on, Ham. We have to go." And turning away, they began running back to Aggie and Tito waiting at the wall.

As they clambered over, Aggie lingered a moment more on the wall. She could no longer see Innes now. All that remained of him was a line of chaos surging through the square. And as the Badger's men came rushing for the wall, she turned and disappeared over the side.

Down the hill they ran, and upon reaching the flats below, they glanced back, where from high above, the Badger's men spied them from the wall. But gliding in off the moors came a cold fog, and the three on the wall could only stand and watch as down below, one by one, they turned and slipped into the mist and were gone.

* * *

The Badger saw him first, then the constable. Then Alastair.

Innes came fighting through the crowd, a trail of men at his heels as he reached Alastair at the foot of the stage. Falling forward, he clutched on to Alastair as the gang of men overtook him. "On Skara Heath," he whispered to Alastair. "The caves south of Mr. Begbie's, do you understand? Due south," he said, disappearing as the men pounded down around him, beating and kicking him where he fell on the cobbles.

Alastair waded into the scrum. "Stop this. Stop this at once!" he shouted, but the surge of the crowd forced him back, and as he was pushed farther away, he looked down and only now realized Innes had pressed something into his hand.

Dropping down from the stage, the Badger rushed into the throng, stripping people off the pile.

"Get him up! Get him the hell up," he called as Constable Tulloch and his men arrived, jerking Innes to his feet.

Innes stood before them, torn and unsteady.

The constable looked him in the face, and a slow recognition came over him.

"Well, now. Innes Mackie. I'd heard you were back on the island." The constable looked Innes over. His clothes mud-soaked. His face bloodied and beaten. "You've looked better."

Through the crowd, the Badger saw Frankie standing at the edge of the fray, catching his breath, his left fist bloody and raw, his right hand purple from the hazelwood shaft.

The Badger pushed through to him. "What the bloody hell happened?" he hissed. "Didn't I say get everyone to the wharf?"

"We did. We're on it. We'll get it fixed," said Frankie just as Munro and some of the crew came shoving out of the crowd. Frankie looked at them standing there, empty-handed. "What the hell are you doing, Munro? Didn't any of you go after the others?"

"We didn't see nobody but him."

"Others?" The Badger asked. "What do you mean, others?"

Frankie started to speak, then stopped.

"Oh, for Christ's sake, what are you telling me, Frankie?" The Badger turned just as the constable was cuffing Innes's hands behind his back. He sighed and slowly stepped over. "Always were the clever one, eh, Innes? I'll give you that." The Badger tilted his head, but Innes kept his gaze on the ground, blood seeping from his hairline, his eye swelling closed. "But we'll find them. Don't you worry. We'll find them." He leaned in quietly. "You know I'm done playing with you now though, yeah? All done." And keeping his fist low in the crowd, the Badger struck him quickly, as Innes doubled over, coughing for air. "Should've stayed away, Innes."

"Right. Let's go," said the constable, and as he started Innes away, the Badger nodded for Frankie and Munro to follow after them.

"Oh, and Frankie?" said the Badger. "Please tell me you at least know where the others have gone?"

But as Frankie stood there with no answer, the three men returning from the wall pressed urgently out of the crowd.

* * *

The Badger hurried back across the stage as the earl cut him off at the curtain.

"I've never been the best with faces, Mr. Croy, but that gentleman being led away there looks familiar, does he not?" Lord Marwick stared hard at the side of the Badger's face. "Now you listen to me, because I will say this only once. If you, or any of your wharf rats, have done anything to jeopardize all this, or me, I promise you that little reward we spoke about earlier will be long gone. And more than that, and hear me now boy, whatever all that trouble in the crowd was, I want it dealt with; I want it gone. Or I promise you I'll put you right back in that hole in the ground where I found you. Do I make myself clear?"

"Yes, sir."

"Then bloody fix it." The earl eyed him a moment more, then headed away toward the dais.

Sweeping the curtain aside, the Badger hurried backstage toward the Rover. He climbed in, and as he backed through the gate, he picked up the radio handset. "Tulloch. Pick up." From his coat pocket, he drew out the cardboard envelope Lord Marwick had given him, and placing it on the seat at his side, he accelerated up the alley as the constable's voice came over the wireless.

* * *

Alastair hurried up the steps as Lord Marwick crossed the stage.

"Well, I don't know what all that was about," said Lord Marwick, forcing a tight smile. "Shall we recommence?"

"What's being done with that man?" Alastair asked sharply.

"I beg your pardon?"

"The man, who was just led away there, where's he being taken?"

The smile disappeared from the earl's face. "Well, I'm sure I wouldn't know."

"But you can assure his safety?"

"*His* safety? I was more concerned with *our* safety there for a moment. From what I understand, that man has a warrant out for his arrest. But perhaps we could get back to the business at hand, yes? Before this storm arrives in force. A great deal of people are waiting?"

Alastair turned and looked out beyond the square, but as the constable's car disappeared from view, something at the back of the crowd caught his eye. It was Jameson, waving for him to come, with Otis and Rat standing at his side.

"So shall we recommence then?" asked Lord Marwick, stepping into Alastair's line of sight. "You'll pardon me for saying so, Mr. Clements, but frankly, I would have assumed a man in your field would consider it an honor to be front and center for such a moment. The world hanging on your every word." He nodded toward the press. "You do realize this is history we're making here?"

Alastair looked out at the press waiting against the ropes, at the cameraman atop the TV truck, at the expectant crowd.

"Yes. Yes, of course you're quite right." He nodded, taking a long look toward the moors. "Unfortunately, I'm afraid a matter of great urgency has come up quite suddenly, and with your permission, I'll be asking Lord Atlee to take over. I'm sure you'll agree it's more appropriate a member of the Order be the one to make the official pronouncement?" And without waiting for an answer, Alastair turned and hurried down the stairs to where Lord Atlee stood waiting at the oaken boxes.

Stepping in close, Alastair drew Tito's unfolded parchment from his coat and laid it down in the chest, its rotting twin affixed above it within the lid.

"Loud and clear for all, John," he nodded, his eyes square on him. "Loud and clear for all." And turning away, Alastair hurried off through the crowd.

XXVII

INNES SAT SLUMPED IN the back seat, his hands cuffed behind him, his eye swollen shut. The constable bumped the car off the last of the asphalt, the village long behind them. Munro sat next to Innes in back, with Frankie in front, their leather coats squeaking in the silence as the car jostled along. Leaning against the window, Innes looked out through the freezing rain at the vast emptiness that swept down and away across Skara Heath, wild and ragged. A hard loneliness overtook him as the dirt road turned into a two-track, then faded away to nothing as they stopped on an open upland overlooking the valley below.

Innes looked up as the others stepped out.

Through the windshield, he could see them talking together, until Munro came around to the side of the car, darkening Innes's window.

Taking him by the elbow, Munro led him to a spot out on the flats. Innes stood alone in the rain as Munro walked back to the car and spoke quietly with the others.

From his coat, the constable drew out a matte-black pistol.

"I don't recommend you use your own for a job like this," he said, holding the gun out to Frankie, grip first. Frankie took it with his broken hand, a deep-purple bloom having swelled from his wrist to his thumb. "And what happened there?" asked the constable.

"None of your bloody business is what." Frankie gingerly tried to grip the gun.

"So will you be shooting left-handed then?"

"Sod off." Frankie paused a moment, then handed the gun to Munro.

"What, me?"

"Oh, would you just take it."

Munro leaned in close to Frankie. "I told you I'd need some advance notice if I was to do this kind of work. We talked about that."

"Yeah, well, I'm telling you now."

"You do know how to use one of those, yeah?" interrupted the constable.

Munro considered the gun a moment, then took it, feeling the weight of it in his hand. Tentatively he stepped out in front of the car. After casting a glance back at Frankie, he turned and raised the barrel of the gun.

Innes lowered his eyes. On the ground at his feet grew a little scatter of moor flowers down among the rocks. Volunteers. He closed his eyes and waited as the frozen rain pattered down.

Munro squared himself nervously, setting his feet.

"Oh, just one quick thing though," said the constable. And as Munro looked back, he saw that Constable Tulloch had leveled a pistol directly at Frankie's head.

"Drop the gun, Munro," called the constable.

Frankie turned and faced him. "And what the hell do you think you're doing?"

Munro swung his gun around. "You'll take that gun off my brother now," he said, pointing the barrel at the constable. "Right bloody now."

"Just shoot him, Munro," said Frankie casually. "We should've done it a long time ago."

"Drop the gun, Munro," repeated the constable evenly.

"You take that gun off my brother or I swear to God!"

"Shoot him, Munro."

Munro shot. Click. Click. He checked the gun. Click again.

"Have you got the safety on?" asked Frankie.

"No, I haven't got the bloody safety on. I told you I needed some advance notice on this."

"Down on your knees," said the constable, keeping his pistol on them. "You're under arrest. Both of you."

"What the hell are you talking about?" said Frankie. "For what?"

"For attempted murder."

"Attempted murder?" Munro looked at his gun. "But there weren't even any bullets in the bloody thing."

"Not murder of me, you idiot. Of my cousin, Otis."

The Duffs stopped. "Your cousin?"

"That's right."

"Otis is your cousin?"

"On my mother's side," said the constable. "Now, get down on the ground, the both of you."

"Oh, would you please shut the hell up," said Frankie. "No one's getting on the bloody ground."

"Down," said the constable. "Do it now."

"And what exactly are you gonna do about it, eh?" Frankie spat in the dirt. "Bloody nothing is what." He started forward toward the constable, but before he took his first step, a blast exploded from the barrel of the constable's gun, ripping the air past Frankie's ear.

The constable recocked the hammer. "Try me again and next time I'll have Munro dig a hole we can roll you into."

Frankie stood a moment, then slowly he and Munro lay flat on the ground. The constable stepped over and plucked the gun from Munro's hand. Then he turned to Frankie. "And I'll be having yours too, Frankie."

"I don't have it."

"Right, you don't." The constable patted Frankie down one side and up the other, and finding no gun, he straightened up and looked at Frankie lying there in the mud. "You know, without a gun, and with just the one hand, there's not really much to you, is there?"

"How about you let me up and try me?"

"Yeah, and I would, you see," said the constable, stepping over to Munro, "but at the moment, I'm a little busy arresting your brother."

"Oh, you go right ahead then, have your little fun." Frankie nodded darkly. "But the Badger will be coming for you after this. You do know that, yeah?"

"Not over the likes of you two he won't."

"And me, I'll be right there with him when he does too," said Frankie. "You can count on that."

"The only place you two are gonna be is on the first boat to Lochinwall," said the constable, cuffing Munro. "Before he even notices you're gone."

"Lochinwall?"

"That's right. My cousin's the constable over there. Or didn't I say?"

"How many cousins does he even have?" whispered Munro, his cheek pressed in the mud.

When the constable was done with Munro, he turned and looked out toward Innes still standing handcuffed in the rain. "Would you mind?" he called, waving him over. But Innes only stood there, staring in disbelief. "Well, come on then. I only have two pairs of cuffs, and you're wearing one of them."

Innes started unsteadily forward, but as he reached the constable, one of his knees buckled out.

"Whoa now, easy does it," said Constable Tulloch, steadying him. "No small thing having a gun held on you, is it?" He undid Innes's cuffs. "Now if you wouldn't mind, could you just cuff Frankie there for me?" He held out the handcuffs, keeping his gun trained on Frankie. Innes stared at the cuffs. "Go on." The constable nodded. "Nice and tight."

Innes took the handcuffs, but as he stepped over, Frankie suddenly kicked back. As he fought to his feet, Innes muscled him back into the mud, giving him an extra shove for good measure. "For laying hands on Aggie." And with the very first tooth of the manacle, Innes clicked the cuffs on Frankie's elephantine wrists, then backed away.

The two stood a long moment, looking at the Duffs lying face down in the dirt.

"So, I ran into Otis earlier, in the square there," said the constable. "Was with another fella."

"Who, Rat?" asked Innes.

"Yeah, no, I believe this fella said his name was Jameson?" The constable holstered his gun. "Seemed like a decent sort. A little chatty maybe. Anyway, I understand I owe you my thanks." Innes glanced at him, confusion in his eyes. "For helping save my cousin's life? I mean, he's not good for much, Otis. But he's kin." Tulloch shrugged. "Family. What are you gonna do, am I right?"

Innes nodded, a little wobbly still. "Yeah, what are you gonna do?"

The two of them stood there awkwardly.

"By the way," said the constable, "did you know there's an old warrant out for your arrest on the island?"

"Is there?" asked Innes.

The constable nodded. "Felony in the first. Resisting arrest, and assaulting an officer of the law while you were at it. And I suppose whatever all else you were running down at the wharf."

"Sounds worse when you say it like that."

"It does, doesn't it?" agreed the constable. "Mind you, it wasn't me that wanted you arrested back then. Was the earl. Once the Badger got him turned on you."

"Yeah, well. It was time for me to leave the island anyway. And I hadn't meant to come back just yet."

"Right." The constable nodded his condolence. "Yeah, I was sorry to hear about your da. He'd had it hard. You all had." He paused a moment. "So look, I'm no angel, mind you. And I'm not forgetting what you did or anything. Punching an officer of the law and what have you. But I do feel like a man's gotta draw the line somewhere, you know, for his own self. I suppose you know Lord Marwick, he wants the Badger to have you shot?"

"Yeah, I'd gathered that."

"Right. And well, what with the circumstances being what they are and all. With Otis and that." The constable took off his hat and knocked the rain from it. "What say we just call it even." He fitted his hat back on his head. "You're free to go."

Innes could only stare as the constable started back toward the Duffs. "But here's some free advice. And trust me on this. I wouldn't go hanging around the islands too very long because the earl, he'll have the Badger looking for you, you can be sure of that." He got Frankie to his feet. "And I can't help you there, lad. Not with them two, I can't."

"So what, he just goes free then?" asked Munro.

"He does today."

As the constable started them toward the car, Frankie called back to Innes.

"No need to bother yourself though, boy. You know how the Badger is, he'll find you right quick. And them others too." The constable opened the door, and Frankie stepped one foot in. "As a matter of fact, he's heading out to Skara Heath right now to deal with them lot first."

At Frankie's words, a chill came to Innes cold and clear. He ran to the edge of the rise and looked out across the valley floor, then back at the constable, who only shook his head.

"Sorry, lad. Like I said. You're on your own with them two."

Tulloch climbed in and closed the door behind him, and Innes could only watch as the car wheeled slowly around and drove away.

XXVIII

THE EARL STOOD AT the dais and waited as Lord Atlee carefully closed the chest.

Lord Atlee exhaled. "Right." He removed his glasses. "So let me first say, purely from an initial reading, my assessment would be in complete accordance with Mr. Clements. It's clearly a document verifying ownership or the transference thereof. I concur, it is a *factum domini*, if you will."

"And so the document confirms it then, the hoard?" asked Lord Marwick, stepping from the dais.

"Well, in a sense, yes. The document actually makes no direct reference to the hoard itself. But given the date, and although you'll certainly want expert translation, I believe I'm quite safe in saying that there is sufficient contextual evidence, more than sufficient really, to confirm that what you have here is indeed the Harald Hoard of Skara Skaill. My congratulations on your discovery, sir."

Lord Marwick clapped his hands once, and as he turned and beamed out at the tent, the press squeezed forward, their cameras clicking above their heads.

"But if the earl will indulge me." Lord Atlee leaned in to the microphone. "If the earl will indulge me, perhaps I might read it aloud here in its entirety, for posterity's sake?"

"By all means," said Lord Marwick, waving his consent, his eyes shining.

Lord Atlee reopened the chest, and down within it still lay Tito's unfolded purse. Putting his glasses on, Lord Atlee cleared his throat and read.

* * *

The wipers flicked maniacally as the Badger navigated the Rover across the open moors. Out from the open radio channel came the amplified voice of Lord Atlee reading aloud to the crowd in the square.

> *"In the year of our Lord, nine hundred and eighty one, by the grace of God and in solemn consideration of..."*

* * *

Over the sodden ground, Innes ran. The freezing rain tore at him, his mud-laden boots slipped heavily as he started up the long slope rising above him.

* * *

> *"...this proclamation goes out to all the northern barons, justices, foresters, sheriffs, stewards, servants, and to all officials and loyal subjects of our realm, a greeting from your grateful king, Harald..."*

* * *

The villagers listened silently as Lord Atlee's voice carried out over the square.

> *"Let it be known to our ancestors foregone and to our descendants to come, to the honor of the Almighty, for the better ordering of these Northern Islands, and in recognition of those to whom our gratitude is given for having quartered myself among them most happily in this furthest corner of our dominion…"*

* * *

The Rover bucked and swayed across the moorland. The Badger squinted through the windshield now, half listening as the voice of Lord Atlee continued through the static.

> *"It is accordingly our wish and command that the people of these islands, its territory being manifest, in issuance for their faithful devotion and kinship freely given me during this my four years in exile…"*

* * *

Up the steepening rise Innes scrambled, and reaching the ridgeline, he looked out, searching the empty sweep of the valley below. Then he saw it. The slightest movement. A cluster of specks tight together, moving slowly across the valley floor. Relief swept over him. But only for a moment. For from the far end of the valley, traveling darkly through the moving curtains of rain, came the Rover, fast closing the distance.

* * *

> *"...that the free people of these Northern Islands and their descendants, who shall be commonly the joint freeholders, guardians and stewards of these lands..."*

From the dais, the smile on the earl's face began to dim in confusion, and looking out, he could hear a murmur rising from the tent as Lord Atlee read on.

> *"... and shall have and keep them in their fullness and entirety, in all things and without limit, ab initio et ad infinitum, from this beginning and for always...."*

Lord Marwick stepped from behind the dais, a slow panic coming into his eyes as he began clapping for an end to the reading, waving his arms for the band in the tent to recommence.

"Thank you very much indeed, Lord Atlee, thank you," and turning his back, he whispered to the man with the clipboard, "Cut the power. Cut it immediately." But as the reporters in the crowd transcribed every word, Lord Atlee's voice continued to ring out over the square like a brass bell, loud and clear for all.

> *"...for the establishment of these islands, from the sky above them to the earth beneath their feet, to be forever the sovereign dominion and birthright of the good peoples of Skara Skaill."*

Lord Atlee looked up from the parchment and removed his glasses.

A stillness hung over the crowd as Lord Marwick, the fifteenth Earl of Skara Skaill, stood staring out at the press, and at the members beneath the tent, and at the camera whirring steadily atop the TV truck.

In an instant, the silence was broken as the press surged forward, shouting questions toward the stage.

Over the din, Lord Atlee leaned again to the microphone. "I believe I speak for the other members, and most importantly the people of Skara Skaill, when I say we wholeheartedly echo the sentiments of Lord Marwick and will guarantee the very fullest scrutiny into the nature of the hoard's discovery, as well as the legal ramifications of the document itself. Of that you can be sure."

* * *

The Rover idled at a dead stop. The Badger stared at the radio as Lord Atlee's voice was drowned out by the crowds in the village square. The radio transmission went dead, and the Badger sat unmoving as empty static filled the cabin. From the glovebox, he pulled out the cardboard envelope Lord Marwick had given him. He held it there in his hand a moment, then let it slip to the floor. Slowly lifting his eyes, he stared through the blur of ice and rain against the windshield. But his gaze narrowed, and leaning forward, he squinted through the glass at something moving out in the gloom. He unlatched the door and stepped out onto the sodden ground. Through the wall of freezing rain, he saw a lone figure standing in the distance, dead ahead.

* * *

Innes stared across at the Rover idling rhythmically, the Badger standing at its open door. The cold rain continued steadily down upon the open ground between them. Slowly Innes raised his hands, holding them empty above his head. The Badger stared a long moment, then stepped back to the vehicle and climbed inside.

In the muffled stillness of the cabin, the Badger could still smell the remains of wet peat from the hoard. Reaching down beneath his seat, a black pistol spun freely from its rag and tumbled heavily onto the envelope, staining it with black grease from the gun.

Innes heard the sound of the engine before the Rover started forward, gathering speed as it came. As the Badger closed the distance, Innes held up his hands, shouting, desperately trying to wave him back. He could see the madness on the Badger's face through the windshield. But the madness became confusion and confusion terror as the Rover suddenly shuddered hard and nosed downward. The mud of the rain-soaked mire that had lain invisible between them began to quickly rise over the hood and up the glass as the wipers twitched mindlessly, not yet knowing their work was done. Like a great beast, the Rover roared and smoked, struggling for its life as the weight of its iron engine drew it swiftly down. Through the narrowing windshield, Innes could see the Badger banging his shoulder against a door already too laden with mud to be moved. Innes ran forward, calling out, but as the Rover slipped beneath the surface, the Badger raised the barrel of his gun. The mud spray from the pistol shot came blasting through the windshield, and rushing in through the exploded glass, the mud filled the Rover's cabin as it dragged the Badger silently below.

Innes ran to the mire's edge but could go no farther. A wisp of engine smoke lingered a moment above the bog before slipping away on the wind. In the stillness, the rain turned again to sleet, then to snow, softly pattering down on the already smoothening earth. After a moment more, Innes turned and walked to the top of the low rise and looked out across the valley floor.

XXIX

THE BLACK TRUCK FRAME moved slowly through the gate. A light snow continued to fall. The flakes blurred into Eustice's dusty hide as the two pigs minced behind, pausing briefly to inspect the contents of the mule's droppings. Beyond the wall, the moors were a sheet of white to the horizon.

A newly cut rectangle in the ground lay alongside two older graves long since grown over. Down within the hole, the earth was warmer and dark as the wind swept across the opening. A sparse gathering quietly assembled. Aggie and Ada. Ham. The two elderly sisters from the fair. A few gray-haired villagers. Tito stood at Rory's side.

At the far gate of the cemetery, the constable leaned against his car, watching the crowd.

The minister stood at the graveside, his hands clasped at his waist. When they had settled, he began.

The Lord is my shepherd; I shall not want.
He maketh me to lie down in green pastures,

Rory glanced back at the gate as the constable, satisfied, slowly climbed into his car and drove away.

He leadeth me beside the still waters,
He restoreth my soul.

The minister raised his eyes and looked up at the gathering.

"We have gathered here today to commit the body of George Harcus Begbie to the ground. May he find peace and rest." The minister opened his book. "And now, a recitation, also read at the services of George's brothers, at their request."

With rue my heart is laden
For golden friends I had,

As Tito listened, his eyes fell upon a headstone one row back, standing alone between the gaps. *Garnet Brown Renfro*.

For many a rose-lipt maiden
And many a lightfoot lad.

By brooks too broad for leaping
The lightfoot boys are laid,

Rory looked over at Tito, who was staring hard at the ground.

The rose-lipt girls are sleeping
In fields where roses fade.

The minister closed his book.

We are all from the dust, and to
the dust we all return.

A thousand years in the eyes of the Lord
are as but a single yesterday.
And swift to its close ebbs out our little story.
For fast falls the eventide.

When all the words were spoken and the coffin lowered down, the crowd began to move off, talking quietly to each other as they started slowly away. Eustice stood unmoving, tied to a post.

"Don't feel much like running off today, eh, big fella?" asked Ham. "Not today." He patted the mule's hard forehead.

At the gravesite, Tito stepped through the row and stood facing Mrs. Renfro's headstone, being careful to stay to one side. He stood a moment, then from his pocket, he pulled out a handful of crumpled paper, little scraps and slips of handwritten notes. He squatted down, and smoothing them a little, he set them at the base of the headstone, holding them there as the wind tried to carry them away. Rory knelt down next to him, and edging Tito's hand aside, he set a stone on top of the bits of paper against the wind.

The two stood a moment more, then without a word, they turned away and headed to the gate.

Ham led Eustice by the reins as the pigs wandered out in wide circles, snouts to the hard ground. In the distance, they could see the fallen yew tree lying within the gray skeleton of Skarahollow Chapel. Someone had begun clearing branches from it for firewood. The white tent was gone.

"So nothing from Innes still, yeah?" asked Ham.

Rory shook his head. "No, but you saw the constable at the cemetery gate?"

"Right."

As they came up the long path to Kettleskaill House, Mr. Begbie's pigs hurried across to the coop to look for fallen eggs. Honey sat fluffed atop the roosting boxes watching them come. From out of the barn, Sir Winston stepped out, stretching his back.

Ham turned to Tito. "And when did he come back?"

"Last night. He just walked up out of the dark like nothing."

Sir Winston twitched his tail at the sight of them, then started off after the pigs.

"Well, he doesn't look any worse for wear."

"That's because Tito won't stop feeding him," said Rory.

Ham released the reins as Eustice plodded forward a few heavy steps, still hitched to his cart. At the front of the house, Aggie stood looking up at the windows and at the front door propped in place, the county notice still nailed to it.

"I don't know about you two being out here. Even if Ham is staying with you."

"I've told them it's just for now." Ham nodded.

"And you have enough to eat then?"

"More than enough," said Rory.

"Ada's bringing some supper by as well," said Ham, brightening. "Plus we have the pigs if it comes to that, eh, Rory?"

"We never would," said Tito, making sure Aggie knew.

"And you're sure it's alright for you to be here?"

"Well, with the Duffs gone," said Rory. "And the Badger."

"And the earl, he's got his hands full just at the moment," added Ham. "More than full."

"And what'll you do for heat?"

Rory nodded toward the barn. Ham's cut us some peat."

"An enormous pile," added Tito.

"Alright," said Aggie, surrendering. "But you're coming for Christmas dinner, yes?"

"Tuesday," said Tito, nodding.

"Tuesday at three. And that's all of you." She turned to Rory. "We've still got quite a lot to talk about, you and I. School and everything else. For after the holidays." Aggie wound her scarf around her. "But that'll keep for another day." She started to leave, then turned to Rory once more. "You know, Rory, I've been wanting to tell you." She looked quietly at him. "You've done quite a thing, you know that? Taking care of Tito, all this time. With no one. You've had a lot to carry." She nodded at him. "But you'll not be alone in it anymore."

Sir Winston followed Aggie halfway up the path. In the distance, they could see strings of white lights twinkling in the village. As Aggie disappeared from sight, Tito turned to Rory at the front step.

"So, why can't we say anything in front of Miss Aggie anyway, about the house?"

"I don't know. I suppose it's OK now."

"Say what in front of her?" asked Ham, looking up, assessing the roof.

"That we paid what was owed," said Rory.

"Owed on what?"

"On the house," said Tito. "On Kettleskaill."

Ham turned to them. "What do you mean, you paid it?"

"I mean we paid it." Rory stepped to the front door. "Actually, Tito paid it."

"Tito?"

Tito nodded, checking his watch. "I wonder if the ferry's gone yet, Rory?"

* * *

Jameson stood at the railing and took a long breath of the chill night air. The ferry's pilot house was trimmed with a strand of garish lights. Below him, the churn of moonlit water raced away toward the low outline of Skara Skaill slowly sinking on the horizon.

Alastair sat inside the little car. The cabin was warm and quiet and smelled of the pies Jameson was bringing home. From below, Alastair could feel the deep thrumming of the ferry's engine. He clicked on the map light, and from his satchel, he drew out Tito's unfolded leather purse. He laid it in his lap. In the small circle of light, he gazed down at the parchment again, its golds and purples and blues illuminating up at him from a thousand years ago as the deep roll of the hull moved beneath him.

* * *

Ham stared at the boys in silent disbelief. "Why you proper outlaws."

"They wanted this too." Rory lifted the little carved elk from his pocket. "But I'm keeping that."

"You know, Ham," said Tito, "you can stay here. Longer than you said. Here with us, at Kettleskaill."

Rory nodded. "Actually, we are supposed to have someone here with us."

"That's the rules," added Tito. "Don't tell Aggie."

"Well, if you're sure. I am a little short, just at the moment, and Alastair did say it could take a couple of months before everything with the hoard was sorted." Ham looked up again at the old house. "You know, I was a carpenter's helper for a time, did I say?"

"You didn't say, no," said Tito.

"Can do a bit of wiring as well. And I've spent more time on a roof than I care to admit." Ham stared up appraisingly at Kettleskaill. "Days are getting shorter now though. But no reason we can't get started on the inside work."

A fresh wind thinned the clouds away as the first cold stars of evening began pushing through the twilight.

"Look," said Tito. "Do you see it?" They stood gazing up at the smudge of light at the far edge of the horizon. "It's almost gone."

Rory watched the comet a moment, before turning away into the dark. "Should we have a fire then?" he asked as he collected the broken kindling that had once boarded up the door.

Tito turned to the yard and whistled for Sir Winston, clean and shrill. As the little dog came running in out of the darkness, Tito gazed up again at the comet.

"And do you still say it's only dust and ice, Rory?" he asked. "Even now?"

Rory stopped and looked up again. "I don't know." In the darkness, Tito could see the moonlight on Rory's face. "But the light does catch it pretty good sometimes. I'll give you that." He knelt down and began gathering up the shattered pieces of wood, stacking them in his arms.

* * *

Aggie clicked on the light. Down the hall, she hung her coat on the rack. The hazelwood walking stick leaned in the corner. Passing into the kitchen, she lit the burner, and leaning against the counter, she stared blankly as the flame hissed blue beneath the teapot. By her hand lay the garland from the fair. She slid it close, and looking up, she noticed a dusty little book, tied with a braided string, set just inside the door. She opened it, and pressed within each page were dried wildflowers, the names carefully written out in a long-faded handwriting. *Stitchwort. Woodsage. Herb Robert. Lady's Bedstraw. Thyme.*

Opening the back door, she stepped quickly out into the night air. On the table in the courtyard sat a fresh mound of mussels, their black shells shining wet in the moonlight. She turned and looked across the yard to the back alley as the faint sound of a neighbor's kitchen radio carried in quietly out of the dark.

* * *

Along the cliffs, the seagrass lay bent in the wind. A square of windowpane flickered orange in the distance.

Inside, a stockpot steamed in the coals. The house smelled of fresh sawdust. Innes sat at the hearth, looking up at the newly cut beams across the ceiling. The white tent canvas, lashed over the opening, shuddered tight against the wind.

Far out in the blackness, the ocean boomed against the rocks below. The little moor pony stiffened his front legs, then wheeled, kicking freely out into the dark as the herd stood in the wind, their winter coats coming in.